THE SUGAR BARON'S GOVERNESS

CHARLESTON BRIDES ~ BOOK 4

ELVA COBB MARTIN

WILD HEART
BOOKS

ISBN-13: 978-1-942265-60-3

This book is dedicated to all those who desire a second chance for love, and to all those who left their faith by the wayside but decide they want to find it again.

If we confess our sins, He is faithful and just to forgive us our sins and to cleanse us from all unrighteousness.

I John 1:9
The Holy Bible, New King James Version

ACKNOWLEDGMENTS

I give a hearty thanks to all my encouraging writer friends and critique partners, but especially Elizabeth Reed, Colleen Hall, and Carlene Brown. Their suggestions have made this story much better.

I am also grateful for my prayer partners including other writers, my sisters Sonya and Phyllis, and my forever hero husband Dwayne. He not only prays for me but puts up with my hours at the computer, quick fix meals, and even pitches in with household tasks, sometimes without even grumbling.

Most of all, I thank my heavenly Father and Lord and Savior Jesus Christ and the Holy Spirit who have been with me, inspiring me, giving me super strength and keeping me on task.

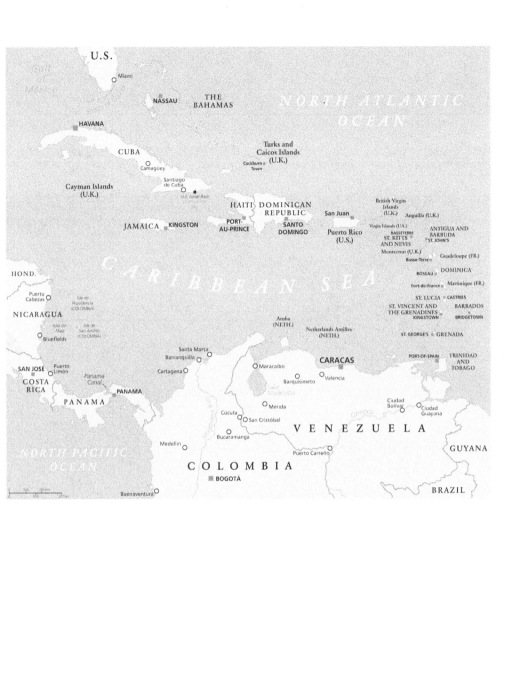

Her employer took his place at the head of the table, she on his right. He looked every bit the wealthy sugar plantation owner, not the pirate-like captain tantalizing her memory.

In that illuminating moment, she knew there were two men in that body—two distinct personalities—one who moved in the planter world as a gentleman, and one who remained hidden, plundering on the high seas. How would she ever fit into this strange picture?

— ABIGAIL WELCH

CHAPTER 1

1785

<small>Between Charleston and Jamaica</small>

*A*bigail Welch awoke in her cabin and sat up, her body stiff, her heart pounding. A cannon blast rocked the ship again. Shouts, stomping boots, and the screeching sound of cannons rolled to gun ports on the deck above sent shivers down her spine. Was the *Marigold* under attack? She rose and gathered her robe about her, unable to control the fitful trembling shaking her. Plunging through the shadows toward the ray of dawn streaming from the porthole, she searched across the white-capped sea. A low sloop, flying the skull and crossbones, pursued them over purple waves. Pirates. She gasped, and her nails dug into her clenched palms.

How could this be happening? Was this to be the end of her dream of a new beginning, love, and security she sought in Jamaica? The *Marigold* left Charleston over a week earlier. Captain Donavan had told her last night at dinner they'd soon see evidence of the island. He assured her the British militia governing the area kept the Caribbean guarded against French and Spanish pirates. Where was the mighty English navy?

The thump of heavy boot steps in the corridor followed by a wallop on her cabin door jerked a knot in her empty stomach. She pulled her robe tight over her chemise, pushed her long tresses back on her shoulders, then called out. "Who is it?"

"I'm from the Capt'n, ma'am. We're under attack by pirates."

She hurried forward and unbolted the door. A crewman she recognized stood there, the whites of his eyes blazing in his stiff, bearded face.

He doffed his hat and reached a gun toward her. "Ma'am, the Capt'n wants you to have this to defend yo'self, in case them scoundrels board us, but we'll fight them to the death."

The flintlock pistol resembled the ones her father had kept in his collection. He taught her how to use the gun when she was fifteen. She reached for the weapon and, forgetful of its weight, almost dropped it.

The sailor steadied her grasp. "It's a wee bit heavy, but it'll sho' stop anyone you want it to, ma'am."

"I am familiar with this gun, sir, and know how to use it."

He nodded. "Thank God for that 'cause I sho don't have time to show you." He pulled a bag of shot and powder from his pocket, thrust it to her, and scrambled back up the passage.

Abigail sucked in a ragged breath, then closed and bolted the door. She loaded the pistol, laid it on her cot, then dressed as fast as she could make her fingers move over the many fasteners of her frock. Shouts, curses, and the deafening blasts of cannons ripped through the air, making her tremble. She could not escape the smell of burning wicks and shot. Whispering a prayer, she dropped onto the side of the bed and pulled the loaded gun into her lap.

Smoke seeped into her cabin and brought on a fit of coughing. Boarding picks crashed on the deck above, and then swords clashing, guns firing, and death cries filled the air. She tried to muffle the formidable sounds with her hands over her ears and bit her lip to keep from fainting. Who was dying? The horrid pirates or the *Marigold* crew?

The ship listed with the waves. Water swished about her feet, and sheer, black fright swept through her. Was the vessel sinking?

Heavy footsteps crashed down the corridor outside her cabin. She stood and wrapped one arm around the bedpost, then gripped the pistol in both hands and aimed at the heavy door.

Father God, help me.

~

Captain Joshua Becket pushed his plumed hat back on his forehead and frowned as he trained his eyepiece on two ships some distance away in the Caribbean. Cannon shots echoed across the waves, and pungent smoke laced the morning breeze. "Lambert, I see an American ship under attack by pirates." He handed the piece to his lieutenant and partner in adventures.

"I think you're right, Capt'n Jay. I see the other flag. The attacker is Spanish." The man returned the instrument.

Joshua strode to the quarterdeck railing and shouted below to his crew, "All hands on deck! Drag on every rag of canvas the sails will hold, lads. Let's help the American vessel."

A swarthy sailor stood forward below and blew a bugle alert. Shouts and mass movement spread across the *Eagle*.

Turning the eyepiece back to the battle, Joshua tightened his lips. Scurrying pirates fled the besieged ship. "They've spotted us, Lambert. Hope we're not too late."

The attacking sloop ripped away their boarding hooks, pulled anchor, and sailed southeast with full sails catching the dawn breeze. Their curses filled the air.

His lieutenant turned to him. "Will we chase them, Capt'n Jay?"

Joshua gazed at the ship with *Marigold* emblazoned on its damaged side. Nothing moved on the deck. "No, let's check on the wounded."

When they drew beside the craft, he and his crew threw hooks and boarded. Fallen sailors littered every space, and blood seeped in rivulets from one side of the ship to the other as the vessel tilted with the waves. His men stamped out the fires as best they could and

3

checked bodies for any sign of life. Joshua found the captain thrust through with a sword and all his crew around him dead.

Lambert strode up. "Capt'n, this ship's been hit below the water-line, and she's taking on water fast. We can't tarry here."

Joshua wiped smoke from his eyes. "Yes, I know." He walked to the entrance and shouted down the cabin hatchway. "We're here to help. Is anyone alive down there?" Was that coughing below or the creaking of the ship's soaked timbers?

He slid down the steps to the second deck into sloshing water and banged on doors, then kicked them open, one by one. Except for the foul-smelling liquid skidding back and forth with the roll of the ship, the deathly silence of the interior made his skin crawl. Perhaps he'd imagined the coughing.

Coming to a larger cabin entrance at the end of the corridor, he pounded on it and kicked, but it didn't budge.

Lambert's heavy tread sounded behind him. "Found one double bolted, huh? Here, let me help." The man slogged back a few steps and rushed at the entrance with his full weight and bull-like strength.

The oak wood split into pieces. Joshua barreled into the room beside his lieutenant.

~

*A*bigail's cabin door shattered from its hinges, and two burly forms armed with pistols and swords charged into her cabin. *Pirates.* She struggled to breathe and tightened both hands on the gun. *Lord, steady my aim.*

She fired the pistol. The ear-splitting charge shook her from head to toe, and acrid gunpowder stung her nose.

One of the men collapsed into the ankle-deep water. His hat flew from his dark hair into the liquid on the floor. The other, of stouter body and boasting a thick red beard, cursed, strode forward, and knocked the weapon from her hands. It landed at her feet and splashed dirty brine over Abigail's skirt. Then the pirate stepped over and knelt beside the injured one. "Capt'n, you hit?" His cold, gruff voice and blazing look he cast back at Abigail sent a chill up her spine.

The fallen intruder sat up, holding his arm. "Just nicked." He pulled a handkerchief from his person and pressed it into his shirt where a red stain spread. Groping for his plumed hat, he clutched it, shook droplets away, plunked it on his head, and stood. Muscles rippled across his shoulders and tall, lank form. The gray at his temples showed some age, but the agile movements bespoke a younger man.

Abigail blinked and swallowed. "You are...English pirates?"

The two exchanged glances, and the injured one grinned at her. "No. Privateers. We just saw your ship under attack and came to help."

Something she couldn't discern laced his deep voice. Was he telling the truth? She stared at him and tried not to be swayed by his handsome face and dark, bold eyes that tripped her heartbeat and made breathing difficult. All her senses flashed an alert. She looked him straight in the eye. "I don't believe you."

~

*J*oshua regarded the striking woman standing stiff and defiant before him, her lovely face pale as alabaster. Fire blazed from eyes the color of the sea in sunlight—a dignified female, the like of which he'd seldom seen since he'd left Charleston. He suppressed a chuckle. If he had to be shot, at least it wasn't by an island doxy.

He gave her a brief bow. "Please come. I'll show you, but we have little time." He indicated the porthole and offered his arm to assist her movement in the unsteady cabin and sloshing seawater.

She refused his gentlemanly gesture, picked up her dripping skirt, and stepped with care to the small window.

He strode behind her and the ship tilted. She fell against him, and he breathed in her womanly violet scent.

She turned, and for a moment, only inches separated their faces. Wide, startled, emerald eyes rose to his and seemed to look into his soul. Pink flooded her pale cheeks, then she reached for the cot post to steady herself, regained her footing, and stretched the space between them.

He pointed out the porthole. "Now, madam or miss, do you see my clipper ship flying the French flag? We're privateers sailing under a letter of marque from His Majesty, King Louis XVI of France." He grinned, when the frown knitting her brows deepened. "We are, however, Americans, sailing from the island of Jamaica. I am Captain Jay. My lieutenant, Lambert, is with me."

She lifted her chin, and her lovely lips softened. "I am Abigail Welch. Can you help me get to Spanish Town?"

"I'll be glad to take you to that port, but we must abandon the *Marigold* before she sinks. Will you come with us?"

The woman took a deep breath and pointed. "My trunk—the large brown one there in the corner—can you please have two of Captain Donavan's crew fetch it?" She moved toward the destroyed entrance.

Joshua caught a worried look from his lieutenant standing in the corridor outside.

He turned to the woman. "Ma'am, you must prepare yourself. The deck is not a pretty sight. Captain Donavan and all his crew, I'm afraid, are...no longer."

⁓

*W*hen Abigail came up on deck in front of the two men, she gasped and her hand flew to her mouth. Tears welled in her eyes and tumbled down her cheeks. Poor Captain Donavan and his men lay strewn about where they'd fallen. Blood streaked the tilting deck, and a terrible coppery odor permeated the air. Unable to catch her breath, she stumbled.

The man behind her who called himself Captain Jay grabbed her elbow in a firm grasp. She resisted to no avail. Was he a British privateer or a murdering pirate like those who'd attacked the *Marigold?* She meant to remove her arm from his forceful grip, but her knees trembled and gave way.

He caught her and lifted her as if she were fluff. Her cheek fell against his solid shoulder, and she breathed in the man's scent of sea and spice. A frenzied thought skittered across her stunned mind. God help her if she'd fallen into the hands of a murdering pirate.

Then blackness enveloped her like the heavy widow's weeds she'd discarded before leaving Charleston.

CHAPTER 2

*A*bigail awoke in an extraordinary cabin. Luxurious silk and satin covered the walls and the bed. She lay in the same dress in which they had rescued her. Sitting up amidst bright-colored pillows, she breathed in the warm fragrant air that streamed from the porthole. Were they in Jamaica? The memory of the brawny arms that had caught her when she'd fainted skidded into her mind and did something to her heartbeat. His crew called him Captain Jay. She looked around the room. Is this what a pirate's private chamber looked like? A bookcase lined one wall, and a desk sat nearby with its red leather chair sitting askew, as if someone had just vacated it. She fingered the silky bed covering. The captain must be a pirate. Why would a privateer have such a bedecked chamber on his ship?

A slight knock sounded at the door, and then it opened. A young black girl peeped in, smiled, and entered, holding a tray. "Hello, ma'am. So glad you've come out of your faint. Captain Jay brought you in from your poor ship. What a shock you've had. I've brought you some tea." The girl spoke perfect English. She set the food on the small table nearby and waited next to the door with her hands folded.

Abigail swung her feet to the side of the cot and stood. Someone had removed her wet slippers and replaced them with dry ones. The smell of tea and bread made her mouth water and her stomach growl. She smiled at the servant. "What's your name?"

"Charity." The brown eyes flashed Abigail's way and then lowered.

Abigail sat at the table. "Thank you for this repast. I'm famished." She unfolded the lace-edged napkin in her lap, bowed her head, and prayed a brief blessing.

"Amen," the girl echoed.

She glanced at the young woman and then fell to consuming the delicious warm bread and butter, following every bite with sips of wonderful, hot tea. When satisfied, Abigail touched the napkin to her lips and looked again at her helper. "Where are we? Is the ship docked?"

"They anchored us some distance from the Spanish Town dock, ma'am. Capt'n Jay doesn't sail the *Eagle* into the harbor."

He didn't sail into the harbor? What could that mean? "What is the rest of the captain's name? I assume he has a surname?"

The girl's brows lifted, then her expression returned to her usual placid look. "We know him as Captain Jay. He doesn't give us any other name. I'm to tell you he has a longboat ready to take you and your trunk into the port as soon as you are ready."

Abigail spied her case in the corner and abandoned her questions. Fingering her hair hanging loose about her shoulders, she glanced at her skirt marked by water at the hem. What a disaster. She turned to the young woman. "I must make my toilette. Can you bring me a bucket of water?"

"Yes, ma'am." The girl picked up the tray and left.

Moving to a tiny mirror on the wall, Abigail wiped the beads of perspiration from her upper lip and inspected her face. She sucked in a tiny breath. Her mouth now sat in firmer lines, the skin stretched more taut across her pale cheeks. Wide eyes stared back at her with uncertainty. "Courage," she whispered to her image. "You're a survivor. Not a victim."

She moved away from the looking glass. How late was she arriving? Would Mr. Scarborough, the agent, still be waiting for her in the Spanish Town harbor? He'd hired her for the governess position while she was still in Charleston. How would she find him and travel to the plantation to begin her work if he'd given up waiting for her?

She sighed and moved to her trunk. Ready or not, this was her new beginning. She'd left Charleston far behind.

Looking through her clothing, she chose what she thought would look best for a governess—a simple dark-green frock of muslin with its high white collar and cuffs.

Would she see Captain Jay before disembarking? A brief quiver rippled through her. She shook her head. No matter.

Charity returned with a steaming pail and set it on the small table.

After Abigail sponged off, the girl helped her into the dress and also brushed her hair and fashioned it into a cool chignon.

Upon completion of her toilette, Abigail affixed her bonnet and walked up to the main deck. The fresh sea breeze offered respite from the hot mid-afternoon sun. Shaggy-dressed members of the crew leered at her and whispered in an unfamiliar tongue. What kind of men did Captain Jay hire? These weren't British sailors. Proceeding to the railing, she observed the island of Jamaica in the distance. Muffled sounds of activity at the harbor floated across the waves.

Captain Jay strode toward her, the plume of his hat dancing in the gentle wind. "I assume you have friends or family to meet you upon arrival?" He leaned on the railing near her, and a smile played at his lips, making his mustache twitch. His dark eyes roved over her, and his spicy scent tickled her nose.

His nearness made her senses spin. She moved a step away. "I should have someone to meet me." She forced her gaze from him and contemplated the Jamaican shoreline. "I want to thank you for rescuing me and helping me arrive here safely, sir."

He gave her a slight bow. "At your service. Is it miss or madam?"

"Madam," she murmured. Then added, "I'm a widow of the American Revolution."

The man's eyes widened for a moment, before his face settled back into its placid confidence. "I'm sorry to hear it. My lieutenant is lowering the longboat with your trunk, and he will accompany you to the harbor. May your stay in Jamaica be pleasant." His voice sounded stilted, and he walked away without looking back.

Abigail watched him stride up the quarterdeck steps, every bit the master of his ship. She moved to the swing that would lower her over the rail into the longboat. Why had she added her status of being a widow, as if to let him know she was not married? That thought plagued her all the way to the Spanish Town dock.

~

*J*oshua watched the longboat carrying Mrs. Welch row away from the *Eagle* toward the harbor with tight lips, and his pulse throbbed in his neck. What a piece of bad luck to run into the new governess while out on a privateering expedition—that many might call pirating. He shook his head. The woman he'd rescued had to be the expected tutor. Her last remark sealed it. Even though he wasn't sure of her name, he remembered Scarborough saying the lady he'd hired in Charleston was a widow from the American Revolution. How many of those would show up at the right time his new employee was due? How would he explain what he was doing sailing on the sea when he later met her at the plantation? Thank God he was in rescue mode, not attack mode, when he met her ship.

His people at Rockford Plantation, and all of Spanish Town, knew him by his real name, Joshua Becket, and his occupation of prosperous sugar planter. They knew nothing of his secondary privateering escapades on the *Eagle*—the secret of his greater wealth. His crew knew him only as Captain Jay. He had always kept his two identities separate. And now this new governess could upset everything. He slammed his fist on the railing.

Something his father, Ethan, had said to him years earlier after exposing one of Joshua's many boyhood pranks flashed into his head. "Be sure your sins will find you out, son. It may take some time, but they will out."

Lambert strode up beside him and grinned. "Sir, you sad to see the lady go? That why you're banging on the railing and frowning like someone stole your last shilling?"

Joshua glanced at his lieutenant. Lambert was the only man who knew about Joshua's double life. "We may have a problem. That woman is the new governess coming to care for Jade."

The man's eyes widened. "You don't say?" He leaned on the railing, nodding his head. "Yep. This is a risky situation. You had no choice but to rescue her, of course. She would've drowned when the ship went down if you hadn't."

Joshua looked out over the rippling ocean. Was there a hand out there somewhere planning everything that happened? He tried to dislodge that thought which might open up a lot of other thoughts he'd avoided for years. But he'd been set up. How else could he have rescued his own governess who could now wonder about his two identities?

"Sir, you could send her back home and never have to meet her at the plantation, you know."

Lambert's words floated to Joshua as through a mist, his mind was grappling so hard with the situation. Abigail's lovely face bounced into his inner sight, a countenance he found most attractive. And not only that, the woman had spunk and courage. A proper lady, very different from his tavern doxies. Something akin to shame tugged at his heart, but he cast it aside as he always did.

Maybe he would send the woman back home. Wouldn't that solve it? He could make up some kind of excuse and have Scarborough attend to it, and then send for another governess. No way could this situation of his rescuing the next governess reoccur.

He took a deep breath. "I *could* send her back. That may be the solution, my man, but I'll have to think about it." He turned and walked to his cabin.

~

*A*t the harbor, a gentleman approached Abigail almost as soon as she climbed from the longboat. He wore a tan waistcoat with lace at the sleeves and on his cravat, white breeches, and knee stockings. A wide-brimmed straw hat sat atop hair gray at the temples. In the blinding sunlight, she couldn't be sure who was beneath the sunhat.

The man doffed the straw head covering. "Hello, madam. You'll remember me. Scarborough. We met in Charleston."

Abigail lifted her hand to shade her eyes and smiled. "Oh, yes, sir. I was wondering if I'd have a problem finding you when I arrived."

"Heard about the pirate attack on the *Marigold*. So glad you survived. Everything is ready for you at the plantation." He motioned to a man standing beside a wagon with a white horse harnessed to it. "Here's Mr. Dykes, who will drive you out to Rockford. You'll make it before the sun goes down, I'll wager."

Abigail looked at a merry little man with tanned, wrinkled skin and pale blue eyes. He wore a faded waistcoat and a tricorn that had seen better days. Ginger hair sprang from under the hat, and his brows and mustache were the same reddish-blond shade.

He walked up to her, clutching his hat. "Yes, ma'am. We'll make it well before sundown with old Dolly here. Be that your trunk on the wharf? Let me load it. You and me and Dolly'll soon be home.

After he pushed her belongings into the back, Abigail let him assist her into the wagon. "Is it far to the plantation?"

The agent, still standing by, answered. "It's a ways out, but I wager you'll enjoy seeing that part of the island." He replaced his hat as the conveyance moved away.

Mr. Dykes clucked his tongue, and the horse trotted down the road between rows of shanty-type houses. The smell of pork roasting mingled with the odor of wastewater in the narrow ditches alongside the street assailed Abigail's nose. Children's joyous cries and goats bleating echoed from yards next to the small houses. As they progressed inland, the houses grew larger and farther apart. The wagon soon left the bustling seaport of Spanish Town behind for fields of sugarcane waving in the warm breeze. Plowed earth and a green scent replaced the smells of the town.

Mr. Dykes took a deep breath of the country air. "Old Dolly'll carry us to Rockford in good time, ma'am, don't you worrit none. Don't let the horse fool you. She's got a little age on her, but she'll be wanting to get home to her stall long before the sun sinks."

Since the man seemed talkative, Abigail could not resist trying to discover something about Rockford Plantation and the people among whom she was going to live. "Where did the plantation get its name?"

"Them folks from England called Rockfords built it many years ago. After several poor harvests and happenings, what was left of the family put it up for sale and went back to England about twenty-five years ago." He turned to glance at her. "There was something about one of them staying on to haunt the place, but I've never seen the ghost myself. You believe in ghosts, miss, or is it madam?"

Abigail cleared her throat. "I am a widow, so it's madam. I do not believe in ghosts, Mr. Dykes, and I hope you don't."

"Well, I've never seen one, Rockford or not, but some of the slave girls say they've seen her on stormy nights. It's supposed to be one of the Rockford ladies that died young from some mishap or other."

"So Mr. Becket bought the plantation when it went up for sale?"

"Not then. I understand it had two or three owners until about five years ago when Mr. Becket bought the entire estate, lock, stock, and barrel, so I was told. We came on after then, but Mrs. Pelfrey, she was there with the Rockfords. It's a sugar plantation, you understand, but I don't have nuttin' to do with the sugar growing. I'm the gardener and me wife Lucy is the chief cook. We got our boy, Jeremy. He's eight. We're indentured for two more years, and we live above the stables."

"Who else works at the plantation?"

"Well, there's the odd house slaves, girls and young men, who take care of things, and the black butler, Walter. He's a pretty good chap. Born a Maroon but got religion now." Mr. Dykes didn't pause long enough for Abigail to ask what a Maroon was. "And Mrs. Pelfrey, the housekeeper. She keeps the house straight and the servants. Then there's Mr. Bishop, the plantation overseer. He sees about the sugar planting and harvesting and oversees about four hundred slaves. You don't want to mess with him. I've seen him deal lots of cruelty toward the slaves."

Abigail's grip on the wagon seat tightened. "But doesn't the owner intervene in such cases?"

"Not much. Mr. Becket's gone a lot. So Bishop has free rein, sorry to say." He glanced at her. "But not to worry. I'm talking out of turn. Mrs. Pelfrey's a great one for order and running the house and gardens well where you'll be staying and caring for little Jade. That is right, isn't it? You're the new governess?"

"Yes."

"I hope you'll stay longer than the last one."

Abigail turned to look at the man. "The last one? How many have there been?"

"Only two. And methinks they was too young to know how to handle a child that's a bit frisky and determined to have her own way most of the time. Or they was not right for the job. Jade's a pretty one and smart too. But you have to keep your eye on her. One has to think it's because of what she's been through."

Oh dear. Might she, too, not be right for the job? Abigail wiped her damp forehead with her handkerchief. Of course, she would be able to care for the child. The Lord would help her. This was why He'd brought her to Jamaica, wasn't it?

"You know little Jade has a sad story, right?"

"Not really. I was just told she was Mr. Becket's child, aged seven, and needed an English governess, since her mother had died." She stared at the man, curious. Surely it would be best to get all the information she could on her new charge, gossip or not.

The man transferred both reins into his left hand and scratched his bearded chin. "Jade's a wood's colt, if you know what I mean."

"Wood's colt?" The driver had her full attention.

"Mrs. Pelfrey found out Jade's mother was a doxy at James Tavern and there was never no ceremony." The man chuckled. "Nothing stays hidden from the housekeeper."

Was that a warning?

"When the mother got shot and killed in a brawl, the tavern owner brought Jade—about age three at the time—and left her on our doorstep. Note said the doxy told him Mr. Becket was the father. I was the one who first found her, making my morning garden rounds. She wasn't crying, just sitting there sucking her thumb, clasping a dirty doll and with a hound dog lying beside her. Mrs. Pelfrey fell in love with the baby and spoiled her right good. That's what she did. Now you got your work cut out for you." He spit over the side of the buggy. "And Mr. Becket never denied she was his. Looks too much like him, if you ask me."

Abigail took a deep breath. A resident ghost and her charge labeled a wood's colt whose mother was a doxy. How many more surprises awaited her at Rockford Plantation? She turned and looked at bright magenta-red blooms climbing and covering the hilly roadside they passed. "What are these beautiful flowers?"

"Them's bougainvillea. You'll see a lot of 'em in Jamaica. I keep some growing on trellises around the house. Easy to grow here. We got lots of flowers I take care of, and I tend the kitchen vegetable garden too. We got a long growing season here. Not a bit like England."

Relieved that she'd gotten the man into his element and away from gossip, Abigail relaxed against the wagon bench. The trip passed quickly as the sun slipped down in the sky.

Passing around a bend, Dolly trotted faster, and Abigail had to hold onto her bonnet and the arm of her seat.

"She knows she's gonna soon be in her stall and eating her oats." Mr. Dykes smiled and let the horse have her head.

They came to a long white stucco wall and then to a wide black wrought iron double gate. A small boy sat on the wall near the entrance. He jumped to the ground and pulled the gates open before Dolly reached them. The wagon entered, and Abigail delighted in her first sight of the plantation great house encompassed with green lawns and flowering hedges. Giant palm trees lined the drive to the three-story structure with its double sets of steps leading to the upper- level main entrance. The setting sun shaded the entire scene in various shades of pink, orange, and purple.

Mr. Dykes stopped the wagon at the first set of brick steps. Servants emerged from the sprawling verandas that encircled the house and came down to them, laughing and clapping. They appeared to be teenagers. A large reddish-blond hound-like dog came with them, barking.

"Pay them young'uns no mind, ma'am. They get excited with every guest. And Potcake knows the difference between a genuine visitor and an intruder. He's Jade's dog."

"Potcake? Is that the dog's name?"

"Yes'm. That's his name and his breed. It's a mixed breed been here loose on the islands for I don't know how long. He's getting older these days, but Jade still loves the critter."

He assisted Abigail from the wagon, and a bright-eyed servant girl came forward and curtsied. "Mrs. Pelfrey is waiting to see you, ma'am. Will you come with me?"

Abigail adjusted her bonnet, smiled, and nodded, then followed the young woman up the stairs as the other servants parted to make a path for them. They stopped chattering until she passed. A glance back assured Abigail that two young men started up the steps, holding her trunk between them.

Potcake rambled up to sniff her skirts. She gasped before she noticed his wagging tail. Thank goodness, the intimidating dog seemed to know she was a welcome visitor. She bent to pat the wide head with its black brows and silver-streaked muzzle confirming his age. "Hello, Potcake. You and I are going to be friends." Hadn't dogs always been her favorite animal friend after horses?

She and the girl entered the wide oak door held open by an African servant standing to attention in the spotless uniform of a butler. Gray highlighted his temples, but muscles bulged in his shoulders. Walter? The man nodded to her, and Abigail smiled.

She looked around the large entrance hall with its colorful tiled floor and polished oak walls. A sideboard with a petticoat mirror at the bottom sat on one side, holding a large vase of the red flowers she'd seen from the wagon.

A tall lady with a white cap on her gray hair and wearing a stiff white apron appeared in an inner doorway. A chain of keys circled her ample waist. More than the chain, her look of authority designated her as the housekeeper. The careful attention she drew from the servants confirmed it.

"I am Mrs. Pelfrey, the housekeeper. I trust you had a pleasant journey from Spanish Town, Mrs. Welch." The woman spoke in a clear, dominating voice.

"Very good, thank you." At least from Spanish Town. But from Charleston to the island…she shuddered.

The woman nodded. "But no doubt tiring. You're needing a rest, is my guess. Come on in. You shall have a good cup of tea in my room while the servants take your trunk up and the girls unpack it for you." She dismissed the servants with a nod of her head, sending the two young men carrying Abigail's trunk and the girls toward the grand staircase that dominated the end of the atrium.

Tea and rest. Abigail sighed. "Yes, delightful." She thanked the woman and followed her down another hall, up a set of narrow stairs, and through a door at the top. Rays of the sunset through a large window bathed the room in soft light.

Mrs. Pelfrey lit a lamp on a desk and showed a padded rocker to Abigail. She pulled a bell rope, then sat opposite her guest in a blue brocaded chair. "I do hope you will be happy at Rockford, Mrs. Welch, and that you and Jade get on. That's the important thing. She's precocious and quick, if I say so myself. I've taken a special interest in her, not having children of my own."

"I'm looking forward to meeting Jade." Precocious and quick. Interesting words. Had the other two governesses not gotten on with the child? Or was the girl undisciplined as Mr. Dykes hinted?

A servant knocked, then entered. "You rang, Mrs. Pelfrey?" A pretty young woman with a soft coffee-colored face and shining black eyes stood before them. She wore a simple muslin dress, and a white kerchief covered her hair.

"Yes, bring us the tea tray I set out, Clarissa, and see that you don't tilt it coming up the stairs. And then make certain Mrs. Welch's room is ready and her trunk unpacked. I'm sure she'll want water brought to freshen up before dinner. Can you remember all this?"

"Yes, ma'am." The girl curtsied and left.

"We have to train these girls from the ground up when they're brought in from the farm. But Clarissa is doing well. I can even trust her to help train the younger ones. I've taught her to read and write too. The trick is to keep her from getting involved with any of the young men on the plantation. She could end up with a passel of children before she's twenty and get dragged down before her time. I've seen it happen." Mrs. Pelfrey leaned back in her chair, nodding.

Abigail removed her bonnet and relaxed. The housekeeper was a woman who would stand no nonsense and who had her own brand of common sense. Dykes's tale of a ghost could cause no concern to such a person. What ghost would dare to inhabit a house of which Mrs. Pelfrey had charge?

A bountiful tea tray with its strong black tea, small, tasty sandwiches, and biscuits arrived and energized Abigail. A few minutes later, trekking up the impressive grand staircase behind Mrs. Pelfrey, shivers of excitement flew up Abigail's back. What grand adventures awaited her here?

The large room Mrs. Pelfrey showed her on the third floor boasted enormous front windows with padded seats from which one could see the front entrance, lawn, and palm trees. A four-poster bed looked comfortable and inviting. The rest of the furniture included a tallboy, chest of drawers, dresser, a small table, and chair. Rugs covered much of the floor, and the boards not covered boasted a high polish. A fireplace filled one wall. Did one ever need a fire in the island's tropical weather?

"We observe dinner at eight, and yours will be brought here to you, or you can have your meal there with Jade in the schoolroom." The woman gestured to a connecting door in the wall as she spoke. Of course, a governess would not dine in the great house dining room. "And Jade's room is beyond that."

So the schoolroom separated her and the child. She gave the housekeeper a warm smile and gestured around the space. "This is a pleasant room. I'm sure I'll be happy here. Where is Jade at this time of day? I'd like to meet her."

"She is outside playing somewhere but knows to come back in before dark."

"And when shall I meet her father?"

Mrs. Pelfrey sniffed as if Abigail had asked an impertinent question. "Whenever he returns, which could be tonight, tomorrow, or a week from now." Then she turned and left.

After freshening up, Abigail sat on her window seat and stared out across the lawn and entrance. The shadows lengthened into darkness. Still, Jade did not appear. Where could the child be? And was anyone, other than herself, concerned?

~

That night on his ship, as sleep escaped him, a familiar voice murmured in Joshua's inner ear. *I'm going to be praying for you, Joshua, no matter how long it takes, that you'll turn back to righteousness.* He knew that voice—his father Ethan's—that long ago day he'd boarded the ship banished to Jamaica for his so-called sins in Charleston.

Bitterness rose in his heart and left a familiar metallic taste in his mouth. Stepbrother Samuel had called his actions crimes that could land him in the noose if he refused to leave Charleston. So he'd left and escaped that judgment.

He smiled. And he'd escape any other threat. He'd made a good life in Jamaica. He had enough gold to buy his way out of any problem now. But Abigail's lovely, straightforward, and honest face floated before his eyes and challenged him. Then an idea of how to handle any of her questions came into his mind, so amazing in its simplicity that he turned on his bed and fell into a deep sleep.

CHAPTER 3

The next day, Joshua docked the *Eagle* in the usual secret cove, and after dividing spoils with the crew, he dismissed all but his lieutenant. The two of them walked toward the small stable secluded in the trees. His servant, who cared for their horses while Joshua sailed on his adventures, had their two Arabians bridled and saddled in the passage.

"Capt'n, you figured out what to do about that nice-looking governess?" Lambert's eyes twinkled and a smile played at his lips.

"Got a great idea. All I have to do is tell her I'm a secret agent for the British authorities to track down pirates and seize their ships."

"That is a good one, sir. I couldn't have thought of a better scheme myself."

"And swear her to secrecy, of course." Joshua grinned at the easy way out of the predicament.

They mounted and galloped toward Rockford Plantation as the sun dropped lower in the west and painted the landscape in brilliant shades of red and amethyst. At the plantation's back entrance, Joshua dismounted and handed the reins to the servant standing nearby. The stable hand walked away with both horses as Joshua bounded up the steps with Lambert behind him. They burst into the kitchen, fragrant with scents of roasting meat and fresh bread baking.

Joshua whipped off his tricorn and hung it on a hook near the door. "What have you got cooking, Lucy? We're a couple of starving men."

The woman standing over the enormous fireplace turned beef ribs on a spit. Her face, reddened by the heat, spread in a big smile as they entered. "We've got one of your favorites, sir. And it'll be ready as soon as you two are."

Lambert sat at the large kitchen table, and Joshua proceeded up the servant steps instead of the grand staircase to his room on the second floor. He washed up and changed into his gentleman's attire, all the while remembering the lovely face and demeanor of Abigail Welch. On the way back downstairs, he stopped by the mirror over his bureau and made sure his mustache was smooth and his black hair still passable in its queue, except for the few waves that always escaped from his tieback. He met Mrs. Pelfrey in the hall.

She stopped and gave him a short curtsy. "Sir, I'm glad you're back in time for dinner."

"Did the new governess arrive?"

"Yes, sir. She did. I was just going to tell her that Jade is now in her room, and I can have both their dinners sent up."

"No, send the governess down to the dining room. She'll dine with me."

Mrs. Pelfrey's eyes widened. "But sir..."

He raised an eyebrow at her, and she stopped her words in mid-sentence. "Yes, sir. I'll inform her." She hurried down the hall, shaking her head, and up another set of steps as he watched.

*A*bigail answered the knock at her door and admitted the housekeeper.

"Mr. Becket has arrived and wishes you to come down to the

dining room for your meal." The woman's voice carried a tone of rebuke.

Determined to be friends with the woman, Abigail looked at her and smiled. "But the maid just informed me Jade was now in her room. I thought we'd take our meal together and get to know one another." Her empty stomach rumbled.

No hint of friendliness arose on the housekeeper's stiff face. "What the master wants, he gets, madam. So make haste. You can see about Jade later, or even in the morning. That, perhaps, would be best for a fresh start."

"Actually, I don't even know where the dining room is."

"I will take you. Are you ready to go?" The woman tapped her slipper.

Abigail glanced in the small mirror over her dresser and pushed a curl back into its place in the twist at her neck. She straightened the skirt of her blue muslin. "Yes, of course." She tried in vain to keep resignation out of her voice. Perhaps it was best to face her employer this first evening, in case she decided...what?

She straightened her back and took a deep breath. There would be no turning back. She needed this position, and a new beginning, and she would have it, God willing. Following the housekeeper down two flights and to the dining room, she set her face in pleasant lines.

On the first floor, Mrs. Pelfrey opened thick double doors, gestured Abigail into a large dining room, and left her.

An exquisite chandelier lit the long table. A servant finished laying out two place settings of brilliant red china, gleaming silver goblets, utensils, and snow-white lace-edged napkins. A tinkling sound accompanied her actions.

Movement near the fireplace on the far side of the room drew Abigail's attention. A man stood with his hands thrust into his pockets and stared into the empty hearth. He wore a dark blue waistcoat with a white cravat. His curly black hair, streaked with gray at the temples, stretched back in a queue tied with a leather cord. Even in the shadows, she was aware of his height and physical prowess, evidenced by the close fit of his coat over wide shoulders. An air of careless elegance clung to him, as though he thought nothing about his clothes but could not help looking well in them.

He turned to face her, and she gasped—the captain who had rescued her at sea. How could it be? The person she had her doubts was a privateer, not a pirate, as he'd claimed.

The man strode to her with his hand outstretched. "Good evening, Mrs. Welch. I hope I haven't shocked you too much. I am Joshua Becket." He leaned closer and whispered, "And Captain Jay as well."

A scent of spice tickled her nose. A tingle ran up her arm when his large hand enclosed hers with its firm clasp. He drew her to the table, and she dropped into the chair he held for her, trying to overcome her shock. What had she gotten herself into coming to Jamaica?

He took his place at the head, she on his right. He looked every bit the wealthy sugar plantation owner, not the pirate-like captain tantalizing her memory. In that illuminating moment, she knew there were two men in that body—two distinct personalities—one who moved in the planter world as a gentleman, and one who remained hidden sailing on the high seas. How would she ever fit into this strange picture?

The servants filled their goblets and served the ribs, steamed cabbage, potatoes, beets, and fresh bread. Then he dismissed them with a snap of his fingers. "Please enjoy the repast, Mrs. Welch. I will soon make all plain to you." He gave her a wide smile and started on his plate of food with gusto without further comment.

Abigail endeavored to taste the food, but her former appetite eluded her.

"I have much to share with you. May I call you Abigail?" Her host spoke between large forkfuls of food interspersed with swigs from the goblet.

Abigail laid down her utensil. "Yes, but might I ask that you call me Mrs. Welch in front of your daughter?" That, of course, depended on if she stayed on as a governess. How could she justify working for a possible pirate?

He chuckled. "Yes, we must maintain the proprieties in front of Jade. I hope you can teach her some appropriate behaviors, Abigail."

He grinned. "But Mrs. Welch it shall be in front of the child and the servants." He continued to enjoy the food.

Abigail found it hard to swallow many bites of her own in his charismatic presence. But what she managed to taste proved delicious.

"Do you like Jamaica and Rockford Plantation? Think you might be happy working here?"

"There's a lot here to enjoy. But I have not yet met your daughter, Jade. I hope she likes me."

"Of course, she'll like you. And she has a quick mind and loves to learn new things. If you can keep her occupied and interested, you'll do well with her. I've no doubt."

Did he say this to the other two governesses?

A servant entered to refill the goblets. He waited until the man left, then swiped his lips with his napkin and leaned toward her. "I've something to tell you, Abigail. And I must ask you to keep it confidential. I believe you are a woman of integrity. James Scarborough spoke well of you when he brought your application to me. Can you do this? I mean, tell no one here at the plantation or in Spanish Town what I'm going to share with you?"

Her heart skipped a beat. What was he sharing with her, and why so concerned that others not know it? "Yes, sir, I believe I can." She wanted to add, *unless it harms someone to keep it secret.* And did he think she'd be spending any time in the town to share anything with anyone? His handsome face turned toward her and made her breath catch. He projected an energy and power that attracted her. She leaned back in her chair to put a bit more space between them.

He smiled. "I'm sure you're wondering how I could be both Captain Jay and island plantation owner. Right?"

She sat her fork on the edge of her plate and dabbed her lips with the lacy napkin. "Well, that question has occurred to me."

"This is how, and it's what you must keep confidential as long as you are in Jamaica." He leaned closer. "I am a secret agent for the British to hunt down and plunder any pirates that dare to threaten our waters." His powerful voice dropped almost to a whisper, and his dark eyes gleamed.

Her thoughts spun. Faces of his crew flashed across her mind. Except for his lieutenant, Lambert, his troops had looked more like pirates than British militia. And he flew a French flag, not British.

He was staring at her. His countenance exuded both strength and cruelty. She took a deep breath. "I see. But why did you fly a French flag if you work for the British?"

He snapped his fingers. "Oh that. I'm authorized to fly whatever flag needed to get whatever job done that needs doing. And that protects the British from involvement and any repercussions. Understand now?"

"I suppose so." What did she know of such things in the Caribbean? The candlelight and his forceful close proximity drew a favorable response from her in spite of her misgivings.

He leaned closer. "Can you do this for me, Abigail? Can you keep my alias secret? My life could depend upon it." His gaze traveled over her face and searched her eyes. His dark mustache shadowed his thin lips stretched in a half grin. There was a maddening hint of arrogance about him, as if he expected her to do whatever he asked without question.

The very air around them seemed to vibrate, and she looked away. A warning voice whispered in her head, but she only half listened. The child had already lost her mother through violence. How could Jade's father expect to stay out of harm's way living such a double life? But whatever her employer did or didn't do was not in the realm of her responsibility, was it? She met his eyes with a calmness that surprised her, since she fought to keep her breathing even. "I have no problem keeping confidences, Mr. Becket. Yours will be safe with me."

He beamed at her, stood, and walked over to help move her chair so she could stand.

"We will get along fine, Mrs. Welch, I'm sure. Thank you for coming to Jamaica. I look forward to Jade's schooling and any improvement you can foster." He nodded toward a servant who appeared to clear the table, and then he strode toward the hall entrance.

Abigail's brows knit. "Sir, do you have any instructions for Jade's studies or the best schedule to follow with her?"

He turned and flashed another of his disarming smiles. "That's up to you, Mrs. Welch. You can ask Mrs. Pelfrey if you have questions. The child needs a firm hand and interesting lessons. We'll talk again after you've gotten to know Jade."

How firm a hand? Had they taught the child any discipline at all? She must have another talk with him once she knew more about her charge.

Abigail found her way to her room. A maid, who said she was Clarissa's sister, Mira, met her in the hall and told Abigail she had just tucked Jade into bed. The young woman had dark, lively eyes and a blue kerchief over her thick, curly hair.

Opening the door to the schoolroom, Abigail traversed the area to the child's bedroom, then toward the cot in the corner. Potcake lifted his wide head from the foot of the bed, sniffed at Abigail, then dropped his muzzle back on his paws.

The little girl moved, then lay still in her bed, her long black curls spread across her pillow.

"Jade," she whispered.

There was no answer. But the child lay there in her bed, her eyes closed—a little too tight.

Abigail bent over her. "I'm Mrs. Welch, your new governess. We're going to be friends."

Still no response. Jade pretended to be asleep.

"Goodnight, young lady."

Abigail turned back to the schoolroom, then to her room and closed the connecting doors. She undressed and dropped into her own bed, exhausted. It had been a long day.

Troubled thoughts and blurred dreams broke her rest that night. She would fall asleep, then awaken, startled. She did this several times, and each time, a segment of her day flashed into her mind. The long drive from Spanish Town to Rockford Plantation and the tales and gossip of Mr. Dykes. The housekeeper's chilly response when Abigail asked when she'd see her employer. But two main images that reoccurred and troubled her were those of Joshua Becket in a satin coat and cravat at his abundant table, dining—and Captain Jay with a jaunty, plumed hat on the quarterdeck of his ship, leading a possible pirate crew. The man was an enigma.

Then there was another issue. When his handsome face grinned at her, she fought a wild excitement—and then trembled under a fearful premonition. What could it mean? How could she be subject to two opposite emotions at the same time?

She finally sat up, reached for her Bible on the nightstand, and read until she could no longer hold her head up. Then she fell into a deep sleep until daylight crept through her window and danced against her eyelids.

Abigail dressed and hurried into the schoolroom.

Jade sat at a table eating from a large bowl of what appeared to be oatmeal. A small jar of honey sat beside her. She looked up at Abigail and smiled, then continued to spoon in the food. The dog, Potcake, sitting at the child's foot, pricked his ears at Abigail when she entered, and then turned his full attention back to the eating in progress.

Mira, standing nearby, approached. "Ma'am, would you like your breakfast brought to the schoolroom?"

"Yes."

The maid hurried out the door.

Encouraged by Jade's smile, Abigail sat across from the child and admired her pretty green eyes when they lifted toward her. Was that why her mother named her Jade? The thick, curly black hair secured in two plaits across her shoulders reminded her of Mr. Becket, as did her facial features in a feminine version. "I'm Mrs. Welch. Were you asleep last night when I came in to tell you good night?" She gave the youngster a generous smile to let her know she wasn't chiding her.

The emerald eyes darkened, then brightened, and the child laughed. "I fooled you, didn't I?"

"Pretty much. But I had my doubts."

A drawing pad lay on the table, and Abigail pulled it over and exclaimed as she leafed through the pencil sketches of animals and flowers. "Oh, my, these are good. Is this your work?"

Jade stood, grabbed the pad, and closed it with a thump. "No one touches anything of mine without permission." She moved the artwork out of Abigail's reach and slumped back in her chair.

Abigail's heart jumped into her throat. The last thing she wanted to do was elicit animosity at their first meeting. Her success as a governess, and her new beginning, depended on this child responding well to her. "I'm sorry, Jade. But I repeat, the work is very good. Is it yours?"

"That's no business of yours. Remember, no one is to touch anything of mine without permission." Her eyes blazed before she lowered them to her breakfast. She moved her bowl to the floor for Potcake to enjoy the rest of her oatmeal.

Abigail's brows rose. "Very well, young lady. I accept your rule. Now let's talk about mine."

Jade's chin lifted and her lower lip protruded. "Your rules? Mrs. Pelfrey makes all the rules here."

An abrupt knock sounded at the door, and Mira walked in with Abigail's breakfast tray and set it on the table. She gave one glance at the child, shook her head, and left. Had she overheard the disrespectful retort?

As soon as Potcake finished licking the bowl clean, Jade jumped up and ran out the door with the dog loping behind her. She carried the drawing notebook with her.

The wonderful aroma of bacon, eggs, fresh bread, and tea made her empty stomach rumble. Food. She needed strength before going after the child, so she lifted the dome over her plate and, in a leisurely fashion, enjoyed her meal.

As she finished her last cup of tea, Mrs. Pelfrey entered the schoolroom, swished over to the table, and sat across from Abigail. She wore a dress of dark blue with her usual white apron. "I saw Jade running past the kitchen window. Did you two get along?"

Abigail touched her napkin to her lips and took a deep breath. "In a way, yes, and in a way, no. I leafed through a drawing tablet she had on the table and remarked on how well the work was done. But she wasn't happy for me to see the artwork."

"Was it a blue tablet with animals and flowers?"

Abigail nodded.

"Well, that's her mother's artwork, and she's very protective of anything that belonged to her mother. So now you know."

"Her mother had artistic talent?"

"Seems odd, doesn't it, for a tavern doxy, but yes, she did from what I've seen in that tablet. I assume Mr. Dykes told you Jade's story?"

"He told me they left her on the doorstep about age three. Is that right?"

"Yes, and she was the prettiest little thing and didn't seem to mind her new place at all, with Potcake lying beside her. I took right to her." Mrs. Pelfrey lowered her eyes. "By the time she was five, I knew I was out of my depth. She could twist me around her little finger. We got to where we couldn't handle her and take care of the house as well. That's when I begged Mr. Becket to hire a governess."

Abigail's spirit took a dive. So she had a genuine job on her hands. Age seven was a bit late to begin correct discipline of a child. But given the child's heartrending history, didn't she deserve Abigail's best effort? With God's help, she would give it.

"Do you have any idea where Jade might have run off to this morning?"

"Well, it being Saturday, she knew there'd be no lessons, so I expect she's gone down to the hut at the edge of our wood. A slave woman who is too old to work, Granny Mae, lives there, and she's taken the child's fancy with her stories and herbs. Some say she practices some kind of root doctoring. Mr. Becket doesn't like her going there, but who can stop her? And the dog goes wherever the child goes, and he'd never let harm come to her."

Abigail went to her room and changed into comfortable walking shoes. She strode out the house's main entrance and reveled in the smells of trimmed grass and flowers in beds as she passed. The sun broke forth from behind a cloud and danced on her arms.

Skirting the side of the great house, she headed down the hill toward the line of trees some distance past the stables and soon found a path to follow toward the woods. The cloud moved over the sun again, and shadows fell across Abigail's way. Birdsong in the trees ceased, and a chill cooled her back. Her steps slackened.

Every tale she'd heard about root doctoring, witchcraft, and voodoo reported on Charleston plantations flashed across her mind. Stories abounded of healers who worked with dolls, herbs, charms, powder made of ground human bones, and substances one could use to prevent attack of evil spirits. She'd always cast the accounts aside as more fantasy and deception than truth. But one fact sent a shiver through her. A lot of the practices, according to her father, originated on islands like Jamaica. And her charge was visiting such a practitioner?

Abigail's breath caught in her throat, and she quickened her pace.

CHAPTER 4

$\mathcal{A}$ bigail shook off her uneasiness as the sun reappeared bright and strong. She approached a small cabin at the fringe of the forest. Jade sat on the porch beside a thin, elderly black woman who had her gray hair pulled into a ball at the back of her head. Curly wisps escaped the bun and framed her face. Across her cheeks, forehead, neck, and chin, a multitude of fine lines crisscrossed like the underside of a leaf. When her dark eyes lifted and she saw Abigail, a wide grin stretched the full, soft lips.

Potcake chewed on a bone at the porch's edge.

The woman spit tobacco juice into a bucket beside her rocking chair, wiped her mouth with the edge of her apron, and stood. Then she gestured to a corn-shuck-bottomed chair. "Come on up and sit a spell, if you'd like, ma'am. Me and the young'un done been in the garden, and I needed to rest me weary bones." She looked up at the sky as a small cloud moved to blot out part of the sun. "We might get a shower 'fore the day's out."

Abigail stopped at the step made of a large rock and smiled at the small, bent figure. She hardly seemed a danger of any kind. "I'm Mrs. Welch, Jade's new governess."

The woman wore sachets pinned to her skirt. She nodded her head and spit again into the spittoon and wiped her lips. "And Granny Mae is what most folks call me."

Jade held a bouquet of flowers and stems, and she leaned forward and extended the plants to Abigail. "Smell."

Abigail breathed in lavender and several other scents she couldn't name.

"Now, Miss Jade, you 'member the names of them plants?" Granny cast her dark eyes toward the child. "I ain't wasting my time wi' ye, am I?"

Jade drew the bouquet close and pointed as she called out names. "Lavender, borage, ginseng, curled mint, chamomile, and gray horehound."

Granny nodded and gave a wide, toothless grin.

Abigail couldn't help being impressed. "That's wonderful you've learned about these plants, Jade. I'm proud of you."

Color appeared in the child's cheeks, and she lowered her head. But a smile played at the corner of her mouth.

"She's learned them names. But don't ask her what they good for yet. We're still working on that." The woman reached a wizened hand out and pinched a leaf off a stem with purple flowers in Jade's bouquet. She held it out to Abigail. "Rub this leaf together and tell me what you smell."

Abigail took the leaf, rubbed it together, and sniffed. "Sage, I believe." A distant rumble in the sky made her look up. More dark clouds gathered above the trees, and a gathering wind shook their limbs.

"Yes'm, and I bet you know folks dry these leaves and pound 'em into powder and put it into breading dishes with meat."

For a moment, a memory of cornbread dressing made by Georgia's Aunt Reba flowed into Abigail's mind. Reba used sage in breading to go with fowl. She'd once seen Reba pounding the leaves into powder. The spicy, woodsy, fragrance filled the kitchen.

A streak of lightning flashed across the clouds, followed by a clap of thunder, and Jade stood from her chair, her face contorted with fright.

Abigail reached toward the child. "Come, we must hurry if we want to miss the rain." How fast storms must come in the tropics.

Jade grasped her hand and jumped off the low porch. Potcake rose, too, with his bone clamped between his teeth, and loped back toward the great house ahead of them.

Granny Mae stood and shouted to them as they hurried away. "You'uns come back and see ole granny when you can. Don't fret. The rain'll stop as fast as it starts."

The wind buffeted them as they sprinted back up the path. Abigail's hairpins worked loose, and her hair fell about her shoulders.

They made it into the stable just before the sky split into a downpour. Abigail took a deep breath and enjoyed the scent of hay and farm animals and the sound of rain pelting the roof. Down the corridor, horses neighed a welcome, but somewhere, hooves struck a wooden wall. She walked to a bale of hay and sat, but Jade stayed close by the barn opening, far enough inside to avoid the sheet of rain falling heavy at the entrance. Abigail pushed her fallen tresses behind her shoulders. "Come sit here with me until the worst of the rain stops."

"No, thank you. I don't like barns and 'specially don't like horses. That's Joshua's stallion you heard kicking. He hates storms."

The child called her father by his first name? "Why don't you like horses? I love riding and bet you would too. I'll be glad to teach you."

"Horses are too big, and they scare me."

Had something happened to the child that brought on this fear? Abigail would need to ask Mrs. Pelfrey.

The thud of heavy footfalls sounded near outside, and a figure burst in from the rain. Jade moved aside as Joshua Becket jerked off his hat and shook the water from its rim.

"So this is where you were. Mrs. Pelfrey was concerned you two were caught out in the flash storm."

His gaze raked over Abigail's disheveled hair and down to her sensible shoes. Warmth flowed into her cheeks. Then he turned his attention to Jade, who still held her bouquet of herbs.

Abigail cleared her throat and tried to force her eyes away from the striking figure he made in what must be his plantation working clothes—tan shirt, breeches, and tall black boots. The shirt, wet with rain, clung to strong, muscular shoulders.

The child shrank from the frown he gave her. "Young lady, what's that you're holding?"

Jade thrust the bouquet behind her and lowered her chin.

Abigail stood and placed her arm about the girl's shoulders."It's only some herbal plants she's collected. We—" She had started to say they had been to Granny Mae's, but Mr. Becket's darker frown stopped further words.

He flashed dark eyes from Abigail to the child. "Jade, you know I've forbidden you to visit that root doctor. Am I going to have to send her off the plantation? Is that what you want?"

Jade's lip quivered, and she blinked three times before answering in a small voice. "No, sir."

Abigail stiffened. Was this the way Joshua Becket conversed with his daughter, intimidating her?

He glanced at Abigail, as if sensing her disagreement. "Now you know, too, Mrs. Welch, if you didn't know before. That cabin is off limits for my daughter."

Abigail did not trust herself to speak. She nodded and placed her hand on Jade's shoulder.

Joshua turned and strode back out the barn door. The rain had ceased as fast as it had begun.

A boy tumbled from the loft just behind them. He rolled in the hay on the barn floor and jumped to his feet, as agile as a monkey. He appeared to be eight or nine. A tuft of blond hair flowed over his tanned forehead. "Hey, Jade. Glad you didn't get soaked."

Jade thrust out her chin and ignored him. Perhaps she guessed that he may have heard her father's harsh words to her.

Abigail smiled at the youngster. "And who might you be? Mr. Dykes's son, maybe?"

"That's exactly who I am." He gave a quick bow. "Jeremy Dykes at your service, ma'am." His gaze flew back to Jade.

The child tossed her head and walked out the door without acknowledging him.

His face tightened as he stared after her.

Abigail laid a hand on his shoulder. "Sorry, Jeremy. Jade's not in a sociable mood right now." She turned to follow the child back to the house.

The boy called after her. "Aw, don't you worry none, ma'am. I've put up with Jade's moods since she was three."

~

*O*nce in the schoolroom, Jade swiped a tear from her cheek and threw the bouquet into the trash.

Abigail bent and lifted the stems from the bin and laid them on the table. "Jade, have you ever learned how to press flowers or plants?"

The girl's eyes turned round and hopeful, and Abigail went to the bookcase and pulled down three of the largest books she could find on the upper shelf.

She had Jade make a list of the plants she wanted to press and save. After showing Jade how to prepare the plants, Abigail retrieved a box of stationery she had in her trunk and helped the girl label the sheets, then place each plant between two sheets, and then between the pages of a book. As they finished the last of five plants, a knock sounded on the schoolroom door.

"Come in," Abigail called out.

The maid Mira entered with a lunch tray. She eyed the table spread with the remains of the plants and looked at Abigail. "Mr. Becket requires your presence at dinner tonight, Mrs. Welch."

"Thank you, Mira. You can tell him I will be there, and you can leave the lunch tray there at the end of the table." The maid left, and Abigail stood and smiled at Jade. "In three or four weeks, you'll be surprised how well your dried plants will turn out. But don't open the books before that. You understand?"

"Yes."

"Ma'am," Abigail reminded the child, as she cleaned off the table and then drew the lunch tray toward the center. The wonderful smell of vegetable soup and cheese sandwiches made her stomach growl.

It was a good thing Potcake was out chasing rabbits. Neither she nor Jade had leftovers.

~

*A*bigail dressed in her blue muslin with its lace collar, the only thing in her wardrobe that could hope to pass for evening wear, and arrived a few minutes early for dinner. Finding the room empty, she sat in the same place at the large table as she had the night before. She reached for the goblet of water sitting beside her plate and almost spilled it as the dining room double doors flew open behind her.

"So you're here. Good. We can get right to business." Mr. Becket strode from the door and sat in his chair at the head of the table. A curl of dark hair hung loose on his forehead, as if he'd walked to the room in a hurry. With a scant glance at her, he spread the white napkin across his knees, picked up a utensil, and chimed on his goblet. Servants entered with platters of steaming food.

Delicious smells of roast pork, greens, sweet potatoes, and fresh bread tantalized Abigail's nose. Hunger rumbled her stomach. After the servants served her and Mr. Becket, they swished back out the door. She placed her napkin in her lap and paused for the blessing.

Mr. Becket stopped the fork heading toward his mouth. "Oh, yes, you prefer to bless our repast, don't you, Mrs. Welch? Will you do the honors this evening?"

Warmth flowed in Abigail's cheeks as she bowed her head and spoke a brief prayer over the food.

Joshua Becket ate with gusto. Abigail gave up trying to keep up her dining with the fast way food flowed from his plate. And the man used perfect table manners. A servant came through the door as if by magic when his goblet needed refilling.

She was only about halfway through the meal when Joshua took a long drink from his goblet and then swiped his lips with his napkin. He leaned back in his chair and studied her.

Abigail's fork slipped from her grasp, but she ignored it and looked up at him.

"Finish your meal, Abigail. I have something to tell you, but you can listen as you dine."

Her name on his lips sent a tingle up her spine. And how could anyone eat a meal with such dark, shining eyes staring at her? With effort, she lowered her attention to the food and continued to push a few bites between her lips.

He leaned forward. "Next week I plan to go away for about ten days on some business. Would that be a bother to you, or do you feel comfortable here with my staff?"

Abigail took a deep breath and touched her napkin to her lips. How she'd like to tell him his attitude with Jade was lacking, but she didn't dare. "I think your staff can answer most questions I might have."

"Good. Tomorrow Jade will spend the day with a little friend at a neighboring estate, and I'd like to take you on a tour of the plantation. You can learn about a sugar estate and meet my overseer. Can you be ready to ride on horseback?" A mocking smile creased his thin lips under his mustache. "You know how to handle a mount, I assume?"

Abigail laid her napkin aside and ignored a twinge of annoyance at his tone and smile. "Yes, sir, I enjoy riding horseback and would love to learn more about Rockford. We don't have sugar plantations in Charleston." She gave him a bright smile at the prospect of a horseback ride, one of her favorite things to do.

"Could you be ready to leave about eight o'clock? We'll want to miss the hottest part of the day. Also, this needn't concern you, but I've informed Mrs. Pelfrey that Rockford will host a soiree to honor our new governor who will arrive soon after I return." He stood and dropped his napkin onto his plate. "Now I must go, but feel free to linger over your dinner. And be sure the servants bring you the dessert they have out in the kitchen. Never miss Mrs. Dykes's chocolate cake, my dear. I've already had a sample." He strode from the room.

Abigail did indeed enjoy the delicious chocolate pound cake, even though his statement that the soiree did not concern her kept flashing through her mind. Of course, they would not expect a governess to attend. That was what he meant. And it was for the good. Her meager wardrobe included only one gown suitable for such an occasion, and it was several years old.

❧

*T*he next morning, Abigail arrived early at the stable in her one riding habit she'd brought from Charleston, bought in a happier time when money was no object. When she had donned it and checked it out in the mirror above her washstand before leaving her room, its excellent lines brought a smile to her lips. One of the main reasons she'd bought it was its design for riding astride, not sidesaddle, which she'd refused to do since her early teen years. The forest-green color and matching, pert hat with veil atop her coiled hair contrasted with her ivory complexion and dark hair. For a moment, she could imagine being at home again, preparing for a wonderful ride through the city park without a care in the world.

Two horses stood in the corridor—the black stallion belonging to Mr. Becket and a sorrel mare with a regular saddle. Abigail smiled. As she approached, Mr. Dykes paused his work saddling the tall stallion and looked at her with surprise lining his lean face. "Hello, ma'am." The horse pawed the ground with one trim hoof and nudged the man. He spit tobacco juice to the side. "For a minute, I didn't recognize you, Mrs. Welch. You look like one of the finest ladies I've ever seen."

Heat rose in Abigail's cheeks. Had she overdressed for an island ride? Perhaps she should dispense with the small hat and veil. Before she could decide, Joshua Becket strode down the corridor. His tan riding pants disappeared into shining black boots, and he wore a blue shirt open at the neck and a short-brimmed straw hat over his dark hair pulled back in a queue.

His glance flew over her, and a grin creased his face. "Well, methinks we have a Charleston belle as our governess, Mr. Dykes. And I can't say I mind."

As their eyes met, a shock ran through her and light words to match his escaped her. "Good morning, Mr. Becket," she managed to say and turned away from his warm stare. She approached the mare. "I assume this is my mount?"

Mr. Dykes responded. "Yes, ma'am. Her name's Arabelle. She ain't as spirited as Haidez here, but she's no plodder. Do you think you can handle her? Sorry we don't have a sidesaddle on the place."

"No worry. I ride astride," she assured the man.

The horse nickered as Abigail walked to her glossy head and extended her palm with an apple slice she'd fetched from the kitchen. The soft muzzle snatched it, and the wide-set, liquid eyes glowed at her. She patted the silky neck and then reached to untie the reins. "Yes, I'm sure Arabelle and I are going to be great friends."

"Here, ma'am, let me give you a lift up." Mr. Dykes turned toward her.

Joshua Becket waved him aside. "I'll be happy to help the lady."

There was nothing Abigail could do but allow him to assist. She placed her boot in the stirrup and stiffened as Joshua's large warm hands encircled her waist and boosted her into the saddle. Was it her imagination, or did his hands linger a tad longer than necessary?

As the man strode back to his pawing stallion, she let out the breath she'd been holding since he touched her.

She reined Arabelle beside Joshua and Haidez as they headed down the dirt road behind the great house at a lively pace. The morning sun dazzled everything around them in golden light, and the sounds of roosters crowing, birds singing, and voices ahead filled the air.

After a few minutes, the talking grew louder as they neared several rows of small houses that perched off the road with narrow paths separating them. Babies cried, mothers called out, and children played in the dusty yards. The smell of bacon and bread cooking drifted on the breeze.

Joshua gestured as they passed. "That's our village for the sugar plantation workers and their families."

Soon they passed a row of men in loincloths carrying farm implements and marching behind a man on horseback. When he saw them coming, he shouted, "Halt." The men squatted on the ground.

Their guard reined his horse near Joshua. He held a whip in his hand and wore soiled clothing that may have once belonged to a gentleman. His scraggly hair hung in greasy strings around his tanned and scarred face. But his hard, glittering eyes were the worst. After greeting Mr. Becket, the man turned his stare on Abigail. She gripped the reins tighter and swallowed her revulsion as he devoured her with that one glance.

"Mr. Bishop is our overseer. He sees to the planting and harvesting of the sugar." Joshua gestured to Abigail. "This is our new governess. I'm giving her a brief tour of Rockford."

Mr. Bishop leaned his head back and laughed. "So you got a new one, have you?"

Joshua frowned.

The overseer wiped the grin off his face. He jerked his hat down and nodded at Abigail. "Glad to meet you, ma'am. May your stay on Rockford be a good, long one."

He turned back to the squatting men. "Git up, you lazy squid. We got work to do." He lashed out at an older man who couldn't stand as fast as the younger ones.

They rode on by and Abigail turned to Joshua. "How much responsibility do you give Mr. Bishop?"

Joshua's lips thinned. "I give him full responsibility over the sugar planting and harvesting. He knows how to get it done, how to handle slaves and snuff out any uprising. "

"With an iron fist and little compassion," Abigail whispered under her breath but mouthed different words to Joshua. "Is there much danger of a slave uprising?"

"Not as long as we have a strong overseer like Bishop. I'm lucky to have him."

They trotted by many fields of sugarcane at varying height and growth. When Abigail asked about it, Joshua explained.

"We stagger the planting to have harvests coming in at varying times. It'd be too much to handle if it all came in at the same time. But I leave it all to Bishop. So far, the plantation has made a good profit each year."

As they passed several buildings, Joshua pointed out the sugar mill, where slaves pushed the mature cane into rollers which squeezed out the juice into pans to sit awhile before being sent to the boiling house. With the sun now high and hot in the sky, Abigail opted out of a walk through the place where the molasses was boiled down, tended by sweating slaves. Moisture trickled down her back and lined her upper lip as Joshua turned Haidez back up the dusty road, but not toward the way they had come. Where was he headed now?

"I want to show you something special at the edge of the estate, Abigail. Ready for a cool respite?" Without waiting for her response, he gave Haidez his head, and the stallion galloped down the road toward the Blue Mountains in the distance, leaving a trail of dust. Abigail clamped her knees on the mare's side, and Arabelle lurched forward to follow the stallion.

They soon left the sandy road and followed a grassy path into the woods at a slower pace. When Abigail caught up with Joshua, he had dismounted and led Haidez to a gurgling, clear stream to drink. She did the same with Arabelle. Somewhere up beyond them, a waterfall crashed, making conversation difficult.

When Joshua led his mount to a tree and tied the reins in a low-hanging branch, she lifted questioning eyes to his.

"Come, I want to show you the waterfall. It's spectacular." He took Arabelle's reins and tied them to another tree nearby. Then he reached out his broad hand to Abigail.

She hesitated.

He grinned. "Abigail, it's a rocky climb. Hold my hand. I'll keep you from stumbling."

Why did her name on his lips please her? She placed her hand in his firm grip, and tremors raced up her arm. They came out on a rocky knoll overlooking the most beautiful waterfall Abigail had ever seen. When she turned to tell him, he drew her into his muscular arms. She froze as her senses leapt to life. His musky scent enveloped her. Blood coursed through her veins like an awakened river, and her knees trembled. He held her close with one arm while he brought the other hand up to lift her chin. Before she could wrench free, his lips pressed down on hers. The roar of the waterfall faded with the drumming of her heart in her ears and her senses whirled and skidded.

When he pulled back, leaving her mouth burning with fire, she raised a tingling hand and slapped his handsome face. He laughed and let her go, then grabbed her shoulders as she teetered on the edge of the cliff. "Now watch it, my dear. I'd hate to lose you so soon, and, besides, you enjoyed that as much as I did."

She shrugged his hands off and stomped back down the path to the waiting mare. Jerking the reins loose from the limb, Abigail mounted before Joshua broke back into the clearing. Urging the mare into her fastest gait back up the wooded path and the dusty road toward the Great House, she flicked away tears. She would have to leave the plantation and Jamaica now that Joshua Becket had shown his true colors.

CHAPTER 5

*A*bigail released the mare to Mr. Dykes and almost ran from the stables to her room, thankful she met no one on the way. She locked the door and threw herself down on her bed until she recovered her breath and peace.

Her employer's intentions were now clear. Was this the real reason the other two governesses had left? Did the man think every woman who came under his roof was his to subdue and claim? Especially a widow like her?

Another thought smote her. Did she enjoy his kiss? Her own mixed emotions shocked her. Why did she let him hold her long enough to kiss her? Why was that kiss still tingling on her lips? Unhappiness cloaked her mind and cramped her stomach. These were danger signals. She had need of her common sense...and above all, God's will.

She dropped to her knees beside the bed.

Lord, I need your help. What should I do?

Images of Jade so happy with her pressed herbs, their relationship just getting off to a decent start, raced through her mind. So did the stark beauty of the island she'd come to love. The once-happy new beginning she'd thought she had in her grasp now slipped through her fingers like sand. Her heart ballooned with a sadness she had not known since losing her little Philip. Before she could get her mind on a fresh track, raw grief over her child's death struck her a blow that took her breath. Tears slid down her cheeks until God touched her and brought peace.

She rose, refusing to give in to the inertia that followed grief. Packing would get her hands busy. The idea lightened her heavy heart. She would pack, then she would write Anna Grace Vargas and return to Charleston to seek a new position. Her friend said her door was always open.

As she walked over to pull the trunk from the corner, a knocking sounded at her door and persisted while she hesitated. She unbolted the entrance a crack, saw the maid, and drew it open.

"Anything wrong, ma'am?" Clarissa stood there as if waiting for an explanation of the bolted door and Abigail taking so long to open it.

"No." Abigail spoke more sharply than she meant to. But she was not going to explain anything to the servant.

"Well, the master is asking for you. He wants to see you right away in the study. He said, 'Tell Mrs. Welch, it is most urgent.'"

"Did he, now?"

"Most urgent, ma'am," Clarissa repeated.

Abigail took a deep breath and nodded.

After the servant left, she rinsed her face with a cloth dipped in the water from the morning basin and arranged her loosened hair. She guessed what this would be about. There would be some kind of complaint. Mr. Becket would give her notice because she was insufficient in some way or other. He no longer needed her as governess. Was this what the other two governesses had experienced when they refused the man's advances? Her heart lurched. What if he even had some kind of trumped-up charge against her that would prevent her getting another position?

How unscrupulous was Joshua Becket?

She would get her word in first. She would tell of her decision to leave before he could dismiss her.

Walking to the study, she whispered a prayer for herself, for Jade, and for Joshua Becket.

She entered and shut the door behind her so gently her employer merely continued his pacing of the width of the room, slapping his riding crop into his hand as a deep frown creased his forehead. He still wore his blue shirt and tan britches pushed into his no-longer-shiny black boots.

She cleared her throat.

He stopped his pacing and faced her. "Hello."

His bright smile stiffened her spine, and she did not return his greeting. "I am ready to pack my trunk, and I'd like to leave as soon as possible."

"Mrs. Welch." His hoarse voice, full of reproach, stole her breath and also sent an absurd thrill through her. Was he going to apologize?

She spoke and failed to moderate a shrill, prim tone. "It's the only course open to me since—"

"Since my terrible conduct this morning." He threw his crop on the desk and looked her full in the face. "Can you forgive me, Mrs. Welch? I'm sure you're generous enough to do that if you think about it. Let's draw a curtain over that incident and go on as before. Can we? For Jade's sake? She's taking to you." He grinned. "And so has Mrs. Pelfrey and even Potcake and Arabelle, and all the servants, I understand." His voice softened. "We really couldn't do without you. Don't let me be the reason you leave."

Was he sincere or mocking her? She blinked. Did she care whether he was, when her heart now sang and relief flooded her inner being? She wouldn't have to leave in disgrace. Nor would she need to write her friend Anna Grace. Her new beginning could still come forth.

She looked him in the eye. "I accept your apology, Mr. Becket. We will forget this unpleasant incident and go on as before." She whirled and walked out of the room.

Only on the stairs did she pause. An apology was so easy, but could she trust him in the future?

rom her window, Abigail watched Joshua Becket and his red-headed partner, Lieutenant Eric Lambert, ride away early the next morning for their ten-day trip. Good. She turned and headed to Jade's room. Today she'd start teaching her to ride.

"No, ma'am. I don't want to ride no horse." Jade poked out her lower lip and sat down for her breakfast.

"Wouldn't you like to please your father? He'd be so happy to find that you have learned to ride."

The child stopped spooning in her oatmeal long enough to glare at Abigail. "How do you know he'd be pleased?"

"Why, every modern young lady learns to ride. And your father is such an avid horseman himself, perhaps you could ride together. We have ten days before he comes back."

With more encouragement, Abigail coached Jade down to the stables with Potcake trotting along. She took pieces of apple and gave some to Jade.

Mr. Dykes smiled and brought out a small, white horse with a yellow mane and tail, a little bigger than a pony he'd already shown Abigail earlier and she'd approved. "Now this'un here will be a fine mount to start Miss Jade with. Her name is Buttercup."

The pony twitched its tail and stretched its muzzle toward the child when she held out the apple on her palm like Abigail had instructed. Jade smiled and jerked her hand back after the pony took the apple.

Abigail asked Mr. Dykes to saddle Buttercup and also Arabelle for her own mount.

For their first riding lesson, she put Buttercup on a leading rein, got Jade in the saddle, and took her back into the paddock. For an hour, they walked around the enclosure with Abigail holding the lead rein. She concentrated on helping Jade gain confidence and grow accustomed to sitting her horse and talking to her mount. Potcake had trotted behind them for a single revolution, then found a shady spot in the corridor and flopped down.

At the end of the hour, Jade sat up straight and hugged the pony's sides with her legs, laughing and patting Buttercup's neck. The first lesson was a great beginning.

They came back into the house to change for tea. Mira knocked on the door, and Jade opened it. The servant walked toward Abigail.

"We got a visitor lady, and Mrs. Pelfrey wants you to serve her tea, please, since the master's not here."

"I'll be down in a few minutes. Can Jade come too?"

The child's eyes lit up. Had she ever been allowed to take tea in the parlor?

Mira looked at Jade and shook her head. "I don't know about Miss Jade, if Mrs. Pelfrey'd like it."

"Well, we'll come and see." Abigail finished plaiting Jade's hair into two long braids and tied them with a yellow ribbon. It was time for the young lady to learn how to have tea in the parlor.

A most elegant lady perched on the sofa before the tea table removing her gloves. Her porcelain complexion, raven hair under a smart, brimmed hat, and penetrating gold-flecked brown eyes must attract men of all ages. Her gown, a pale amethyst, composed of yards of chiffon, spilled over the divan. Abigail straightened as if pushing back her shoulders would help enhance her simple muslin dress.

Mrs. Pelfrey set the loaded tea tray on the table and introduced them. She eyed Jade standing beside Abigail but didn't order her to leave. "Lady Harcourt, this is our governess, Mrs. Abigail Welch, and Mr. Becket's daughter, Jade."

The woman's amber eyes glanced at the child, but lingered on Abigail as if taking in every detail of her dress and form. Abigail shook off discomfort under that scrutiny and gave a brief curtsy.

Jade did the same.

"Lady Harcourt owns the estate joining ours on the north side," Mrs. Pelfrey added before leaving the room.

Abigail, followed by Jade, took chairs opposite the settee. The well-laden tea tray boasted small sandwiches, biscuits, jelly, wedges of chocolate cake, and a small, ornate silver teapot. The guest must be one that needed to be impressed.

Lady Harcourt smiled at the child, showing even white teeth. "So this is the daughter I've heard so much about but never met. Is she doing well in her studies?" Her amber eyes swept from Jade to Abigail.

Abigail poured three cups of tea. "Yes, she works hard. Today she has even learned to ride horseback."

A smile played on Jade's lips.

The woman reached for her cup, added four cubes of sugar, stirred it, then brought it to her lips. "How interesting." She took a cucumber sandwich, then a scone. "And I understand you are from Charleston, Mrs. Welch, and a widow?"

Who had told her that?

"Yes." Abigail took a bite of a tasty scone and watched Jade stuff two into her mouth.

"I am a widow, too. My late husband had several business associates in Charleston, so I've traveled there often. A lovely city to be sure, but, in my opinion, foolish to force out the British." She lifted her chin and sipped her tea. "Which side were you on, my dear?"

The mention of the Revolutionary War struck the usual heartrending cord in Abigail. As always, the memory of Philip's death and the later loss of their young son flashed across her mind with raw pain—like the space between a broken bone, a hollowed out space the rest of the body must work hard to heal until the throb subsides and the break can be mended. She set her cup back on the tray. "With the patriots, of course." Even to her ears, her voice sounded clipped, tight. Perhaps the woman would get the message and drop the subject.

"Really? Do you think the colonies will survive without England's wise oversight and power, my dear?" Lady Harcourt's hard eyes blazed a challenge.

Abigail swallowed the bile rising in her throat. "The colonies will do well with their own oversight and power of hard won liberty is my firm opinion, Lady Harcourt." She had a much stronger guard up now.

Something like a snort came from the guest but a movement beside Abigail drew her attention.

Jade took sips from her cup, Abigail prayed she'd not slosh it, or, God forbid, drop it. The child placed her cup back on the tray with care but brushed the silver teapot with her elbow. It tottered, then crashed to the floor.

Jade jumped up with a sob and ran from the room. Abigail reached down and replaced the pot on the tray, thankful it had been almost empty. The servants would have to clean the spilled tea from the rug.

"Tsk, tsk. The girl still has a bit to learn, doesn't she?" The woman finished a wedge of chocolate cake and touched her napkin to pink lips. She pulled her skirts aside to keep from touching the tea table, or the spilled tea, and stood. Pulling her gloves on, she turned self-assured eyes on Abigail. "I'd hoped to see Joshua. He asked me to plan his soiree for the new governor in about two weeks. Please let him know when he returns, I came by, and the plans are going forward well. And I'll see him soon."

"Of course."

Abigail saw her to the door and to the coach with its four liveried footmen waiting in the drive. Exactly what was the lovely Lady Harcourt's relationship with her employer? She was a neighbor and a widow. He'd asked her to plan a soiree for him he was hosting at Rockford. He'd evidently even told the woman about her own arrival as a widow from Charleston. Surely if they were that close, she would've known he would be out of town ten days. So what had been the purpose of her visit? Walking up the stairs to find and comfort Jade an answer tripped into her mind. To see what the new governess was like?

~

Joshua surveyed the chests of silver, gold, and royal plate spread out on the deck of the conquered Spanish ship. He smiled. This could be the biggest haul he'd ever taken in his privateering career. Why not let it be his last? Even after the dividing up among his crew, his take would still be a sizeable fortune. Why keep tempting fate? He had enough wealth to do anything he wanted, including sailing back to Charleston in style. Wouldn't his father and stepbrother Samuel be surprised?

The Spanish captain corralled in a corner of the deck with his offi-cers stepped forward and spat, then ground out a statement in butchered English. "You pirating devils. You Captain Jay, whoever you are, you'll pay for this."

Lambert gestured at the angry officer with his musket. "You should be more thankful our captain spares all your lives." The man moved back to his crew.

After Captain Jay dropped the Spanish off with provisions on an island in the circuit of the treasure ships, he lowered his French flag, raised the British colors, and headed back to the *Eagle's* home port, Rockford Plantation dock.

They came in at midnight, as usual, to avoid any suspicion. All the crew but two slithered off into the moonless night happy with their fortune and their lips sealed.

Standing on the dock, Joshua called to Eric Lambert, still busy unloading his and Joshua's part of the treasure, three crates each. Two crew members loaded Joshua's crates on a wagon, then Lambert's on a second wagon. "You coming home with me or you got other plans, friend?"

"I've got some other plans this time, Captain Jay." Lambert grinned.

"That's fine. Maybe you've got a doxy waiting for you?" The night before, Joshua had shared with him that this might be their last venture. The man didn't seem surprised or upset.

"No, I've got one better. A Spanish Town merchant's daughter has caught my eye. With our take tonight, I might catch her and her papa's eye."

Joshua walked closer and out of the hearing of the two men help-ing. "That's great, Eric. I'm glad to hear it. Sounds as though you're going to settle down. It's been good, but there comes a time." He held out his hand, and his lieutenant shook it.

Lambert's eyes danced. "What about you? Got any idea of matri-mony? I've heard about the widow lady whose estate joins yours. Some talk is that she's looking your way. Any truth to it?"

An image of the luscious Lady Harcourt flowed into Joshua's mind, and he smiled. But then the prim face of Abigail after the wonderful stolen kiss at the waterfall replaced it. Could he return to her good graces? Did he want to? "Who knows, friend? Right now, I don't know what the future holds, just feels like it could be good."

They parted, and Joshua climbed aboard his wagon and headed down the dark road to the great house with two of his men. In the late night stillness, they unloaded the crates into a storage building at the back of the house, and the two helpers hopped back on the wagon, turned it around, and left.

∼

*A*fter the evening meal, Mrs. Pelfrey invited Abigail to her rooms. She poured out cups of tea for them both, then sat back in her rocker with a conspiratorial look. "What did you think about our neighbor, Lady Harcourt?"

Abigail raised her brows. Was Mrs. Pelfrey about to share a fact about the woman, or was this her way of introducing some piece of gossip? She didn't want to encourage tittle-tattle. Perhaps the house-keeper felt a governess was more her own class to share such things. "She's an attractive woman. I can say that for sure." Abigail smiled at the housekeeper and took a sip of tea.

"That woman has plans for Mr. Becket, mark my words. Her husband is not even cold in his grave, but she's not wasting any time. Wants a handsome man like our master by her side and in her bed. Not to mention, to join his estate to hers." She sniffed. "In fact, I have it from a good source, she was after him even before her husband passed."

Abigail's breath caught in her throat at the candid words. And Mr. Becket had asked Lady Harcourt to plan the soiree? How close were they? And had their friendship, or whatever it was, truly started before the husband's death? She shook her head. It was none of her business.

In her bedroom, Abigail battled restlessness by straightening the room, which didn't need it, and selecting clothing she'd wear the following day. She blew out her lantern and, on an impulse, walked to the small window facing the back of the house and pulled back the drape. Moonlight flowed into the room and warmed her spirit. She would keep her mind on her work with little Jade. No child could need her more.

Movement near an outbuilding below her drew her attention. A lantern hanging on a wagon revealed Joshua Becket dressed like a buccaneer with a sword at his side and guns stashed in the sash across his chest. He and two men carried trunks or boxes into the outlying building. The others were not Africans. Their baggy pants, swords, and guns strapped to their sides marked them as pirates. A chill ran up her spine. Where had Mr. Becket been the past many days when absent from Rockford? With what kind of employer had she cast her lot?

CHAPTER 6

*T*he evening of the soiree, Jade burst into Abigail's room with a secret. "We don't have to miss the ball. We have a peep to see down into the ballroom."

Abigail looked up from the mending she held in her lap. "What is a peep?"

"Come, I'll show you."

Laying aside her work, Abigail followed the excited child up two levels of stairs and through several corridors in a part of the house she'd never been. Music, conversation, and laughter floated up to them but grew softer on the last floor.

Jade stopped at an insignificant mahogany door. "This is the room above the chapel." She led Abigail into a wide room with only one window on one side and curtained alcoves on the other, decorated to match the wallpaper so that one not would notice them unless they were looking for them. "There are two peeps in this room. Look." Jade pulled aside a drape. Three chairs sat there, and Jade pointed to an octagonal opening in the wall.

Abigail bent to gaze through it—to the chapel below.

Jade clapped her hands. "Mrs. Pelfrey told me when the ladies of the house were too ill to attend service, they'd come here to sit and watch it."

"How interesting, but what does this have to do with the ball?"

Jade had already run to the far side of the room and disappeared behind another drape. "Come in here and you'll see." Her muffled voice drew Abigail closer.

She pulled aside the dusty curtain and moved beside Jade to peer into the peep, wider than the first one. Her breath caught in her throat. Musicians sat on the temporary dais playing, and guests danced or stood around talking in their gorgeous gowns, silk waistcoats, and white wigs. Music and the cadence of conversation floated up through the opening. One man, more pompous than any in yellow silk from his neck to his polished, buckled shoes, seemed to be the focus of attention. His white wig, with thick, long curls cascading about his shoulders, outshone all the others. Ladies who approached him curtsied, and men bowed. The new British governor of Jamaica?

She searched the other men's faces for Joshua's strong, tanned visage. A flame-colored gown and wigless, long black hair caught her eye. Lady Harcourt. Even in the brilliant gathering of expensive gowns and evening attire, the woman shone like a lighthouse, her white shoulders draped by her thick hair held back by a diamond tiara. More diamonds sparkled about her person.

Joshua stood beside her, the only other person in the gathering without a powdered wig. The ribbon that secured his queue matched his blue silk waistcoat. A snow-white cravat extended at his neckline. Tall, over six feet, he stood out in the gathering with his usual air of careless elegance.

Lady Harcourt leaned over to whisper something in Joshua's ear. He nodded and smiled. Abigail swallowed and stepped back. Why did the thought of the two of them together make her uncomfortable?

Later in her room, Abigail pressed her lips together and admitted her strange feelings were akin to jealousy. She undressed and threw herself on her bed. What was she to do? Maybe she should have left when the waterfall incident occurred. But she wanted to help Jade, didn't she? And wasn't she master of her own emotions? With God's help, she could resist whatever she needed to resist. Any relationship between her and Joshua Becket, alias Captain Jay, the pirate, was hopeless.

Long after the muffled ballroom music stopped filtering into her room, she spiraled into a fitful sleep and troublesome dreams. She awoke amid a heavy darkness and tried to expunge the last nightmare from her mind. The hall clock struck two o'clock. In the dream, she'd been running from Lady Harcourt, her face contorted into a witch's toothless grin, and Joshua Becket stood afar off, watching. Then she'd found herself enclosed in his arms with his mouth claiming hers as he'd done at the falls.

Abigail threw off her hot sheet and shuffled to the water basin. She took a cloth, wet it, and washed her face and neck. Then she lit a candle, sat in her rocker, and reached for her Bible. The Word of God was the only way to battle in the spiritual realm. Hadn't this been what saved her sanity after losing her little Philip? She'd been remiss the past few days in her Bible study, but she would be more diligent from now on.

When she closed the book and crawled back into bed, the heaviness in the room had evaporated, and sweet sleep overcame her.

~

*S*he rose early, and with only a few hours of good sleep, still had energy. Today was Saturday. No classes for Jade. Why not take a horseback ride? What a wonderful way to clear the air—in her heart and mind.

She dressed in her riding habit and sailed down to the kitchen for a piece of cheese, bread, and a cup of tea. Then she hurried to the barn with an apple slice.

Mr. Dykes and Jeremy looked up from cleaning out stalls. "You up early today, Mrs. Welch. You wanting to ride Arabelle?"

"Yes. Would it be too much trouble to saddle her for me?"

"No trouble for me, but trouble for the mare. She's done thrown a shoe, and it'll be Monday 'fore the blacksmith can come."

"Oh." Abigail could not keep the disappointment from her voice.

The man leaned on his shovel. "You've still got two choices—Buttercup or Haidez. Course, ain't nobody much ever ridden Haidez but Mr. Becket. But I doubt he'd mind if you think you can handle him. Somebody needs to keep him exercised. The master ain't sent no word about riding today after being up most of the night at the ball… and maybe elsewhere."

Of course, the house servants and stable workers knew about the ball's late ending. What else was common information in their midst? Did Joshua accompany Lady Harcourt home?

She cast that thought aside and took a deep breath. Buttercup would be a boring ride. "Let me try Haidez."

When Dykes brought him into the corridor to saddle him, he sniffed in her direction, then nickered. She came forward and gave him the apple slice on the palm of her hand.

A few moments after mounting the stallion, she knew the two of them would get along fine. She loved horses with spirit. His smooth gait gave her a pleasant seat without a jolt. They started down the dirt road behind the great house at a fast clip. Abigail reveled in the fresh air and the willing horse beneath her. The sun, though bright, did not beam down on them the heavy heat that would come toward midday.

As Abigail rounded a bend and came in sight of the slave village, a terrible scream pierced the sunshine, then another. Haidez's ears twitched, and he slowed his pace. Abigail reined him toward the source of the third scream between the rows of small houses. On a raised platform, a young woman tied to a post cringed away from the overseer wielding a whip. Blood stained the torn places of her thin dress. Abigail's heart jumped into her throat, and bile filled her mouth.

She forced Haidez closer, and he snorted, stopped, and pawed the ground. He rolled his eyes at the man brandishing the whip and at the gathering of people standing around. Angry mutters punctuated the air.

The man, dressed in gentlemen's clothing that had seen a better day and needed laundering, turned to glare in her direction. His dark eyes widened upon sight of the horse, then he squinted at Abigail. "Miz Governess, you need to trot right back where you come from. This here is none of your business."

"I'm making it my business, Mr. Bishop. Why are you beating the girl?"

"Like I said, this is none of your business. So you best be off."

A louder, heated murmur erupted from the bystanders.

An older woman stumbled from a doorway. She looked at the man with fear in her eyes but then looked at Abigail with pleading and hope. "She ain't done nothing, ma'am. I'm her mother. She's a good girl. Too good for…" She cast a quick glance at Mr. Bishop, and her voice trailed off.

Abigail dismounted and held Haidez's reins with a firm hand. She patted his nose and whispered gentle words to him. Then she addressed the overseer. "Sir, untie the girl. Let her mother tend her wounds. And be assured, I will report this to Mr. Becket. I'm sure you'd better never try to whip her again. I will keep check."

The man cursed and spat tobacco juice on the ground. Then a devilish grin creased his leather-like face. "Well, Miz Governess, I'm going to do what you ask, but I'll also report you to Mr. Becket. He's given me, not you, rule over these no-good slaves, and there's half a dozen other planters who'd love fer me to come work for them if that wuz to change."

He untied the girl, and she stumbled into her mother's arms. Both cast thankful glances toward Abigail and hurried into their small abode.

The other bystanders nodded at her. Some smiled until the overseer glared at them.

Abigail mounted with anger boiling inside and swallowed the bitter taste filling her mouth. What kind of planter was Joshua Becket that he allowed this evil overseer complete rule over the plantation slaves? And did what the mother say mean what Abigail guessed it meant, that Bishop was trying to force the girl to his bed?

She rode to the waterfalls, tied Haidez to a limb, and sat until her emotions cooled down. She'd heard of the terrible plight of slaves, but this was the first time she'd witnessed it firsthand. Her family and her friend Georgia's family treated their servants with respect and kindness. A prayer gushed from her heart.

Lord, show me how to handle this with Mr. Becket. Turn his heart to righteous dealings with his people. If he's not a Christian, please save him.

~

*J*oshua Becket traveled by coach from the Harcourt Plantation to Rockford. The bright sunlight hurt his eyes. Exactly what had happened the night before? Too much drink and too much temptation in a flame-colored gown. He'd escorted Lady Harcourt home at her insistence. That was a mistake. A black cloud of conviction, along with a rum haze, pressed against his mind.

Hopefully, he'd promised her nothing. All he remembered was falling on her sofa and passing out about four in the morning. His father Ethan's voice rose over the pain in his head. *Joshua, don't tempt the mercy of God. Change your ways. Find the right path and walk in it before it's too late.*

The man must be praying for him without ceasing.

At Rockford, he stumbled out of the coach and into the great house. His butler, Walter, pressed his lips together and shook his head as he helped him up the stairs to his room. "Sir, I'll get that concoction that always helps you and bring it right up."

"Yes, thank you, Walter. And some hot water and fresh clothes." Thank God he'd not run into anyone on the way to his room. Especially the child or her governess. Those were small blessings he could be thankful for.

By three o'clock that afternoon, his recovery from his night of excess had progressed enough for him to sit in his study and check the mail. A knock sounded at the door.

"Enter."

He sat back as Abigail Welch walked up to his desk. She wore her riding habit, and her pretty, stiff face hinted at some kind of trouble.

He smiled. "What can I do for you, Mrs. Welch? Won't you have a seat?"

She didn't sit, and she wasted no words. "I rode down the plantation road early today and heard a woman screaming. I found your Mr. Bishop mercilessly whipping a young woman tied to a post in the village."

He frowned. "It's not been my habit to interfere with Bishop's handling of the plantation workers, Mrs. Welch. I've learned that's been the best policy for running this estate. He knows how to keep them under control and prevent uprisings. Believe me, all the planters on the island live in fear of another uprising."

Abigail's lips tightened. "This was not preventing an uprising, sir. This was beating a young woman who...who would not do his ungodly bidding. Her mother intimated that much to me."

He sat back in his chair and regarded her. "And what, may I ask, did you do about this beating when you saw it happening?"

"I told him to stop and to untie the girl."

Mr. Becket leaned forward. "And what did Bishop do?"

"He laughed, but he did what I asked and told me he'd be reporting my interference to you, that you had given him complete control over the plantation workers." Her pinched features confirmed her opinion of this rule, as did her flashing emerald eyes.

His earlier headache started back with gusto, and his father's gentle face popped into his mind. His father would be angrier than Mrs. Welch in this situation. He took a deep breath. "That description of his control is true." He stood up. "But it may not continue to be true." That last tumbled out of his mouth before he realized it.

Abigail stepped back with her jaw slackening. "Do you mean it? You will make sure this man stops mistreating the workers?"

He looked at her through the haze of pain in his head. "I'll do what I can. You have my word."

She spun on her heel and left. He slumped back into his chair. What he needed was to get out of the sugar plantation business altogether. He glanced at the calendar on his desk and blew out an exasperated breath. The Assembly met tonight. Since the last governor had appointed him to serve, he'd tried not to miss a meeting. It was the best way to keep up with what transpired in England and in the Caribbean.

Another knock sounded at his door. Had the woman come back? "Enter."

His overseer walked in wearing clean clothes and without chewing tobacco in his mouth.

"Sir, I 'spect that governess done told you what happened this morning."

Joshua suppressed a groan at having to deal with the man while still battling the pain in his head from his own misbehavior the night before.

"Yes, she's been in. What's your side of the story?"

"It was just a girl that done got sassy, and I knowed if I didn't put a stop to it, it could spread, and soon who knows what'd be happening around here."

Joshua banged his fist on his desk. "Bishop, I don't want you whipping women, no women of any age. Do you understand?" He made his voice as stern as he'd ever made it on ship to lazy crewmen who then changed their actions pronto.

The man's mouth tightened, and then he threw out his chest. "Well, sir, there's a few planters who'd like to have me as overseer, and they'd never give me no instructions."

Joshua didn't relent. "I'm sure there are. I would like to keep you, but there'll be no more whipping of women. That's my rule."

Bishop's nostrils flared. "Well, I guess you and me are gonna part company as of the end of this week, sir. You can count this as my notice." He stomped from the room.

Joshua made a note to put a watch on the man to make sure he took nothing not belonging to him when he left the plantation. At the assembly meeting tonight, the other planters would laugh at him for losing Bishop, if they found out. Then they'd fight over who could hire him first. And how would he find an overseer this far into the planting season with harvests coming up? It would take a miracle, and who believed in those?

CHAPTER 7

*T*he next day being Sunday, Abigail rose and dressed for services at the small Baptist church she'd glimpsed at Spanish Town weeks ago when she'd arrived. That was something else she had to get back to doing—attending church.

She walked into Jade's room during her breakfast and persuaded the child to accompany her. Mira, who came to clean up, was happy to take a note to Mr. Dykes to have the small carriage ready to go into the town.

At nine-thirty, the conveyance stood at the main entrance, driven by Mr. Dykes' son, Jeremy. With a freshly scrubbed face and clean clothing, the stout young man looked proud and able holding the reins with a straw hat atop his head of ginger hair so like his father's. Abigail and Jade climbed in, and off they clattered down the drive. Glancing back at the great house, Abigail gasped. Joshua stared after them from the upstairs front parlor. Was it her imagination, or did his countenance seem drawn, unhappy? Had he confronted Mr. Bishop yet?

She turned her attention to their young driver. "Jeremy, we're glad to have you drive us. Are you planning to attend the service with us?"

"Yes, ma'am."

"That's wonderful."

The boy grinned, clucked to the horse and it increased its pace.

The morning sun cast golden, warm highlights along the roadside flowers and on the carriage. Abigail opened her fringed parasol over her head, thankful she'd brought it to alleviate some of the tropical heat. Her heart rose in anticipation of a good day ahead.

"What do you do at a church, besides dress up?" Jade turned her face toward Abigail. The bow of the bonnet, Jade's first experience with such, was already a little askew under her chin.

Had the child never attended church? Abigail righted the bow and sighed. They definitely needed her at Rockford Plantation. "Well, you go with other people into the church building, and you sing hymns and listen to prayers, and then the pastor will speak on some subject from the Bible." She tapped the worn book in her lap, her mother's treasured Scriptures.

"Are there pictures in your Bible?"

"There are some good illustrations."

"Can I see them?

"By all means…when we get back to Rockford."

When they arrived at the small, stucco church, Jeremy guided the horse to a hitching bar, giving plenty of space to the horse and carriage beside them. He jumped down and tied the reins to the metal hook on the bar.

Beckoning to Jeremy to follow, Abigail led Jade by the hand into the cool sanctuary and found an unmarked pew toward the back. The scent of lemon oil filled the building, and the wooden pews' glossy shine confirmed someone cared for God's house with love.

A woman played a harpsichord on the left side up front. Soon the building filled. When the singing began, Abigail joined in with a full heart until people turned to look her way. She softened her tone, but her heart still overflowed.

A handsome young man in a white robe walked behind the pulpit and gazed out at the congregation. Tendrils of his thick brown hair escaped his queue and curled around his tanned forehead. His gaze seemed to pause on the three of them. Warmth rose in Abigail's cheeks, and he looked away.

When he opened the Bible and began to preach, she no longer thought of him as a fine-looking man, but as a genuine servant of God, opening up God's Word to her understanding.

As they left the church, the minister waited at the door, smiling. "Hello, I'm Mark Gardner." He held out his hand, and Abigail shook it. "It delighted us to have you visit our service this morning. Do you live in the city?"

His dark eyes danced with intelligence and interest, and his hand warmed hers.

"No, I'm Abigail Welsh." She gestured to the children. "This is Jade Becket. I'm her new governess at Rockford Plantation. And this is Jeremy Dykes who drove our carriage very well."

The youngster tried to hide his grin, and the minister tousled the reddish blond head, then turned his attention back to Abigail.

"Rockford? I've wanted to ride out that way for some time. Do you think I'd be welcome?

Abigail didn't know what to say, so she just nodded. Why wouldn't he be welcome?

Others waited in line to speak to him. He glanced at them, smiled, and released her hand.

On the drive home, Jeremy broke the happy silence. "Ma'am, you sure showed 'em you know how to sing. Sounded like a regular bird to me."

"Well, thank you, Jeremy. When people started turning to look to me, I guess they thought it might have been a bird that had gotten trapped in the back of the church."

Jade giggled.

Walter clanged the midday meal bell soon after they walked into the great house, and Abigail dined with Jade in the schoolroom. Where did Joshua spend his Sundays? Would he follow up with her on the situation with his overseer? He'd given her his word to deal with it. But her employer never made an appearance, and Abigail enjoyed a peaceful afternoon and evening.

~

*A*bigail did not see Joshua until the following Monday after her lessons with Jade. He sent for her to come to his study late in the afternoon.

When she strolled in, he gestured to a chair in front of his desk, and she sat. Was this going to be her dismissal for intervening with the overseer? His countenance held no clue. Or did it? Shadows darkened the skin beneath his eyes, and his mouth pressed into a thin line under his mustache. She forced her glance from him to the tall, thick books lining the shelves behind him. Were they law books? They reminded her of the ones her father had kept in their library at home.

He leaned back and cracked his knuckles twice. "I talked to Mr. Bishop and informed him there'd be no more whippings such as you witnessed."

She swallowed. "Thank you." Her employer rose several degrees in her estimation.

He sat forward and frowned. "Bishop gave me notice. He's leaving at the end of this week."

She suppressed a gasp but almost in the same instant found her shoulders relaxing. "Is that so bad? Can't you find another overseer who will treat your people better?"

He stared into her face and sucked in a breath. "That, dear Mrs. Welch, is the immense problem. Capable overseers are most difficult to find on an island like this. There are no unemployed ones available, and ships only bring in prospects before planting season, not at harvest time like this. And it's critical to get our sugarcane harvested when it's ready." The corner of his mouth twisted.

She bit her lower lip. "Oh." Truly, a lame answer. She dropped her gaze to the floor and whispered a prayer. Only one further response came to mind. She twisted her hands in her lap and looked into his face. "Mr. Becket, this may sound weak, but it's not. I will pray that God will send you the best overseer and in time."

He slammed his fist onto the desk.

She jumped.

His nostrils flared. "Didn't mean to scare you, but that sounds just like something my father would say."

"Your father?" She knew nothing of his background.

"You couldn't tell it, but my father was, *is*, a pastor in Charleston." He lowered his head.

Her mind whirled. A pastor named Becket? Could Joshua be related to Ethan Becket, the minister in her friend Anna Grace's family?

"He couldn't be…Ethan Becket, could he?" Her voice came out in a whisper.

His head shot up. "Yes, do you know him? Have you met my father?"

She took a deep breath. "Yes. He's related to my best friend's— Anna Grace Vargas's—family. In fact, he performed her wedding ceremony with John Vargas last year. I was there."

"My nephew John. It's hard to believe you've met my family." Joshua stood, ran his hand through his hair, and paced back and forth to the window, muttering under his breath. He finally stopped near her chair. A frown contracted his dark brows, and his face had paled under his tan. "Do you want to hear a sad story, Mrs. Welch? My story. One I've told no one on the island and haven't even thought about for years?"

She looked into his troubled countenance. "If you want to share it." Her heartbeat quickened, as did her interest.

He moved behind the desk and slumped into his chair. He stared out the window as he began in a low voice.

"John's father, Samuel Vargas, and I grew up together as stepbrothers. His mother is Marisol, whom my father married after Samuel's birth. She has quite a story herself, but I'll stick to mine. Ethan, my father, treated us two boys with equal love and justice. I was older, but like an idiot, I took a dislike to Samuel and aggravated him as much as possible growing up." He stopped and gazed at her as if to gauge her reaction.

She didn't move a muscle.

"The worst thing I did, when I was the worst kind of fool, was to kidnap Georgia Ann Cooper and..." He hesitated and turned his face away, but not before she saw the tightness that gripped his countenance.

"I hoped to force her to marry me, but she loved only Samuel. He came and rescued her and threatened to turn me over to the British authorities for some other shenanigans I'd pulled if I didn't leave Charleston right away. That's how I came to Jamaica about twenty years ago, banished from Charleston, my family, and my law practice. The black sheep of the clan."

Her mouth fell open. "Law practice?" How many more secrets did the man possess?

"Yes, I practiced law and still caused trouble on the wrong side of the law." He looked in her face and searched her eyes.

His powerful perusal caused a tremor in her middle and heat to rise in her cheeks.

"What do you think of your employer now, Mrs. Welch? Can I trust you with these dark secrets?" He moved to sit on the edge of the desk near her.

Abigail blinked and took a long-needed breath. "My father once said confession cleanses the soul. And he was one who ought to know. He gambled away our family fortune and then died in a duel and left my mother and me penniless. Mama died of a broken heart."

He winced. "I'm sorry. You and your mother deserved better."

Was that sympathy in his voice? There was more to her unhappy history. "Want to hear my story?"

"Do you have one too?" He took his seat behind the desk, steepled his hands under his chin, and gave her his full attention.

She balled her fist on the arm of the chair. "Mine is...more of sadness." A raw and primitive grief rose in her as it always did when she remembered—like an old wound that ached on a rainy day. "I married Philip Welch just as the Revolution started. We had two wonderful weeks together, and he left with Washington's Continental Army." She swallowed the inevitable lump that rose in her throat. "He lost his life in a battle three months later. He's buried somewhere in Virginia."

Joshua frowned. "I'm so sorry."

"That's not all. I had his son later that year, our dear little Philip, named after his father, a happy bundle of joy and a living, breathing reminder that God was still on His throne—and that He still loved and cared for us even during the horrors of war."

Her employer leaned forward, his dark eyes widening. Was he surprised she'd had a child?

The lump proved too hard to swallow, and moisture gathered in Abigail's eyes despite her effort to prevent it.

Anger flashed across the man's face in front of her as she tried to make her voice work.

"Don't tell me. Something happened to your child too?" He ground out the words.

She nodded. "Yellow fever when he was two."

He started to slam his fist on the desk again but stopped short of the surface. Instead, his nostrils flared. "How can anyone still believe in a God who'd let that happen, Mrs. Welch?" His voice had hardened to gravel.

Abigail forced a breath into her lungs. He was taking it all wrong. "I don't believe God had anything to do with the death of my child. We live in an evil world that often turns its back on Him. Because of the evil, bad things can happen, even to good people. And folks get mad at God. But Jesus told his disciples who is doing the bad things. He said, 'The thief does not come except to steal, and to kill, and to destroy. I have come that they may have life, and that they may have it more abundantly.'" She swallowed a sob rising in her throat. "I believe God has my little Philip now in His loving care, and I'll see him again one day."

Joshua's lips thinned. "Have it your way, if that helps you." He continued to study her face. "Are you all right, Abigail Welch?" When she gave a small nod, he continued. "Thank you for sharing your story. At least you weren't busy doing bad things as I've done."

She stood and studied his handsome face. A special peace flowed over her. "We all have some unhappy parts in our past—things we've done ourselves, or things that happen to us through no fault of our own. But what we do with the future is more important than living in and regretting the past. Don't you agree?"

His taut countenance relaxed. "Yes. I plan for my future to be different. I think it's time. But are you ready to flee Rockford and go back to Charleston after hearing my story?"

She collected her wits. "No, not if you meant what you said, about a different future." Did this mean he would not practice pirating and call it privateering?

He smiled with a maddening hint of arrogance about him and cocked his chin at her. "So I can trust you with my dark secrets, Mrs. Welch?"

An invisible warmth from his gaze wrapped around her, and she stepped back. She needed to leave. At the door she turned and answered him. "Yes, you can."

The glow accompanied her as she walked up the steps to her room. She would pray for the new overseer as she'd promised. And for her employer.

~

*J*oshua stared at the door long after Abigail had left. Who was this woman he'd just poured his soul out to? Had he lost his mind? She was at least fifteen years younger. Could she possibly have more wisdom? That was a new idea. A woman who had true wisdom. He'd seen precious few of those. Perhaps it was just a dream, a mirage that the next day's light would dissolve. But he did feel lighter than he'd felt in a long time. If he didn't have the overseer position to worry about...

As he left his study, a servant handed him a note.

Darling, will I see you tonight? -Geneva

He crushed the missive in his palm. No thank you, Lady Harcourt. He bounded up the stairs, threw the wadded note into the trash, and changed into his riding breeches. A pleasant ride over the plantation, perhaps all the way to the Blue Mountains, would be the best thing to help him to get a good night's sleep and start his search for an over-seer in the morning.

～

On Tuesday, while Abigail sat in the schoolroom finishing her class with Jade, a brief knock sounded at the door.

Clarissa entered with wide, excited eyes. "Ma'am, there's a preacher here to see you, and this is his card."

Abigail read on the small stiff card,

Reverend Mark Gardner, Spanish Town Road Baptist Church.

"Put him in the first-floor parlor and tell him I'll be there in about five minutes."

"Yes, ma'am." The girl turned at the door and smiled. "He's one of the handsomest ministers I've ever seen."

Abigail dismissed Jade and Potcake for a romp and hurried to her room to freshen up. Most ladies would agree with the girl's observation, but Abigail thrust the remark out of her mind. To her he was simply a good minister who knew the Word of God and whose friendship she might enjoy while on the island.

Mark Gardner stood from a side chair when she entered. "Good afternoon. I hope I'm not coming at an inopportune time." He wore a black waistcoat and breeches, with white stockings and shoes with shiny buckles and clutched a brimmed hat in his hands.

"No, Jade was happy to finish her grammar lesson and romp with her dog." Abigail sat on the sofa across from where he stood.

Once she was seated, he took his former chair. "I guess you wonder why I've come. First, to let you know how welcome you are to visit Spanish Town Road Baptist. We were happy to have you and the two children."

"I was blessed. Your message was timely."

He grinned. "Next, I've heard by the grapevine that Mr. Becket is looking for a new overseer. Is that correct?"

Abigail sat forward. "Yes, do you know of such a man?"

70

"I do. And a good Christian man, he is. I met him on the ship coming to Jamaica, and we've been friends ever since."

"You mean he's not already employed as an overseer at some plantation?"

"No, no, he's not. I'll tell you a little about him. He's a freed African, and the family who freed him gave him enough to buy a small plot of land on the little-used part of the island. That's land the other planters don't care for. They thought it wouldn't grow sugar. But this man has done wonders. He knows how to handle sugarcane, and I believe the blacks would work for him. If you're open to it, I'd love to take you to meet him and see what he's accomplished. I've got my carriage outside." A sparkle lit up his eyes.

"But Mr. Becket is the one who needs to meet this man and see what he's done. I'm not sure where he is this time of day, but let me send a servant to check. Do you mind waiting?"

The minister leaned back in his chair and crossed one knee. "Not at all."

~

Thirty minutes later, Abigail rode with the two men, with Joshua driving the carriage, to meet the possible overseer. She tried to beg off going, saying only Mr. Becket needed to go, but neither would have it. Joshua's skeptical agreement to come and his silence on the way shot a sting of worry through her. Was he only coming to mock her and the pastor when the man turned out to be unsuitable? Had he only agreed because he was desperate?

As they entered a part of the island that seemed deserted, the road turned into more of a rut filled with bumps and holes. Joshua slowed the horse to keep from bouncing them out of the carriage. Gullies and low spots not conducive to cultivation filled the outlying areas. Finally, small plots of tall sugarcane waved in the breeze between the low areas. A group of black men worked at the edge of one.

"Stop here, Mr. Becket," Reverend Gardner called, and Joshua halted the carriage.

The minister climbed out of the conveyance and walked toward the Negroes. One dropped his hoe and came toward the visitor. The tall, thin man's brown face creased into a smile.

The pair clasped hands and then fell into an earnest conversation that Abigail could not discern. The minister turned and gestured toward the carriage.

Joshua jumped down and examined the field of sugarcane nearby. The two men walked toward him.

"Mr. Becket, meet Isaiah Brown." Reverend Gardner introduced them and moved back. The black man nodded and looked down and then lifted his bright eyes to Joshua when spoken to.

They were close enough to the carriage for Abigail to hear the conversation.

"You plant and grow this cane?"

"Yes, suh."

"It looks good. How many years you been working this plot?"

"Three, suh.

"Mr. Brown, what kind of success have you had? Make a profit?"

"We've made a good profit the past two years, and I believe it'll be even better this year."

"You're a freed man, got your papers?"

"Yes, suh. I have my papers, and before you ask, the men you see in the field belong to me to help work this harvest. They know sugarcane just like me."

Abigail's eyes widened. A freed man owned slaves?

Joshua glanced at Reverend Gardner. "Did the minister tell you what I'm looking for?"

Mr. Brown responded. "He told me, but no one's ever done it on this island before as far as I know, a black man made overseer on a plantation like yours. How big is your estate?"

"I have four hundred acres and one hundred workers who need a good overseer to get the harvests in. We can come to terms about salary. Are you interested?"

Isaiah Brown stepped back, crossed his arms, and closed his eyes for a moment. When he looked up, a frown creased his forehead. "Mr.

Becket, your neighbors might take real offense to my being your over-seer. They might try to run me off or worse."

Joshua's nostrils flared and he balled a fist. "I can handle any inter-ference and take care of any who'd dare to come on my property uninvited."

Isaiah nodded. "I'll come tomorrow and bring three of my men with me."

Joshua reached out and shook Isaiah's hand.

In the carriage, Abigail expelled her held breath and whispered a prayer of thanks.

~

*T*he following week after the assembly met, one of the biggest plantation owners on the island, Richard Williams, and Governor Smith himself cornered Joshua in the hallway.

The governor, a corpulent man of medium height who was never without his long curled brown wig and extravagant clothing, pompous for the island, pointed his chubby, ringed finger at Joshua.

"You've taken a dangerous step, my man, putting in a black overseer."

Another younger planter who lived a few miles from Rockford, Andrew Campbell, stood just beyond the group, his ear cocked in their direction.

"Yes, a perilous one, not only to you but to all of us." William's long nose flared, and his bushy brows met in a frown.

The man spent most of the year in England and only stayed on the island when it was time for harvest money to flow in. His estate was in the hands of an overseer and a financial manager. Joshua refrained from smiling. The two employees probably kept half the owner's profits for themselves.

Joshua refused to cower before the men and threw his chest out and looked them in the eye. "Well, now, you both heard I needed an overseer to get my harvests in. And you know there's not an experienced overseer to be had on the island this time of year. So I did what I had to do. And, I might add, it's working fine."

Elbowing into a place next to Joshua, Andrew Campbell spoke in a clear, firm voice. "Becket, you're just begging for your people to decide they don't need to work at all and choose your new overseer to lead them in an uprising to take what they want. Then the Maroons in the mountains will join them, and this island can end up in a blood bath like we've had before."

The young peacock. Joshua gave him a scant glance before pushing his way out the door of the Government House. Regardless of his neighbor planters' worries, he had taken the only choice he had to make sure his harvest came in. Not a hint of a problem had surfaced so far. He'd take care of whatever arose.

At Rockford, he ran into Mrs. Pelfrey in the hall, her face tight with anxiety.

"What is it?"

"Jade. After supper, she went out to walk with Potcake and never came back." She wrung her hands. "We thought she'd be safe with the dog. We've looked everywhere. Mrs. Welch and Jeremy are still out searching."

Joshua started for the stairs, speaking over his shoulder as the interchange in town still dominated his thoughts. "Never fear, Potcake won't let anything happen to her."

"But...sir." The housekeeper's tone froze him on the first step. "Potcake came back half an hour ago. Without her."

CHAPTER 8

$\mathcal{A}$s she followed Jeremy astride Buttercup at a brisk pace, Abigail kept a firm grip on Arabelle's reins. Fearful images bombarded her mind—Jade fallen into a river, or down an embankment, or lying somewhere crying for help. With effort, she forced them away and prayed.

Potcake led for a while, then dropped back, winded. Their fast gait he could not keep up with, revealed his age.

Abigail looked up at the gathering shadows of twilight and whispered a prayer. *Lord, you know where the child is. Please help us find her before dark, and let her be unharmed.*

They left the road when it became only a path into the woods she had traveled on her earlier ride with Mr. Becket. But Jeremy didn't go toward the waterfall.

He called to her as he took another path. "Don't you fret, now. I bet I know where she is."

The horses slowed their pace through the shadowed trees. Potcake loped ahead of them and disappeared. As they arrived at a clearing, Potcake growled up ahead—and Jade's voice told him to behave!

Abigail's heart leaped. Jade sounded like her normal, commanding self. *Thank you, Lord.*

Jeremy dismounted. She did the same and followed him, leading her horse. Suddenly, a large, black man dressed only in ragged breeches came from the trees carrying Jade with one arm as if she were so much fluff. He wore a soiled cloth tied around his dark head. Setting Jade down near Abigail, he bowed and stepped back toward the trees.

The child took a deep breath. "I fell and hurt my ankle trying to get to some herbs I saw on a cliff. When I knew I couldn't get back home on my own, I started singing. Loudly. This man came and helped me. Potcake would not let him help, so I had to tell him to go home."

Abigail found her voice. "Thank you so much, sir. If you tell me your name and where you live, I'm sure her father will want to give you a reward."

He shook his head. "No reward. No tell about me." Then he melted into the shadows of the forest and disappeared.

Abigail suppressed a gasp. Jeremy moved close to her and whispered. "He may be a runaway or one of them Maroons that live up in the mountains."

"Whoever he is, Samson is very nice." Jade lifted her hands toward Abigail and Jeremy. "I might still be on that cliff where you'd never find me if not for him."

Jeremy helped her mount Buttercup, then swung up behind her. "How did you find out his name?"

"I didn't. I just called him Samson, since he seemed strong like the man in the Bible story you read to me, Mrs. Welch." Abigail smiled as she gathered Arabelle's reins, then Jade sighed. "I'm so tired. Can we go home?"

As they rejoined the dirt road, Joshua galloped toward them on Haidez.

When he came up to them and saw Jade was fine, he expelled a hot breath and glared at her. "Young lady, what on earth led you to come out here alone? You know that's forbidden without one of us. Look, it's almost dark. What if we hadn't found you? Do you know what could happen to a child away from the great house after dark?" Haidez tossed his head and snorted as his master's harsh voice blasted through the twilight.

Jade seemed to sink a foot in the saddle. Tears slid down her cheeks.

Abigail reined up closer to Joshua. "Sir, she's so tired, she can't sit alone in the saddle. Perhaps if you carried her with you?"

In one sweep, he pulled the child from Buttercup and placed her in front of him. Haidez pawed the ground but calmed with one word from Joshua.

As they started back down the road toward Rockford in the gathering darkness, Jade pressed her head against her father's shoulder and sighed. Abigail smiled. Had the man ever held the child close? Probably not.

〜

Two weeks passed with every slave and Joshua hard at work harvesting the sugarcane. One day, he invited Abigail to go with him to check on the progress. They rode horseback and passed a field where Isaiah led a team cutting off the tops and stripping thick leaves from the canes using machetes. Then they chopped the bottom thick section, which Joshua explained was full of juice, and threw it in piles for another team to stack on wagons.

They followed a wagon to the mill. Abigail stayed at a distance on Arabelle rather than move any closer to the big presses into which slaves fed the cane as fast as they could. Cane juice flowed into a vat on the other side.

When she asked why a man with a machete stood beside the revolving metal rollers, Joshua grimaced. "I hate to answer that, but since you asked, harvesting sugar out of cane is a dangerous business, but particularly at the presses. He's standing there in case one of the men gets a hand caught in the rollers. He's there to chop his arm off and save his life."

"Oh." Abigail turned away, nausea rising in her throat.

"But don't worry, that's never happened since I've owned Rockford."

Next, they passed the boiling house where Joshua explained the roaring fires beneath the vats cooked the syrup down to thick molasses.

Abigail wiped the moisture from her face with her handkerchief and whispered a prayer for the servants working in such heat.

"You about had enough touring, Mrs. Welch?" Joshua grinned at her.

"I think so, but how does the molasses end up becoming the white sugar we use?"

Joshua pointed to the next building. "That's our curing building which turns the molasses into golden-brown muscovado sugar." He indicated a stack of barrels. "Those are hogsheads of raw sugar we ship to Europe to further refine into the white sugar crystals you're familiar with."

He reined Haidez back to the main plantation road, and Abigail followed, her mind full of the things she'd seen and learned. Growing sugar was no easy or safe task.

"Do you enjoy being a sugar grower?" She had to ask that question.

"I'm not overjoyed. One day, I may sell out."

Her heart quickened its beat. "Where would you go?"

He twisted in his saddle to glance at her. "Back home to Charleston, of course."

And where would that leave her?

~

One day as the harvest season ended, Joshua called for Abigail to come to his study. He sat behind his desk with his arms crossed. A special light she had not noticed before shone from his features. "Have a seat, Abigail."

She swept her skirt beneath her and sat, her heartbeat quickening as it always did when he spoke her name in that warm tone.

"Jamaica celebrates the harvest with its biggest ball. I'd like you to attend as my guest. Government House hosts the event at Spanish Town in three weeks."

The man could get right to the point without preamble, but a ball was out of the question. "Sir, sorry, but I must decline. I have nothing in my wardrobe suitable for a ball."

"I've thought of that, and right now I'm sending a trunk to your room that I... uh, have at my disposal. It's full of what I assume to be fine gowns. I'm sure you'll find something suitable among them. Would you give it a look?"

Abigail's heartbeat increased, and her breath caught in her throat. A ball like those in her coming-out days in Charleston—and in a lovely gown? Was it possible? Would she dare? But Joshua Becket was a pirate, wasn't he? Was this plunder from a ship he'd taken?

He drummed his fingers on his desk. "Come on, Mrs. Welch. You'll have a great time. You deserve to attend at least one ball while you're here. This is the best one."

She swallowed. "All right. I'll check out the gowns, but I'm not making any promises." What if they were awful or horribly out of date or nothing fit her? And if she did find the perfect dress could she keep her wits about her attending such an event on the arm of such a man?

He smiled and stood. "Good. Let me know tomorrow."

~

*I*n her room, Abigail gasped as she pulled one lovely gown after another from the trunk. What lady of quality lost her wardrobe?

A gown of azure-blue taffeta rustled in her hands. She lifted it out, and pleasure rushed over her like a warm breath. Double rows of exquisite white lace lined the off-the-shoulder neckline, and the snug waist came down to a delicate point in front. The skirt encompassed yards and yards of the shining blue fabric. She held the dress up and turned to gaze in the mirror on the door of her chifferobe. Excitement tripled her heartbeat. Her one exquisite piece of jewelry —a gift from her mother—the teardrop blue sapphire pendant with its silver chain would be a perfect ornament. But would the dress fit her?

A knock sounded at her door.

She moved the gown to her bed. "Come in."

Clarissa breezed in and stared at the dress on the bed, then at the trunk. "I see you have received a gift from the master, ma'am. I heard he'd sent a chest to your room."

Heat climbed up Abigail's neck and spread to her face. "No, not a gift. Just a loan, Clarissa. Mr. Becket was good enough to let me see if I could find a suitable gown to wear...to a ball." She should've hidden the trunk and the blue dress. She pursed her lips and stared at the maid, daring her to ask more questions.

"Would you like me to help you try on that blue one?"

Abigail relented. She'd need other hands to help tighten her corset and lace the eyelets at the back of the dress.

In a few minutes, she stood before her mirror and stifled a gasp. The beautiful dress fit her as if it'd been made for her. She grasped the folds of the skirt and twirled around, then her gaze fell on the neckline. Was it too low? She tucked her lower lip between her teeth.

Clarissa stepped forward and patted the full skirt. "Ma'am, I ain't never..." Her eyebrows rose an inch. "You gonna be the belle of any ball, is what I think."

Abigail ducked her chin. "Thank you, Clarissa. Now help me get out of it and back into my muslin, please." Perhaps the gown would do for this one ball. Besides, who would be interested in anything a governess wore that night when all the planters, their wives, and their daughters arrived in their finest?

The following morning, a Saturday, Abigail walked to the stables and asked Mr. Dykes to saddle Arabelle. A good jaunt in the fresh air was just what she, as well as the horse, needed.

She was no sooner in the saddle than Joshua Becket strode up and commanded Haidez to be readied. "You don't mind if I ride along with you this morning, do you, Mrs. Welch?"

She took a deep breath and forced her voice to sound light. "Of course not, if you'd like to come." She wanted to add, "It's your plantation, sir," but didn't. Her idea of a quiet, contemplative outing dissolved like a bubble in the morning sunshine. And she didn't like the way her heartbeat increased in the man's presence.

Dressed in tan riding pants, black boots, and a green shirt open at the neck enough to show curly dark hair, he exuded his usual magnetism. He wore no hat, and the gray at his temples only made him look more handsome. She turned her glance away, and he smiled. Her cheeks heated. He'd caught her staring.

She trotted Arabelle behind Haidez out to the plantation road.

"There is one place I'd like to show you that's pretty interesting. I don't think you've seen it before." He turned to face her as he talked.

"Yes, and what is that?"

"We've got what folks call healing mineral waters on the island. It's a special spring that comes from the mountains."

Arabelle matched her gait to Haidez's, and Abigail came even with the man. "Sounds interesting, Mr. Becket. Is it far?"

"Oh, we'll be back for the midday meal, Abigail." He grinned as he used her given name. "You won't mind, will you, if we skip the surnames while we're away from Jade?"

"Very well, Joshua." She smiled at him. "If you insist." His name felt good on her lips.

They cantered for a time until Joshua turned Haidez onto a worn path off the road that led across a field and toward the mountains. Soon they traveled in the forest's shade. A breeze rustled the leaves, and birdsong echoed amid the limbs. Somewhere distant, the sound of a waterfall echoed. "The healing spring has a story about its history. Want to hear it?"

The path narrowed, and Abigail had to ride behind Joshua. "By all means, but let's wait until we get there so I won't miss hearing it."

They came out to a clearing and just beyond, a glassy pool shimmered with the contrast of sunlight and shadows from the mountain behind it. Boulders surrounded the spring. Joshua dismounted and tied Haidez's reins to a limb. She did the same for Arabelle.

Joshua sat on one of several rocks that seemed to be lined up around the pond and gazed at it. He moved over and patted a place for Abigail to sit. She selected another rock.

He shook his head and smiled, then began his narrative. "The story is told that many years ago, a slave named Jonathan Ludford discovered this place when he ran away from his master after being beaten. It seems he stepped into these waters, and the minerals there soothed and healed his wounds within a few minutes. When he returned to his plantation, his owner saw his fast-healed wounds and promised he'd never beat him again if he'd reveal the pool's location."

Joshua stood.

Abigail stared at the bubbling spring. "Do you think the story is true?"

He moved toward her. "Folks here believe it, and you see the rocks they've drawn up around it. They come here and take a dip when they have a wound that needs to be healed."

"Interesting tale. Thank you for sharing it." She rose, but that put her much too close to him. Her stomach dropped. When she tried to step aside, she stumbled and fell toward him.

He encircled her in his brawny arms and looked into her countenance. "You know, you have the brightest eyes I think I've ever seen."

She couldn't think or move as she breathed in his scent of spice and manliness. The heart-rending tenderness in his gaze washed over her. It filled her with surprise and turned her knees to jelly. With effort, she pushed back from him and searched for a level spot to place her feet and escape his embrace. When she turned back to face him, he bent and planted a kiss on her forehead.

His lips on her brow burned with warmth that tingled down to her toes.

The next second, he removed his hands from her shoulders and stepped back. "Don't worry, Mrs. Welch. My intentions are honorable." His mustache twitched and a grin spread across his tanned face. "I admit, temptation tried me when you stumbled my way. It's not that often I have a beautiful woman fall into my arms."

She averted her warm face. Twisting aside, she traversed the rocky path toward the horses. How about Lady Harcourt? Did he say such things to her?

As they mounted, he shot her a question. "What about the Spanish Town Ball? Will you attend with me? You saw you can trust me to behave—when I have to." He chuckled.

She pressed her lips together to resist a smile. "I found a suitable dress in your offering, so I'll be happy to accept your invitation."

~

A few days later, about five o'clock, Joshua sat in the study mulling over government papers for the British Council meeting that night. A plantation worker rushed into the room with Walter and Mrs. Pelfrey steps behind him. Joshua glanced up and frowned. All he needed was some kind of crisis to hinder him getting to the meeting on time. He'd missed the past month's meeting.

The sweating black man Joshua recognized as one who worked with Isaiah Baker whipped off his dusty hat. "Suh, I hates to tell you, but three mens come up on us while we wuz cutting the cane, and theys told Mas' Baker they had to teach him a lesson, that no black man, slave or free, could be no overseer." The man gushed words out between deep gulps of air while he twisted his hat in shaking hands. "And they beat him. They got him pretty bad."

"What?" Joshua stood so fast his chair tilted back and fell. He walked toward the worker who was still trying to get his breath. He laid a hand on the man's thin shoulder. "You did right coming to me. Did you recognize any of them?"

The man stiffened, lowered his dark eyes, then shook his head.

Walter placed the chair upright.

Joshua grabbed his hat. "We'll need a wagon to go to the field and bring Isaiah to the house." He shot a glance at Mrs. Pelfrey. "Get hot water ready and our medicine chest."

He hurried toward the stables with the plantation servant trotting behind him. As he strode into the corridor, Joshua yelled, "Saddle Haidez and harness a wagon for this man to drive. And throw some hay in the back." His voice rang through the barn, and Mr. Dykes and Jeremy rushed down the steps from their living quarters above and hurried to prepare the horses and wagon.

Cantering to the field where Isaiah Baker had been working, Joshua fought a fiery rage rising up from his middle. Bishop most surely had instigated the beating, and the servants had recognized him but were still so fearful of the former overseer they couldn't speak a word to stop him.

Pray for Isaiah's life.

The words seemed to whisper on the breeze stirred by Haidez's gallop. Or did Joshua imagine them? He ought to pray for the man to survive, but it'd been too long since he'd prayed. And why would God listen to a sinner?

They arrived at the canebrake, and he slid off his horse. One of Isaiah's men stooped beside him, holding his hand, as he lay prostrate on the ground. The other slaves stood with furrowed brows and mournful eyes, in a circle, as if in a death vigil.

They parted like the Red Sea as Joshua strode forward and bent down beside the overseer. Anger flowed like hot lava through him as he assessed the battered face and blood seeping from several wounds on Isaiah's head, shoulders, and arms. He swallowed bile and touched one of the man's large, callused hands. "Sorry I didn't believe you when you said they'd come after you, Isaiah. I'll make sure they pay for what they've done."

A swelling eye blinked up at the late-afternoon sun, then at Joshua. The bruised lips opened on a grunt, followed by a confession. "It were Mr. Bishop and his two men what always run with him. He threatened that any of these who tried to help me would get the same. He had a gun." Isaiah closed his one good eye and sighed as if that much talk had taken the last of his strength.

Joshua looked around at his people. Yes, they still feared Bishop. Why had he kept the man so long? Dare he arm some of his slaves? "Come, let's get him in the wagon."

Several of the men spread a blanket and gently rolled Isaiah into its middle, then they picked up the four corners and laid him inside the wagon bed strewn with hay. Joshua rode Haidez beside it toward home.

Halfway back to the plantation, a tiny figure with her wispy gray hair stuffed under a triangle of blue cloth stood in the middle of the road waving long thin arms. The wagon driver shouted, "Whoa."

Joshua rode forward and confronted the elderly woman. "Granny, what are you doing here? Go back to your cabin."

"Sir, not before I gets the injured man brought home with me."

"What do you mean? Get out of the road."

"I'se gonna nurse him back to health. Yo white doctor'll let him die."

Curses formed on Joshua's lips, but before he could utter them, a loud groan issued from the wagon bed.

Joshua turned Haidez back. Isaiah looked more dead than alive, lying there. The man lifted a large shaking hand toward him. "Suh, let me go with the woman. She's a healer. I knowed her years ago." His arm plopped back down on the hay.

Joshua shook his head as he scoffed lightly under his breath, but he motioned to the woman, and she climbed into the wagon beside the driver. Joshua pulled aside as the wagon moved away.

Striding back into the great house a few minutes later, he met Abigail descending the staircase. She approached him, gentle creases on her smooth brow and her full lips pressed tight. "I heard about the beating. Is Isaiah going to be all right?"

"If your prayers and Granny's herbs work, he will be." He left her standing at the bottom of the steps, staring at him speechless.

CHAPTER 9

*T*he last to arrive, Joshua slid into his seat at the British
Assembly in the Government House and adjusted his
waistcoat and cravat after his hasty ride on Haidez into town.

Governor Smith sat at the head of the table in a blue satin waistcoat and long white wig. A young liveried servant waved a palm leaf
to stir the air around the king's appointee to Jamaica. The leader
acknowledged Joshua's arrival with good humor. "Glad you made it,
Mr. Becket. We're just getting started." He shuffled papers before him
on the table.

A servant placed cool drinks at each of the council members'
places.

Wealthy planter Richard Williams sat at the right hand of the
governor. He returned Joshua's nod with the slightest tip of his blond-
wigged head, as did most of the other men present. Andrew Campbell
ignored Joshua, even though he sat across from him. Campbell had
wanted Bishop to come work for him in the past. The word on the
plantation was that he'd hired the overseer as soon as he left Rockford. After the session, Joshua would confront him about Isaiah's
beating.

But as the planters stood around the table at the end of the business meeting and Joshua approached Campbell, the younger man strode to the door. Joshua caught up with him. "Sir, I'd like to have a talk with you, if you don't mind."

Pompous in green satin and a shoulder-length brown wig, Campbell turned a sallow face with thick jowls toward him. "I don't want to hear anything you've got to say, Mr. Becket, since you hired a freedman as overseer." He pulled a lace handkerchief from his cuff and touched his nose as if Joshua exuded an odor. His dark, beady eyes hardened. "That is, unless you're going to tell me you've come to your senses and fired him, or that the man has…"

"Died? Is that what you were going to say? I know Bishop is working for you, isn't he?"

"That's none of your business."

"It became my business when he came over today and beat my overseer."

"Did he? And how is the freedman?" Not an ounce of sympathy emerged on the man's face.

"He didn't die, for your information, despite Bishop's barbarism."

Campbell flicked his handkerchief. "If you'll excuse me, I have to be off." He turned on his heel to pass.

Joshua blocked his path, his nostrils flaring. "Be warned. If Bishop ever comes onto my property again, I'll have his hide and also bring charges against both of you."

～

*A*bigail chose a good time two days later to visit Granny when Jade was busy elsewhere. She found Isaiah lying on a pallet on the little porch. The tall man almost reached from one end of the space to the other, with just enough room remaining for Granny's rocker. The woman sat there shelling peas from her garden.

"You come to visit my patient?" Granny spoke in a low voice and smiled.

Abigail stopped at the edge of the porch. Isaiah's face remained swollen, but the wounds on his face and bare shoulders appeared clean and not inflamed. A soft snore escaped from his nose and mouth every few moments. "Yes, it seems he's resting well. Your medicine must be working."

Granny's wrinkled face brightened. "I cleaned and coated his wounds with goldenseal and aloe, and I give him valerian to help him rest."

"Ho, there." A warm, hearty voice caused Abigail and Granny to look back toward the path from the great house. Reverend Mark Gardner walked toward them, smiling. He stopped at the edge of the porch beside Abigail and nodded to her.

Dressed in a neat brown waistcoat stretched over his wide shoulders and with his brown hair pulled back into a queue, he presented a picture of pleasant, powerful manhood. Strength of character flowed from his countenance, confirming a person void of hypocrisy and artifice.

As he looked down at Isaiah, his expression sobered, and his voice lowered. "I hate to see my friend like this, but at least he's resting." He glanced up at Granny and held out his hand. "I'm Mark Gardner, the minister from the Baptist church in Kingston. Isaiah and I are the best of friends."

Granny stared at him for a moment, then dropped the peapod she held into her lap, wiped her hand on her apron, and shook his. "I'se doing all I know to do. He's gonna be fine in a few days."

The minister's smile returned, lighting up his handsome face. "That's good news." He reached inside his waistcoat pocket and pulled out a card. "Here's my name and address. If you need anything, will you please send a message to me?"

Granny didn't take the card. "I can't read, mister minister, so you can keep yo card. But iffen I need anything, I'll send word by the governess here, if that's all right." She nodded toward Abigail.

"Of course, it will be fine, Granny. Shall I tell Jeremy to come by each day and see if you have a message?"

The woman nodded.

Isaiah groaned, and Granny placed a bony finger to her lips and motioned Abigail and Reverend Gardner away. "Let 'em sleep."

Abigail headed back up the path toward the great house with Mark Gardner's reassuring presence behind her. As they neared the entrance to the garden, he touched her elbow.

"Abigail—if you might allow me to call you that—I'd love to see Rockford's garden. I've heard Mr. Becket has an excellent gardener. I love gardening myself. Do you have time to show me?"

She smiled at the friendly sound of her name on his lips. "Yes, I think Mr. Dykes is an accomplished gardener, and I'd be happy to show you the grounds, Reverend Gardner."

He stopped and folded his thick arms. "Just one thing. Please call me Mark."

She nodded and led him through the gate and down the path past various flowers in full bloom. Their glorious fragrance filled the air, especially one with long tubular white flowers. She stopped to enjoy the plant's beauty and breathe in its exceptional scent. "I don't know the name of this one, but it has the most glorious smell."

"It's Jamaican Lady of the Night. Its delightful fragrance beats most roses."

Abigail turned to him. "Why is it called a lady of the night? It looks great in daylight."

He grinned, and Abigail liked the way a dimple showed up in his chin. "The fragrance intensifies at night, that's why."

Amazingly, Mark seemed to know the names of most of the plants in the garden. He pointed out the Bougainvillea that climbed over trellises, native orchids, and Jamaica's beautiful Blue Mahoe tree with its straight trunk, broad green leaves, and hibiscus-like blossoms. He touched one on a low limb. "These blossoms change colors as they mature. From this bright yellow, they'll go to orange, red, and finally, to crimson."

"But not to blue?" Abigail tilted her chin.

He tapped the trunk. "The blue in the name comes from the blue-green streaks that appear in the wood when it's harvested and polished. I've studied a good bit about plants and the meanings of their names. It's like a hobby with me."

He gestured to the bench on the other side of the tree and sat beside her. The man's clean, musky scent tickled Abigail's nose.

"The most important thing about flowers and any other growing thing is how much they have to tell us about their Maker."

Abigail turned to face him. How pleasant to have a talk about spiritual things. She'd missed her friend Anna Grace and their wonderful conversations. "What sort of things?"

"Mysteries, truths hidden from all but the most diligent of seekers." His dark eyes glowed.

"Mysteries? Why would God not want everyone to know all they can about Him when they look at His beautiful creation?"

Mark bent and scooped up a handful of dark soil from beside the bench. "For the same reason that most of the garden's wonders lie underground for all but a short time of the year. Only those who love gardening enough to dig, plant, water, and watch for growth learn the messages."

"But wouldn't everyone enjoy and admire the beauty of this tree, for example, or the scent of the Jamaican Lady of the Night whether or not they planted them? Don't you like them for these same simple reasons?"

He grinned at her. "Yes. Of course, I do. But I love them most of all for the deeper truths they have to tell us. The glimpses of eternal things they give us. Many miss seeing these."

Like Joshua Becket and the busy Mrs. Pelfrey. "You may be right. I doubt many people would think about eternal things if they took time to walk in a garden."

"God's growing things contain more mysteries and lessons than we'll probably ever know." He opened his palm. "What do you see?"

"Soil."

"Do you see the colorful blossoms or smell the perfume of flowers?"

Abigail shook her head.

"Have you ever wondered how a lovely flower or even a red tomato can emerge from what I hold in my hand? Dirt. Something most people try to keep off their hands and out of their houses. Yet, when water is added, it is the very transmitter of life for everything that grows. That's a genuine mystery. It hints to me of how God can take a broken piece of lost humanity and make something beautiful arise out of the ashes with the water of His Word." His voice, though deep, was crisp and clear.

Abigail took a deep, satisfying breath. Amazing. The man had stirred up quite a few new thoughts in her mind.

"There are many truths we can see if we have spiritual eyes. For example, The Jamaican Lady of the Night exudes a stronger fragrance at night when there is no warmth from the sun and no adoring glances to appreciate her blossoms. Isn't that a great lesson God gives to us, to shine in darker times, to exude the fragrance of faith in the face of lack or crisis?"

Abigail stood and smiled. "You can get a sermon out of that, I'm sure." She glanced back up the path, the sun now higher in the sky. "This has been most interesting, Mark, but I must get back to the great house."

He dropped the soil on the ground, wiped his hand on his breeches, and then followed her to the garden entrance. "Will you ever think of soil the same way, Abigail?" he called to her.

She laughed out loud. "No, I don't think I will."

$\sim$

*J*oshua Becket rode up on Haidez as Abigail and the reverend emerged from the garden. What could they be talking and laughing about?

The minister greeted him. "Hello, Mr. Becket, I came to check on Isaiah, and Abigail was good enough to show me your garden. Next to pastoring, gardening gives me joy."

Was Isaiah the only thing the good reverend had come to check on? Joshua nodded at the man, but the satisfied expression on the minister's face and the tender way he glanced at Abigail as he talked sent a streak of surprise up Joshua's back. His governess's cheeks were a rosy pink. So that's the way things were. "How did you find Isaiah?"

Reverend Gardner crossed his arms. "He was resting well, I'm happy to say, and the elderly woman there seems to know how to help him."

Abigail stepped forward. "Granny says he'll be recovered in a few days."

"Good. He's a strong one."

Joshua reined Haidez toward the stable. After he dismounted, he released the reins to Dykes and headed back to the house. Abigail and Gardner strolled well ahead of him, still engrossed in conversation. They paused to say their farewells at the steps, the minister briefly taking her hand.

Of course, it was fine if Abigail became attracted to the minister and him to her. They were of a similar age and interests. But why did the idea sit heavy as iron across Joshua's middle?

～

*E*arly the following morning, Joshua walked to the north field with Isaiah's machete slung across his shoulder and his team of men following. Good thing he'd never hesitated to get his hands on the actual work of sugar planting when necessary, but sailing the waves was so much more interesting.

He joined in as they stripped the leaves and chopped the cane. He soon discarded his shirt. By noon, they finished cutting the main part of the field and piling the cane onto the wagons for transporting to the mill.

Joshua took a long drink from the water jug as the men loaded the last stalks. He flexed his shoulder muscles. Maybe they were a little sore because it'd been a while since he'd done any cutting, but they still served him well. He pulled his handkerchief from his breeches, dipped it in the water, and wiped the sweat from his face and neck. Horses approached—Abigail and Jade coming down the road on horseback. He stepped over to the wagon wheel and grabbed his shirt. He got it on, but not stuffed into his trousers before the two stopped a few yards from him.

Jade laughed. "I've never seen you so dirty, Father."

"Sugarcane cutting is hard, grimy work, daughter," he responded, but his gaze flickered to Abigail. How lovely she looked in her green riding habit, with her thick, dark hair in neat coils under a net.

The woman lowered her lashes and lifted the basket balanced in front of her. "Would you mind coming to get this, Mr. Becket? Mrs. Pelfrey has sent you some food."

He smiled and came forward. "I hope there's enough for the workers too."

A servant behind him spoke up. "No, suh. We's all have our own food our womens bring to the mill. We'll just get this last load finished and go meet 'em."

Jade's face lit up like a lantern. "That means we can have a picnic. Where's a good place? Will you have a picnic with us, Father?"

His daughter's wheedling tone and wide eyes smote him, then Joshua turned to Abigail. He placed his hand on her horse's mane. "I know a cool spot, but it's a bit of a ride. Would you mind if I mounted behind you on Arabelle to travel there, Mrs. Welch? I'm afraid Buttercup would never hold me."

~

*A*bigail stared, tongue-tied, as Joshua's eyes filled with fierce sparkling. Able to do no more than nod her consent, she took a deep breath. How could she mind? The horse belonged to him.

He placed his hand on the saddle and swung up behind her with ease. She struggled to keep the basket balanced with one hand and the horse's head under control with the other until he reached around her and grasped the reins. His muscled, tanned arms enclosed her. His stiff torso close behind her emanating heat, a spicy scent, and honest sweat exploded a gamut of perplexing emotions through her.

Arabelle tossed her head but soon adjusted to the extra weight and rider.

Joshua turned the horse and started down the road.

Abigail concentrated on holding the basket tight and keeping her own balance while not leaning against him.

He snorted. "Mrs. Welch. Forget trying to avoid leaning into me, or we may both lose our seats." He tightened his arms around her until she rested against his chest, close enough to feel the beat of his heart. Then he clicked his tongue and Arabelle picked up her gait.

Abigail, busy trying to breathe and slow her racing heart while in his grip, didn't remark when they left the plantation road. They veered down a narrow path toward a patch of woods with the Blue Mountains looming beyond. The steady heartbeat of the man behind her mocked the hammering in her chest.

When they came to a shady spot next to a stream, Joshua pulled back on the reins and slid off Arabelle. Then he lifted the basket from Abigail's grasp and set it on a rock. Walking back to her and Arabelle, he reached up to lift her from the horse. She couldn't rally quickly enough to protest. He placed his hands around her waist, brought her down, and steadied her as her boots touched the ground.

"Thank you, Mr. Becket." She moved away as soon as possible.

Jade jumped off Buttercup, tied her reins to a limb, and ran to the stream. "This looks so cool, Father. Can I kick off my boots and wade?"

Joshua assessed the stream as he strolled a few feet up one side. "Maybe if you stay right by me. First, I am going to wash off a bit of this field dirt." With that, he cast off his shirt and scooped water over his face, head, and arms.

Abigail helped Jade pull off her boots, trying not to look at the man washing in the stream. His brawny build and tanned upper body proved he was not the average plantation owner who led a gentleman's life and never lifted a finger in actual work.

Moments later, Joshua joined his daughter, and Jade's laughter at the cool water flowing over her dancing feet echoed through the trees.

Abigail spread a cloth on a large rock and pulled cheese, bread, and apples from the basket. Jade brought the water skin tied to her saddle. They sat and ate. Somehow the simple fare had never tasted better.

After finishing, Abigail cocked her head to one side. Why was there no birdsong?

"You're wondering about the birds?" Joshua's voice was steady but lower in volume than before. "I want you to get the stuff back in the basket. I'll get Jade's boots on." His last words carried a warning tone.

She stared at him. His lips had tightened and a muscle worked in his jaw.

"Do it now, Abigail, as fast as you can, and don't look around."

Jade protested, but he shushed her and helped her get back into her boots and up on Buttercup while Abigail shoved plates and napkins into the basket. He turned the horse to the path and whacked its rump. Buttercup trotted fast back the way they had come.

Abigail stood near Arabelle. In one swoop, Joshua lifted her, basket and all, onto the horse and slid up behind her.

He placed his arms tight around her, clutched the reins, and whispered in her ear. "Hold tight. We're going to run for it." He clamped his legs into Arabelle's sides, and she lunged forward into a gallop.

Joshua didn't speak again until both horses arrived at the entrance to the stables. He slid off Arabelle as Mr. Dykes and Jeremy appeared to take the horses.

Abigail tried to catch her breath.

Jade turned to her father. "What did you see, Papa, that scared you so and made us have to leave fast?"

"I just decided we needed to get on back home, little lady." He helped the child off Buttercup and sent her on her way to the great house.

Abigail dismounted before he could assist her. "Can you tell me what you saw?"

"I saw some painted Maroon warriors coming down the mountain before they saw us. That's why the birds ceased chattering." He spoke to Dykes. "Saddle Haidez as fast as you can."

The man hurried into the barn.

Joshua stepped inside the entrance and lifted a waistcoat from a hook. He slipped into it and came back to Abigail. "I must ride into town and tell the governor what I saw. Something could be amiss with the Maroons. Tell Mrs. Pelfrey where I've gone, and keep Jade in the house until I return. Will you?"

Was there some danger? "Of course, I will." *If I can,* she felt like adding. Jade could scoot out of sight faster than Potcake.

Dykes returned with Haidez. Joshua gave the man some instructions, then mounted. He twisted in the saddle toward Abigail and gave her a dark, layered look. "You stay in the house, too, Mrs. Welch. Dykes will station guards around the place until I return." He clamped his knees on his mount and galloped down the drive.

CHAPTER 10

Clutching the picnic basket, holding only the used plates and utensils now, Abigail trekked up the cobbled path to the great house and caught her lower lip between her teeth. The sun's warm rays and myriad kinds of birdsong in the trees did nothing to soften her irritation. Joshua's last command before he galloped off toward Spanish Town stuck like a splinter in her thoughts. Of course, she'd stay in the house. How could she keep Jade in the house without being there herself? Was the man truly concerned about her safety? But overriding every other concern, the ride back home double-mounted on Arabelle, encircled by his arms, continued to make warmth flush her body.

Determined to settle her countenance into its normal tranquility, she sucked in a deep breath, strode into the house, and sailed up the grand staircase.

She found Mrs. Pelfrey in the schoolroom with Jade. The woman stood with her arms folded, staring at the child. "Are you sure your father didn't tell you why you had to hurry back?"

"No, ma'am. He just said we needed to get home."

Abigail walked to the bookcase and pulled the heavy book down that held the pressed herbs. Setting it on the table, she smiled at Jade.

"Honey, I think it's time for you to check on your herbs. Would you like to get your journal list and make a note beside the appropriate herb name of how it looks now at two weeks? Would you do that and do it with care while I go wash up a bit in my room?"

"Yes, ma'am, I'd love to see my pressed herbs." The child sat in front of the enormous book, her green eyes dancing.

Abigail motioned to Mrs. Pelfrey to follow, and they left Jade busy and humming a little tune.

Once in her room, Abigail related what Joshua said he saw coming down the mountain.

Mrs. Pelfrey's eyes widened. "Did you see them, too, madam?"

"No, I was too busy finishing lunch...and keeping watch over Jade." She lowered her eyes. At least, the child was the main one who'd claimed her attention. She would not admit that sitting so near to Joshua Becket on the warm rock had also kept her senses in a stew.

"Let's sit a spell and I'll give you the facts." The housekeeper marched to the chair facing Abigail's balcony and sat. "Not being from Jamaica, you wouldn't understand the import of this, but I will try to help you see." Abigail sat beside her and gave the woman her full attention.

"I was here about twenty years ago when the last Maroon uprising took place. It's now referred to as Tacky's Revolt. Those were hard, scary days for all the plantations, believe me."

Abigail leaned forward. "But who are these Maroons, and where did they come from?"

"They're former slaves, and some are descendants of the Spanish colonists who didn't flee the island when the British captured Jamaica. Instead, they made settlements high in the mountains. Runaway slaves and freedmen often join them. At times, they've come down and raided and burned plantations, killed the owners, stole weapons, and made demands."

"How terrible." Abigail hung on every word of Mrs. Pelfrey's.

"The first Maroon War was before my time here, back in the 1730s. It concluded with a treaty, but some never agreed to the treaty. Later, the man Tacky, a slave overseer on one of the plantations, led a group of enslaved Africans to kill the owners and take over the plantation. The revolt spread to other plantations, and warriors from the mountains joined in. They gained confidence from Obeah men, Caribbean witch doctors, who helped inspire the revolt. But the British militia and some Maroons who were on the side of the planters finally helped put the revolt down." She took a breath and her face hardened. "But many plantations were burned, their owners murdered. Today slave revolts are still the worst nightmare of the plantation owners. If what Joshua saw means anything, you can see how it would worry folks."

Abigail's eyes widened. "Was Rockford burned?"

"No, it was one of the lucky ones, but the revolt scared the Rockford family so badly, they sold out and sailed back to England."

"You didn't want to go with them?"

Mrs. Pelfrey sighed. "Well, at the time, I had some friends here, so I didn't want to leave. Course, they've gone to their reward now or moved away." She stood. "I'll go make sure the rest of the house servants know about the sighting and lock all the outer doors. Walter'll see to that. You know he's from the mountains, a Maroon himself."

"Really?"

"Yes, but he got religion as a young man and left the settlement and came looking for plantation work. Rockford's old English butler took him in hand and taught him how to be an excellent butler. Now he's got a family in the slave village and is even a grandfather by now, I understand."

Abigail repressed a shudder when Mrs. Pelfrey finished her explanation about the Maroons. Would Walter's connections and Joshua's alertness be enough to spare them from future danger?

~

*J*oshua arrived at Government House in Spanish Town, tied Haidez's reins to the hitching post, and wiped the sweat and dust from his face and neck. Beyond the impressive white stucco building, a militia squad in their bright red-and-white uniforms marched to the staccato beat of a drum. He bounded up the marble steps to the massive oak door. The unfamiliar soldier standing guard there moved to block the entrance.

"Move away, soldier. I'm Joshua Becket and a member of the assembly here to see the governor." Why did the British militia post new recruits at the main door?

"Sorry, sir." The young man jutted out his jaw, clicked his heels, bowed, then moved aside.

Joshua strode down the wide, tiled hall to the governor's office. The secretary, a young soldier in British uniform, stood as he recognized Joshua, and told him the governor was in a meeting.

"Well, maybe I need to break into his meeting." Joshua headed toward the conference room door.

"Sir, you can't do that." The secretary hurried to intercept, but he was too late. Joshua opened the door and entered before the man could prevent it. He stepped inside beside Joshua.

The governor looked up and frowned at his secretary. Andrew Campbell sat across from the statesman's desk. Both men wore full, curled wigs and satin waistcoats.

"What is this, Jones? I told you no interruptions."

The young man's face turned bright red as he faced his superior. "Sir—"

Joshua moved forward before the soldier could finish his response. "Governor Smith, I need to talk to you about what I saw in the mountains today. It may mean nothing, but it could also mean something important."

The man exhaled an aggravated breath, then sat forward. "Very well, Mr. Becket. This better be significant."

Campbell started to leave, but Joshua spoke to him. "You need to hear this too."

Joshua came fully into the room and stopped in front of the men. "Today I saw three painted Maroon warriors marching down the mountain, closer than I've ever seen them descend since I've owned Rockford."

"Painted, you say?" The governor took a cigar from a box on his desk and lit it. "What significance does that have?" He inhaled and then blew pungent smoke into the room.

Campbell stirred in his chair. "Sir, they put on war paint when they are thinking about going into war."

The governor coughed and his face stiffened. He snuffed the end of his cigar in the ash tray and glared at Campbell, then Joshua. "I heard horror tales about these Maroon warriors in England, but I thought all that was settled with a peace treaty years ago."

Joshua nodded. "There have been several treaties, but there're always a few who don't want to abide by the treaties."

The governor narrowed an eye at Campbell. "What do you think? You've been on the island longer than Becket here."

"I've never seen a revolt, but I know some who are scared even of the word being said." He tilted his head toward Joshua. "Maybe these warriors you saw were painted up to fight another division of Maroons. You only saw three, you said. I heard they fight among themselves most of the time." Anger stiffened the man's bearded face before his next words. "Hiring a black overseer like you've done, Becket, might help start a revolt. Maybe we'll blame it on you if one does come."

Joshua frowned. "Who I hire at Rockford is none of your business, sir." His voice was controlled but cold. "And if your plantation is burned, you won't be worrying about who to blame if you're murdered in your sleep."

The governor made a scolding sound and leaned back in his chair "Joshua, that's not the kind of talk I want to hear. We've got a well-trained militia, and I think they can protect us. I appreciate your keeping me informed. Do let me know if you see any more warriors." He stood, came around the desk, and laid his hand on Joshua's sleeve and smiled. "And don't forget about our ball coming up at Government House. I was just telling Campbell we will host a special guest, Lord Halton, the King's emissary, being sent here to check up on reports of pirating in our waters."

Joshua's chin jerked up and his face tightened. Maybe he'd decided to give up his swashbuckling adventures at the right time.

The governor patted his arm. "But that has nothing to do with you, my planter friend. Are you bringing the luscious Lady Harcourt to the soiree?"

Joshua expelled a harsh breath. Why had he even bothered to ride Haidez into a lather to alert the governor about what he'd seen in the mountains? "No, sir, I'm not bringing the lady. Thank you for the audience." He turned and strode out of the office, then from the building.

A king's emissary, headed to the island. What could his investigation turn up? Nothing to link Joshua to pirating. He'd been too careful, and besides, he had now given up his escapades by sea.

After finding a watering trough for the horse, he rode back toward Rockford at half his earlier pace. Were the warriors he saw preparing to fight another group of Maroons, or were they spying out the territory for a revolt against the plantation owners? Why did his gut tell him it was the latter?

～

On the day of the Government House ball, Abigail finished tutoring Jade early and hurried to her room at three o'clock. Joshua had told her he'd have the carriage at the front entrance at six o'clock. Surely, three hours would be enough time to get ready. She pulled the bell rope and asked for hot water for her bath.

Mira soon came with a steaming bucket. She eyed the blue gown spread out on the bed. "Ma'am, would you like me to dress your hair? I know how to do hair for ladies—just ask Clarissa or Mrs. Pelfrey."

Abigail pulled her long dark tresses out of the way as she unbuttoned her frock. It wouldn't hurt to see what the girl could do. And she had the pearl comb Anna Grace had given her the last Christmas she'd spent in Charleston.

By five o'clock, she sat in front of her mirror fully dressed, turning her head from side to side, admiring Mira's work. The maid had transformed Abigail's thick hair into cascades of curls. Leaving a few to frame her face, Mira had piled the rest into coils on top of her head and secured them with the gleaming pearl comb.

"Thank you, Mira, you've done wonders." Abigail leaned forward as the maid fastened the blue sapphire pendant with its silver chain around her neck. How perfectly the gem matched and enhanced the dress. And she'd managed to raise the low neckline a tad with her needle and thread without destroying its lines. Hopefully, eyes would be drawn to the sparkling necklace. She pulled on her long white gloves and fitted her fingers into them snugly.

A quick knock sounded at the door, and Mira admitted Clarissa carrying a small tray with a cup of tea and slice of cake. The girl glanced at Abigail and gasped. "Oh, my, you most surely will be the belle of the ball, ma'am." She deposited the tray on Abigail's small table. "Here is some tea and Mrs. Dykes's raisin bread to tide you over."

As inviting as the fragrance of the tea and food might be, how could she partake of anything with excitement spiraling through her middle as the hour for the ball approached? She turned to the servant. "I'm not sure I can take any refreshment, but thank you for bringing it."

Clarissa drew closer. "But ma'am, it will be eight or nine o'clock before the dinner at the ball will be served, so there's a long time to go before you'll get more to eat. That's how things are done here."

Abigail took a deep breath and stood. Maybe part of the discomfort in her stomach was because it was empty. The midday meal was long past. Her bouffant satin skirts rustled as she moved to the table. "All right. You've convinced me." She pulled off one snow-white glove and took sips of tea and then bites of the delicious cake. Her maid was right. Fresh energy flowed through her body.

Clarissa grinned, and she and Mira left together. Whispers and soft laughter trailed in their wake.

A wave of warmth touched Abigail's cheeks. She could almost hear the two sisters in the servants' hall conjecturing with the others about whether a new relationship had begun—or was about to begin—

between the master of the house and the governess. Most definitely not. She would never fail the way the other governesses might have, eventually leaving in shame. This employment was part of her new beginning, and she must keep it or return to Charleston in defeat. She straightened her shoulders. She would make sure that didn't happen.

Jade emerged through the schoolroom door and came forward to stare at her with widened eyes. "Ma'am, I never imagined you could look like a fairy princess." The child reached out and fingered the satin skirt, then looked up at Abigail's hair. "And you oughta keep wearing your hair like that."

"Thank you, Jade, but this hairdo and this gown would never do for everyday wear." She smiled. "But it is nice to dress up sometimes." She bent and attempted to draw the child into a quick hug, but Jade pushed her away and ran from the room. So much for trying to show the little one affection.

At six o'clock, Abigail descended the grand staircase with a silver reticule—another surprise from the trunk—hanging on her wrist. Her steps faltered when she lifted her eyes to find Joshua Becket watching her with a bold, assessing gaze. He stood in the entrance hall with his muscular arms folded, bulging in his clothing. Dressed in a black silk waistcoat with a stiff white cravat and breeches, the man's good looks made her pulse pound.

When she reached the bottom step, he extended his hand and shook his head, smiling. "Well, Mrs. Welch, everyone will wonder who my lovely guest is."

As their eyes met, a shock ran through her, but she responded, "Just your child's governess, of course, Mr. Becket." She accepted his gloved hand, and he led her out to the waiting carriage.

He assisted her inside the conveyance with its Rockford crest emblazoned on the door, then entered and sat across from her. He knocked on the gold-velvet-covered top of the coach, and the horses moved forward.

The drive to Spanish Town turned out to be most pleasant...and something else—riveting. Joshua's proximity and his continued perusal unnerved her, as did his broad knees pressed against her skirt.

She wanted to say something, anything, but her breath hitched in her throat.

With complete confidence and ease, Joshua broke the silence. "You can see we dusted off the best coach for this annual trip to the Governor's Ball." He glanced around the interior. "How do you like it?"

The sudden vibrancy of his voice in the confined space caught her off guard. She looked around the fresh-looking, exquisite gold-and-red upholstery. "It's lovely. Was it once owned by the original Rockfords?"

"Yes, but it had fallen into disrepair. I had it redone a year ago." His eyes suddenly filled with fierce sparkling. "Looking forward one day to having a princess sit across from me going to a ball."

The man had to be joking, and she searched for a response. "Well, sir, can you tell me if I need to worry about it turning into a pumpkin at midnight?"

He laughed out loud, and the cheerful sound filled the coach with well-being. "A pumpkin? Where did you ever get that idea?"

"From a French writer, Charles Perrault, who wrote fairy tales. My mother read them to me as a child. In one of them about a poor girl hoping to marry a prince, her fairy godmother made her a coach out of a pumpkin and horses from mice to ride to the ball. She warned the girl the magic coach would revert to a pumpkin if she failed to return home by midnight."

Joshua chuckled. "Are you reading these tales to Jade, Mrs. Welch?"

"Well, I haven't yet, but this gives me an idea. The stories, written in French, provided an excellent incentive to me to learn that language."

"You do that, Mrs. Welch. If Jade learns French, I'll make a coach out of a pumpkin for you." Smiling, he looked out the window and tapped his fingers on his knee.

Abigail's opinion of her employer adjusted up another notch. Joshua Becket had a lighter side that had nothing to do with his secrets or his sugar-planter role.

*A*t Government House, the herald announced them, and they found their way into the ballroom. A pompous-looking gentleman in a yellow silk waistcoat and a long white wig approached. After a quick introduction and bow to Abigail, the governor whisked Joshua away. He cast a look at her over his shoulder and mouthed an apology.

She nodded and withdrew her fan from her reticule. Finding a secluded spot near some tall ferns in the vast ballroom, she spread her fan and took in the startling scene before her.

Never had she imagined she'd find a glittering gathering like this on the island of Jamaica. It looked like an English soiree on its best behavior. The ballroom itself extended farther than she could see through all the well-dressed guests in their elaborate, curled white wigs. Servants in blue-and-white livery flowed among the guests with trays of thin-stemmed glasses filled with sparkling liquid. Romantic strains of violin music filtered through the room, and oversized, sparkling chandeliers supplied with scented candles worked their magic with fragrance and soft light. The lovely gowns of the ladies in the many colors of the rainbow shimmered as they swept by in the dance.

To Abigail's right, where non-dancing couples congregated, one gown stood out from the rest. Its shapely owner flitted like a bold-colored butterfly from guest to guest. The ruby-red color of the dress, plunging neckline, and sparkling diamonds at the throat and earlobes of its owner caused heads to turn as she moved about in effortless elegance. Lady Geneva Harcourt. Only she could have worn such a startling color and carried it off with finesse. The woman was surely the most beautiful in the room. The princess Joshua Becket might seek? Or the one who wished she were?

"Why, hello there."

Abigail turned to find Reverend Mark Gardner's gentle presence a few feet from her. How had he slipped up without her noticing? Handsome in his creamy white waistcoat and smart black cravat, he wore his curly dark hair without a wig. His lips stretched into a sunny smile. "I almost didn't recognize you, Abigail. You look stunning."

Abigail waved her fan. "Meaning, most days I look drab?" She smiled as surprise lit his face and red crept up his neck.

"No, I didn't mean that at all." He cocked his chin. "You know how to strike down a simple man trying to pay an honest compliment, don't you?"

She laughed. "No strikes intended, sir."

He looked around. "Are you alone or with a partner?"

"I came with Mr. Becket, but someone drew him away the moment we arrived."

"Good, would you give me this first dance—if your card is not already filled?"

She smiled into his shining brown eyes. "I didn't bring a card. Are you sure you want to dance with a lowly governess? I see a row of eligible, probably wealthy, young ladies there with their dowagers." She gestured with her fan to young women, some standing, some seated, near the far wall, all looking hopeful. They had their dance booklets clutched in gloved hands.

A frown flitted across his brow, then disappeared. "Mrs. Welch, if there's one thing you don't look like tonight, it's a governess. So play the part of a princess and no one will know the difference. Now about that dance..."

"Why not? I'd be delighted, sir." She placed her fan in her reticule and slipped the small strap onto her wrist.

He took her hand and led her toward the middle of the floor where other dancing couples moved in a slow, revolving dance she'd seen only once in Charleston. She hesitated. "What is this dance called? I don't think I know the steps..."

"I'm not sure what it's called, but looks easy to learn. Come, trust yourself to me." He drew her onto the floor, placed his hand at her waist, and lifted his opposite one for her to grasp.

She took his broad hand, and he moved the two of them across the floor. She breathed in the clean smell of him laced with lemon oil. Had the man polished pews before coming? Her gown rustled and glistened in the candlelight, and she found it easy to follow Mark's steps. She closed her eyes for a few moments and savored entry into a magic world. A place where one could be a princess for an evening, even with Mark's occasional missteps. It had been a long time, through the entire American Revolution, since she'd danced, and she savored every moment.

"Excuse me, sir. I'd like to dance with Mrs. Welch." A deep voice spoke to their left.

She knew that voice, and her eyes shot open. Her make-believe world disappeared like dew sucked up by the morning sun.

Joshua Becket tapped Mark's shoulder, and he released her into her employer's hands with a bow.

Abigail's breath swooshed out of her lungs when Joshua drew her into his arms and swung her around the floor with a smooth elegance that could have come only from much practice. She'd never dreamed of being held thus in an exciting dance with a master partner. Other dancers made space for them when Joshua led her into more and more intricate steps while she gasped for breath.

Then he pulled her aside with slower movements and mixed with the other couples. He spoke his first words to her. "Want to know why I interrupted your dance with the reverend?"

"Why did you?" She glanced across the room at Mark, who stood next to a tall fern, watching them.

Joshua drew her closer and his spicy scent enveloped her. "I thought I'd better rescue you before you swooned in his arms," he whispered into her ear.

She swallowed and drew back. "I was not about to swoon, thank you."

"You had your eyes closed."

"That was...for another reason."

"What reason?"

An exasperated breath escaped her lips. Why didn't the man give it up? "Maybe I needed a glass of punch."

He stopped dancing right away and led her to the corner table with a gigantic glass bowl filled with some kind of yellow liquid. A servant stood behind it with a ladle. Joshua spoke to the man. "Two glasses, please."

The man ladled two servings into crystal glasses lined around the bowl, and Joshua handed one to her, then picked up the other. He led Abigail into a side room that looked like a parlor, and they sat.

She sipped the golden liquid and, to her pleasant surprise, found it to be apple cider.

Joshua drank his. "Want something stronger? Believe me, there's plenty of rum and port and about anything you can name here for the guests. In fact, this place will get a little wild after dinner. You can count on it."

Wild? The last thing she wanted was to be in a drunken crowd. Could they leave early?

"No, this cider is fine, thank you." Abigail finished hers, set the glass on a small side table, and opened her reticule. She withdrew her handkerchief and dabbed at her lips. In the corner of her eye, red satin flashed, and she looked up as Lady Geneva Harcourt glided into the room. Her strong perfume floated around her like an aura.

"My dear Joshua, I've found you. Come, we're to lead the line to dinner behind the governor and his wife." She cast a quick glance at Abigail and then took Joshua's hand and pulled him from his chair. She turned back to Abigail. "My dear Mrs. Welch, you won't mind if I borrow your employer for the dinner, will you? We planned these things far in advance, and it's rather an honor to follow the governor into dinner. Joshua will not want to miss it."

How could a governess mind anything Lady Harcourt wanted? Abigail looked into the lovely, flawless features and hard hazel eyes. "Of course not. I'll be fine. Take your prisoner away." She smiled the warmest smile she could muster at both of them and turned her face aside—before they could see her expression sink into something not fine at all. Added to it, her stomach knotted. Abandoned. Again.

Joshua's lips thinned into a frown, and he seemed about to say something, but the woman drew him away.

A moment later, Mark Gardner entered the room and strode over to her as she tried to get her face and emotions back to normal.

"Will you be my dinner partner, most lovely lady?"

She cocked her head at him. "How did you know I might need a partner?"

"I could say the Lord revealed it to me." He grinned. "But maybe I ran into Joshua accompanying a blaze of red out of this room, and I put two and two together."

Yes, those were a twosome she needed to put together and keep her heart and mind free. But Mark had said *maybe* he guessed she needed a partner. She stood and looked him straight in the eye. "Is that really why you came in here to offer to be my dinner partner?"

Mark pressed his lips together, then nodded. "Fine, the minister must tell the truth to the nice-looking lady. Joshua Becket beckoned to me and asked me to take care of you."

How kind of her employer. Be a rogue at heart but throw in a half ray of sunshine when possible.

Abigail took Mark's arm, and he led her toward the dinner line. As they entered the large dining hall with its head table and many smaller tables, the succulent smell of cooked pork filled the air. Abigail caught a flash of red at the head of the line of guests. Lady Harcourt stood in the buffet line with Joshua. She hung on his arm as though she owned him and let him place her choice of foods on the small china plate she held. Joshua often bent to hear something she leaned to whisper in his ear.

Abigail bypassed the roasted pig but partook of several fruits, bread, cheese, and a piece of chocolate cake. Mark led her to a table in a corner where she waited while he returned to get apple cider for them both. She glanced across the room at Joshua, without Lady Harcourt, talking with the governor and an important-looking man, if pompous satin clothing and prideful attitude translated into rank. The king's emissary? Mrs. Pelfrey had told her about Lord Halton and his mission to eradicate piracy in the Caribbean.

She lifted her shoulders and mused. What else might this night of revelry reveal?

CHAPTER 11

*J*oshua regarded the royal emissary bragging about what he planned to do about piracy. He sipped his drink. More power to the king's little man. "I tell you, I plan to search these waters and rid them of any pirates who dare to continue operating here," Lord Halton declared to the governor. The official dressed like a popinjay, but his words and steely eyes revealed a man of power and one who knew how to wield it. "We will find them, and we will blow them out of the water if they refuse to surrender. We will give no quarter." He took another sip from his glass of sherry.

The governor smiled. "That's exactly the attitude we need, wouldn't you say, Joshua?"

Joshua's face warmed, and he took a deep breath. "If you can find them, my lord, is the first problem."

Lord Halton swiped his damp forehead with a lace-trimmed handkerchief and frowned at him. "Of course, we'll uncover them. I've three ships to sweep through these waters and three hundred trained soldiers."

The governor placed a placating hand on Lord Halton's arm. "Certainly you will, and we'll be happy to have our waters safe when you do. Becket here has a plantation near the Blue Mountains, and close by is a secret cove where pirate vessels have hidden out."

Lord Halton looked at him with fresh eyes. "Is that so? I'd like to talk to you, sir." He glanced around. "Is there a garden we might walk in and get a breath of cooler air?"

"Of course." Joshua bowed before turning to speak to the governor. "Would you mind giving Lady Harcourt my apologies when she returns?"

The governor laughed. "I'll be glad to spend some time in the lady's presence. Never fear. Take your time."

Joshua led Lord Halton through the balcony entrance and down the steps. He would have to be very careful about what he told the king's emissary. He often hid his own ship in the mentioned cove. Thank God the *Eagle* was not there now but docked in his plantation harbor, ready for the legitimate business of shipping sugar once the harvest was completed. They stepped into the dark garden—such a contrast to the many candles lighting the ballroom, they had to step carefully until their eyes adjusted.

A sliver of a moon sailed like a ghostly galleon through murky clouds. The air, though still warm and humid, proved cooler than inside the ballroom. They strode down a shell-strewn path between rows of tall gardenia bushes. Joshua drew a deep breath of their sweet fragrance filling the night.

Lord Halton ceased wiping his brow and turned to Joshua. "Now tell me about this cove. All you know, sir."

He drew a breath, but a rustling movement behind them stole his response. Before he could look to see what it was, two powerful arms gripped him, and a thick, foul-smelling hand of another assailant covered his mouth. A pointed thrust in his side stiffened him.

"Be quiet." A deep voice spoke into his ear. "Or you'll get more of this."

A knife's razor-sharp tip nicked Joshua's skin through his clothing.

"Halton?" he garbled through the hand and tried to twist away from his captors to check on the emissary. Scuffling and grunts issued from the man's position.

"Quiet," snarled one of his assailants and pricked his side again, this time drawing blood. Warmth trickled down Joshua's side. One of his captors forced his hands behind him and tied them tight. Another jerked his cravat from his neck and tied it around his mouth, preventing any sound and barely permitting breathing. At least three men gripped him, and the foul odor of their sweat assailed his nose.

They forced him down the long garden path and across a field to the edge of the Government House property bordered by an old seldom-used road. Lord Halton groaned and stumbled along beside him with three other captors dragging him.

At their approach, mules harnessed to a wagon stamped their hooves. Two men moved from the shadows to place their hands on the animals' muzzles. How many kidnappers were there? At least six, maybe eight or ten. Their dark skin and scant clothing blended into the night.

The rough hands guiding Joshua dropped him face down onto the straw bed of the wagon. They tied his feet together and then connected the rope to his wrists behind him. Trussed up like a pig, he turned his head on the straw and sucked in air. A heavy thump beside him alerted him that Lord Halton experienced the same treatment.

No sooner than the two of them lay stretched out on their stomachs in the wagon bed, a blanket descended over them, and the wagon lurched forward.

They bumped along for a long time, often turning right and left over uneven terrain, and once even making a circle, it seemed to Joshua. His and Lord Halton's groans followed the severe bumps and bounces the minimal straw did little to cushion. Three men conversed in whispers on the driver's seat while several others ran alongside, their breathing heavy.

When the wagon finally stopped, Joshua flipped onto his back, groaning with the effort. Perhaps he could surmise something from the stars. But the clouds masked even the feeble light of the quarter moon. He could see nothing, not even the faces of his captors when they gripped his feet, untied his ankles, and pulled him from the wagon. They stood him up and pushed him into the darkness. He shook his head to dislodge dizziness. Had he lost that much blood? He bumped into something that snorted and moved—a horse or mule.

The same man who had pricked his side came close and cut the ropes from Joshua's hands. He pushed him toward the mule. "Climb on," he commanded. White rimmed his dark eyes in his brown face. His shirt and breeches hung in rags. Were his captors the feared Maroons?

Joshua hesitated, and the knife stung against his ribs again. He lifted his fist to plant it in the man's fierce face, but two sets of hands struck him from behind with brute force. He landed in the dirt, almost under the animal. It lurched away. A boot kick landed in Joshua's middle, and his breath gushed from his lungs.

"Don't be foolish or you die. Slow. And the king's man with the wig." The speaker laughed—a low, horrible sound—and other voices echoed it in the darkness.

Joshua clamored to his feet, clutching his middle. They brought the mule around for him to mount. He saw neither stirrups nor saddle.

"Get on." The man waved a cutlass at him.

Joshua put his hands on the animal's straggly mane and hauled himself up. His grunt of discomfort as he landed on the sharp back-bone of his poor excuse of a mount brought out laughs and jests around him.

"Quiet," the man with the machete hissed, and his accomplices fell silent.

Lord Halton slumped on the mule they had made him mount. His curled white wig no longer sat atop his head, and dirt or blood stained his satin waistcoat and britches. He wobbled and almost lost his seat. A captor at his side swung up behind and held him in place.

"Halton, are you all right?" Getting no answer, Joshua turned to the man giving orders. "Who are you?"

"Quiet. Or I cut off your arm."

The speaker motioned, and Joshua heard scuffling sounds of other mules being mounted. A lead rope was hooked to his mule's bridle, held by a rider ahead, and two men came to run alongside Joshua's mule as the entire group moved into the darkness at a trot.

Mules and men hurried down paths between vast, waving fields of cane, and then across hilly areas and flat savannahs. Clouds still covered the stars, preventing Joshua from grasping any sense of direction. Soon, without a saddle, he was so sore that he gave up wondering which way they headed. It took all his concentration, gritting his teeth, to stay on the sweaty back of the mule, while every movement increased his pain.

They climbed a sharp ascent. The mules slipped and lunged across the uneven surface. Once, Joshua almost fell off, but the man running alongside heaved him back up.

Thunder rumbled as they continued to climb, and lightning blazed across the dark sky, but the men and the mules pushed onward.

Joshua—drenched with sweat, his mouth parched, and weary beyond words—grew stupefied with misery. When the rain fell, he lifted his face into it with his mouth open. Though it somewhat relieved his thirst, it revived the pain of sitting on the ridge of the mule's spine. When he thought he couldn't stand another moment, the group came to a halt.

The gurgle of water flowing over rocks reached Joshua's ears. His mule made sounds like a donkey that ended with a whinny and pushed toward the stream. Other mules echoed him. The poor animals were as thirsty as any would be after such a night, forced to travel with loads in tropical heat.

The man holding the mule's lead rope jerked it, and the mule stopped, snorted, and swung his head so hard Joshua lost his grip on the scanty mane. The two men still at his side kept him astride the animal.

The apparent leader of the kidnappers spoke. "You cross river behind me. Try anything, you die, and king's man."

Fingers of dawn streaked across the eastern sky and shed light on the kidnappers and the Blue Mountains before them. They stood at the base of a cliff with a fast-moving stream in front of it. Joshua's nostrils flared when he finally discerned his captors. Maroons. All wore ragged clothing and cutlasses strapped to their lean, muscular sides.

The mules lowered their heads to drink, and then the entire group crossed the river. The mountain stream turned out to be about waist high until the middle where the mules had to swim.

Stories still passed around the taverns of the past Maroon wars flashed through Joshua's mind as the cool water rose to his knees astride his mount. Why had the Maroons chosen to kidnap him? Were they also planning to burn Rockford?

The danger to Abigail, to Jade, and to the plantation stabbed his conscience. Some of his father's sad last words to him when he'd left Charleston echoed in his ear. *Joshua, be sure your sins will find you out. Sin pays wages you will hate.* Was judgment of his wicked ways going to tumble down over his plantation and all the innocent ones there?

He cast the heavy, pricking thoughts aside. Perhaps it was Lord Halton the Maroons had been after, and they had only brought Joshua along since he accompanied the emissary into the garden. That had to be it.

On the other side of the river, his captors, some mounted, some walking, trailed along the cliff side until they came to a wide area under a rock overhang. The Maroons dismounted. Joshua slid from the mule and worked hard to make his strained legs hold him up. Behind him, Lord Halton crumpled from his mule to the ground. A guard pulled him to his feet.

A rope ladder shimmied down the rock and hung swinging in the air. A face leered down at them from the high ledge, illuminated by a lantern. Voices—only speaking a few English words—and a savory scent also filtered down from above.

"Climb." The leader of the Maroons they called Cudjoe poked him toward the ladder. Joshua, every stiff limb protesting in his wet garments, grabbed the rungs and climbed with the man swinging up behind him.

When he emerged onto a rock surface, Joshua fell on his face, gasping. A hand pulled at him, to make room for the climber emerging behind him. He gritted his teeth from exhaustion and forced himself to crawl on all fours toward the back of the ledge. So much for the haughty, self-satisfied being who had danced around the ballroom in silk and satin clothing many hours earlier. He'd never wear the ruined clothes again. He sat up and clenched his jaw in fresh determination. He'd make it through this some way. But would his partner?

Lord Halton's pale, distraught face appeared next at the cliff's edge with a warrior behind him, pushing him up. Joshua crawled forward to assist the man onto the ledge. When up, he, too, rolled over, groaning. A gash, covered with clotted blood, crossed his forehead. When he opened his eyes, he stared at the overhanging roof above them.

Joshua leaned toward him. "Sir, are you all right?"

Halton's cracked lips moved. "If being only half dead is that, I am."

The man needed encouragement. Joshua leaned closer. "My lord, once we eat something, we will think of some way to escape."

Halton closed his eyes. "My ships will blow this mountain to pieces. You can depend on it, Becket." He sat up with a groan.

Joshua nodded. Good. Lord Halton would stay strong as long as revenge enflamed his mind, energized his body.

CHAPTER 12

*A*bigail begged to sit out the next dance, and Mark Gardner led her to a chair. When he left to get them both cool glasses of cider, she fanned her face and looked around the ballroom. Where was her employer, her absent escort? Gardner had been most kind to keep her occupied since dinner, but wasn't it time for Joshua Becket to make some kind of appearance, especially as it would soon be time to leave? He was tall enough to be seen over most dancers, but his curly black head and handsome face failed to appear in the crowd. Perhaps if she concentrated on looking for a red dress, she'd find him?

"Here you are." Mark handed her a cup of cider, and she drank half the glass.

"Did you, by any chance, see Mr. Becket in the refreshment hall?" She tried to keep her voice from betraying emotion. Just a simple question.

The man took a deep breath. "Sorry, I didn't." He smiled. "But I'm not too sad about it." He looked into her eyes. "Abigail, I'm having a great time, and I hope you can say the same."

She looked away and scanned the fewer dancers on the floor and those gathered on the sidelines. The crowd had thinned and not a red dress flashed among them. She turned back to him. "I've had a great time, Mark, and really appreciate your...standing in for Mr. Becket. But it's about time to leave. What can detain my employer?"

"Oh, I'm sure he'll be around soon. He is a gentleman." Mark finished his cider.

Was there a shade of mockery or bitterness in the man's voice? She looked into his face. It couldn't be. Yes, Joshua was a gentleman. He would not abandon his duty to her. He escorted her to the ball and would escort her home.

"Shall I take our cups back and we dance another round?" His blue eyes gleamed above his smile, and he stood.

"Actually, I think I'm a little tired. Would you do me a favor, Mark?"

"Anything you need, my lady." He bowed.

"Would you look around for Joshua and mention to him I'm ready to leave?" Why didn't she tell him just to look for the red dress? It would be quicker, but pride reared its head in her heart.

"Glad to. Just sit here and rest, and I'll be back with that tardy gentleman before you know it." He strode away with their two cups.

He came back in about twenty minutes with a frown knitting his forehead. He sat beside her and leaned forward. "I'm sorry to say, I looked everywhere I could think of, including the balcony, and even checked the side parlors—and there're lots of those in this Government House—but I found no sign of Mr. Becket. Would you like for me to approach the governor and ask if he knows where he could be? He was in one of the rooms."

Abigail drew in a tight breath. "Answer me one more question, Mark, before we think of approaching the governor." She clenched her fist in her lap and swallowed her reluctance. "Did you, by any chance, see Lady Harcourt anywhere?"

Mark's lips tightened, and he tapped his knee with his fingers. "No, no I didn't." His voice was low, sympathetic.

Abigail stood. "Mark, would you see me home? I'm sure Mr. Becket won't mind. Who knows what government business might have detained him?"

Mark stood. "Of course, I'd be happy to. And if it's any connection,

I didn't see Lord Halton either." He left to request his horse and carriage.

All the way back to Rockford, as if sensing her mindset, Mark didn't carry on a conversation. Abigail seethed. How could Joshua Becket treat her so disrespectfully? Gentleman, he was not. Of course, he'd gone off with Lady Harcourt. Even before the ball, she'd heard the servants talking about their long relationship. The least he could've done was to let her know he had other plans and arrange for Mark to escort her home.

They arrived at the plantation about midnight, if the sliver of moon sailing in and out of clouds high in the sky was any sign. Mark assisted her from the carriage in the cool night air laced with the rich fragrance of Jamaican Lady of the Night blossoms, but the heady scent offered no relief to Abigail's emotions.

When he escorted her to the door, he squeezed her hand before releasing it. "I can't tell you what a wonderful evening this has been, Abigail. I hope you find out what hindered Joshua, but I can't say I'm sorry." He gave her a wide smile.

"Thank you, Mark. You've been the perfect gentleman, and I appreciate it." She managed a small smile. "We can't say that about everybody."

She flew up the stairs and into her room before tears clogging her throat flooded down her cheeks. She fell across the bed and muffled her cries with a pillow. She'd never been so mortified in her life. How dare Joshua Becket ignore her the entire evening, except for one showy dance? She'd have been abandoned but for Mark Gardner's kindness. Worst of all, Joshua had obviously left the ball with Geneva Harcourt without so much as a word. Insufferable man.

She sat up, walked to the washstand, and splashed tepid water on her tight face. As she undressed and readied herself for bed, she lectured herself. Nothing would be the same for her at Rockford. Out with silly daydreams of Joshua Becket. He was a man who lived for himself and for pleasure. She was his employee, a governess for his daughter. Now she knew her place.

~

O n the cliff shelf, Joshua wiped weariness from his face and looked about for the source of cooking. Amid smells of wet stone, animal scat, and wood smoke, a scent of food stewing made his mouth water. Across the rocky terrain, a slovenly woman stirred a large pot hung on a tripod over a fire. Another female dropped vegetables into the vessel.

Several warriors, including those who had forced the two of them on their horrible journey, sat in the cave on their haunches, close around Cudjoe. For the moment, none of them paid any attention to Lord Halton or himself. They murmured, excited and interrupting each other in marked contrast to the silence enforced on their mad dash across country. The men spoke in their native Creole language that Joshua could not understand. But he discerned exultation in their tone. Their voices mingled with the crashing of a waterfall nearby. That explained the dampness on the rock floor. His equally damp clothing made him shiver in the late night cooler breeze high up on the ledge.

He examined the walls of the cavern, lit by lanterns. The cliff shelf on which they sat was perhaps twenty yards at its widest and about seventy-five yards long. With the ladder drawn up, nothing could reach them. Water dripped from cracks above, and darkness loomed at one end, as if a cave went deeper into the mountain. The dim light flickered over weapons stashed against the far wall. If he could grab just one gun...His heartbeat increased.

The leader stood suddenly and walked to the women at the fire. He spoke to them, and they served up liquid into two wooden bowls.

Cudjoe approached and handed both of them a container but no utensils. "Eat, then write letter."

"Letter?" Joshua took the bowl and sipped the broth. What was the man thinking? Would they demand money for his and Lord Halton's release? But the leader returned to his men.

Lord Halton blew on the stew and downed his serving as fast as

Joshua did. "These Maroons will be most sorry they meddled with the king's emissary."

"Look, you see those guns over there? I'm going to watch for an opportunity to grab one. Then everything's going to turn around." Joshua kept his voice low, and he spoke between slurps from his bowl. His spirits rose as his stomach filled with the warm broth.

Cudjoe returned with a piece of paper, a book, and the stub of a pencil. Another man brought a lantern near. The leader stopped in front of Joshua. "You write letter." In the closer light, the man appeared taller and heavier built than Joshua had imagined. He was not entirely Negro. His skin was the color of creamed coffee. He wore a dirty blue shirt and loose, ragged black trousers with scuffed, buckled shoes on his wide feet. A cutlass hung at his side.

Joshua set his bowl on the rock floor. "A letter to whom?"

"Letter to governor." The man's words, though in English, carried the island accent with a thickening of vowels and a slurring of consonants.

A second man came forward from the shadows. His face, covered in white paint, drew an intake of breath from Halton. The thin, black figure wore beads and what appeared to be a snakeskin around his neck, and a strange red hat sat atop his head. His clothes were unkempt, but he grasped a shiny sword in his right hand.

"Who or what is this, Becket?" Halton whispered.

"An obeah man, Jamaican witch doctor," Joshua responded, not taking his eyes off the fine sword. Where had the witch doctor found, or stolen, a Toledo sword?

"Be quiet," the leader hissed and thrust writing material toward Joshua.

He accepted the paper, book, and pencil. "What am I to say in the letter?"

"Tell governor you want treaty with seal on it. Treaty granting us our own settlement lands, our freedom, our pardon from all past acts."

"The Governor will never do that."

The obeah man pointed the sword at Lord Halton. "Then we send him his ears. Then we send him his nose."

Halton turned white, and Joshua swallowed hard. It was a horrible thing to contemplate.

Cudjoe spoke. "He the king's man. Governor will do it."

Joshua sat and propped the book and paper on his knee but hesitated. The witch doctor stepped forward and pushed the tip of the sword against Joshua's chest. The point pierced his clothing, and he recoiled.

"You write or I prick his eye." He nodded toward Halton.

The emissary shrank back against the rock wall, his gaze glued to the witch doctor's horrible, painted face, even more grotesque in the lantern light.

"I'll write." Joshua put the pencil to the paper. How was he to write? *Dear Governor?* Or *Your Excellency?* He decided on *Your Excellency. Maroon warriors hold Lord Halton and me.* He looked around. *Somewhere in the Blue Mountains. For our release, they demand a treaty guaranteeing their settlement lands as freedmen and pardon for all their past acts.* He signed the missive, *Your obedient servant, Joshua Becket.*

Cudjoe and the man with the cutlass peered over his shoulder at the writing. Others pressed forward, trying to see.

When Joshua handed the letter to the leader, a chattering debate started.

Halton leaned forward and whispered, "Can any of them read?"

"Not likely. They are probably discussing who is to take the letter to the governor. That Maroon will risk his life, of course."

The leader turned back to Joshua, holding up the letter. "What you say here?"

It wouldn't matter what he read aloud since they had no way of knowing, but Joshua read what he'd written. Cudjoe and the witch doctor studied his face. Then the chatter began anew, but in lower voices.

Joshua shook weariness from his body and mind. He eyed the distance to the guns propped on the wall of the cave. Could he scramble and grab one while the letter held their attention? It was worth a try. He stood and lurched forward five steps. Three warriors reared up in his path and flattened him onto the hard ground. They pummeled him and drug him back to his place beside Halton. He lay still, dazed, and bruised from their fists.

"Good try," Halton spat out and sighed. Then he stretched out beside Joshua. "I'm so weary, I believe I can sleep on this rock."

Sometime later, Joshua sat up with a groan. He must have dozed. Every muscle in his body ached, and with each movement, he discovered new bruises. Their captors moved about and chattered. Halton stirred beside him. The moon, no longer obscured by clouds, made their predicament clearer. Far below, the dense forest growth trailed the river. When Joshua turned his head just so, he could hear the distant sound of the tide on rocks. The Caribbean had to be near this mountain hideout, or he was imagining things. "This must be Cockpit Country."

"Cockpit Country?" Halton raised up and followed Joshua's gaze into the treetops cloaked in shadows beyond their rock cliff.

"Yes, I'd heard of it but never traveled here. Few white men ever have, to my knowledge. It's like an independent republic in the northwest of Jamaica. It's been here since the British took over the island, inhabited by survivors of the Indian clans and runaway slaves. I understand several attempts to subdue this area ended with disaster until a treaty came forth about fifty years ago."

Halton gestured to the group beyond them. "Is this all that's left of them?"

"No. This is their warrior elite, I assume, who have executed our kidnapping. Their settlements exist hidden in these mountains."

Cudjoe came toward them. "We send you." He pointed to Joshua. "Me?"

"You go to governor. Take letter. We keep king's man, and he die slow death if you fail. And plantations burned."

Halton stiffened and grimaced. "Lord, I hate to be left here with these...devils." He spat the words out but kept his voice low.

The leader glared at Joshua, and the obeah man moved to stand beside him, both with their chests thrust out and faces grim. Cudjoe gave Joshua an evil grin. "We burn your plantation first as warning."

An invisible hand gripped Joshua's windpipe. Was the man

speaking of the future, or was Rockford already under attack? "How do you know my plantation?"

The leader stepped closer to Joshua. "I once slave on Rockford. You allowed bad overseer to beat me. I run away but not forget." He pulled up his shirt and turned. Terrible scars crisscrossed his dark back.

Joshua inhaled a shaky breath and tried to remember any runaway. Abigail's and Jade's faces and those of others at Rockford swept across his mind. Would they have any warning or be able to escape? This was no idle threat. He clenched his fists and looked into the man's face. "I'm sorry. That overseer is no longer in my employ."

The leader gestured toward two brawny warriors, and they came forward and grasped Joshua's arms. To resist proved futile. They drug him to an open space against the rock cliff where a rope hung down from a tree root above. They stretched him until he stood on tiptoe and tied his hands to the rope over his head.

"You will know my pain." Cudjoe spat out the words. Another tall warrior with muscles bulging came forward, snapping a whip in his hand.

Somewhere in Joshua's memory, he heard his father's voice. *Son, call on God. Repent. God will always hear that kind of prayer.* But would God hear a prayer from someone like him?

The warrior arched back with the whip. A single drum sounded, and agreeing voices rose in cadence with the beat.

CHAPTER 13

Sunlight played across Abigail's eyes, and she opened them and sat up in bed. Mercy, how late was it? She arose, washed her face at the side table bowl, and patted it dry. The reflection of her puffy eyes rimmed by dark circles in the mirror above reminded her of her pain the night before. She shook all those thoughts away and dressed as fast as she could. She was pulling the spread up on her bed when a soft knock sounded on the connecting door to the schoolroom. Then it opened.

Jade bounced in with Potcake close behind her. "Oh, I'm glad you're finally awake. I looked in before but let you sleep." She plopped on Abigail's bed as if it were her own. "I know how late you came in."

Potcake crouched on the rug and looked from one of them to the other with big tired eyes.

"Is that so?" Abigail tried to appear stern. She sat in the chair to slip on her boots.

"Yes, I saw you and that minister drive up in the carriage from the schoolroom window."

"What were you doing up so late, young lady?"

Jade ignored Abigail's question and toyed with a lace border on the bedspread. "Why did my father not bring you home?" She turned serious eyes on Abigail.

Abigail leaned down and pulled on one boot. "Because he had something else important to do." She kept her voice indifferent. "So I was happy to have Reverend Gardner drive me home." She pulled on the other boot and stood. "Have you had breakfast?"

"Hours ago." The child eyed Abigail's boots and riding skirt. "Are we going riding today?"

"Would you like to?"

"Sure." Jade ran to the bedroom door. She and Potcake started down the hall, and Abigail followed to the kitchen. The smell of fresh bread and tea made her mouth water.

Lucy Dykes looked up from peeling potatoes as they entered. "There you are, miss—I mean, madam. Would you like a piece of bread and butter? And I've plenty of tea."

Jade ran to the back door and called out, "I'll have Mr. Dykes saddle up our horses."

Abigail nodded. "All right, but be careful, Jade, and don't think of mounting until I get there."

She turned to Mrs. Dykes. "Yes, that would be wonderful. Sorry I missed breakfast." Abigail sat at the large wooden table and partook of Lucy's delicious bread, fresh butter, and a hot cup of tea.

Mrs. Pelfrey entered the warm kitchen, frowning. She stopped in front of Abigail. "Mrs. Welch, there is a courier calling from the governor's headquarters. It seems he thinks Lord Halton came home with Mr. Becket last night, or at least, he's asking if he did." She folded her arms. "The king's man has not reported back to the governor, and no one has seen him. The messenger asked to speak to you when I told him Mr. Becket was...not available."

Abigail almost choked on the bite she was swallowing. He'd asked to see her? "I'll be glad to speak with him, but I know nothing of the whereabouts of the king's emissary." She took a last sip of her tea, stood, and brushed her lips with her napkin. Her mouth thinned. She had an idea where Joshua Becket might reside this morning. But surely, he hadn't taken Lord Halton with him to Lady Harcourt's.

The housekeeper touched Abigail's arm. "Mr. Becket has not slept in his bed. Do you know anything about it?"

When Abigail's face stiffened, the woman's cheeks turned pink, and she rephrased her question. "What I mean is, did he bring you home from the ball?"

Heat climbed up Abigail's neck. "I understood Mr. Becket had some kind of business to take care of, and Reverend Gardner brought me home."

Mrs. Pelfrey's eyes widened. "I see."

What did the housekeeper see? Did she guess that Joshua Becket spent the night at Lady Harcourt's or in some other lover's arms? The woman undoubtedly knew about her employer's shenanigans.

The young courier, dressed in his red British uniform, white stockings, and wig, stood as Abigail entered the parlor. He clutched his black tricorn in his hand and bowed. She introduced herself as the governess.

He smiled. "I'm from Governor Smith's office, madam. He is inquiring if Mr. Becket brought Lord Halton home with him last night."

Abigail shook her head. "I think not. Our housekeeper says Mr. Becket did not...arrive home last night. And she'd surely know if he did and certainly if he had brought a guest."

The courier's brows knit together. "But, ma'am, I was told Mr. Becket escorted you to the ball, so surely he..." He stopped speaking, swallowed, and tugged at his cravat.

Abigail's face tightened. "He accompanied me, but he did not escort me home, sir. Reverend Mark Gardner did so about midnight."

"And you know nothing about Lord Halton's whereabouts...or Mr. Becket's, I assume?" His face turned beet red.

Abigail took a deep breath. "No, sorry, I do not. I really didn't see either of them hours before I left the ball." Then her conscience tweaked her. Could she somehow ease this serious situation? What if Lord Halton was in trouble and Joshua knew where he was? "I understood Mr. Becket had some kind of business to take care of, possibly connected to Lady Harcourt, so you might check with the lady. She owns the neighboring plantation."

The man bowed, clicked his heels together, and then plopped his hat atop his white periwig. "Yes, I know of Lady Harcourt's plantation. Thank you for your time." He marched to the front door and out of it as soon as the butler opened it.

Abigail watched from the window as the courier mounted his horse and galloped away. No doubt Mr. Becket would have a surprise and some explaining to do when the courier arrived at Lady Harcourt's. Served him right.

She hurried back to the kitchen and out the back door. Walking into the cool recesses of the stable, she found Arabelle saddled in front of her stall. But where was Jade? Down the corridor, Mr. Dykes appeared carrying a shovel he'd been using to muck out a stall. She approached him. "Hello, have you seen Jade?"

"Yep. She climbed on Buttercup and took off as soon as I had the pony saddled."

"Oh no!" Abigail ran for Arabelle. Why had the girl disobeyed her?

⚬

*J*oshua clenched his eyes shut and prayed a silent prayer. *Father God, You know how wicked I've been in so many ways. I ask Your forgiveness, and I accept Jesus Christ. Please help me.*

The whistle of the whip sang in the air behind him, and he grimaced and stiffened. But no pain seared across his back. He opened his eyes, turned his head, and saw the obeah man standing before the man with the whip. He'd caught the man's wrist before he could lash Joshua's back. Gruff words he could not discern flew from several mouths. But a decision seemed to be made.

The witch doctor came forward and slashed the ropes off Joshua's hands, and he fell to his knees. Standing, he rubbed the taut muscles of his arms and shoulders, made his way back to where Halton sat gaping, and dropped beside him.

"That was close, Becket. Wonder why they stopped?" Lord Halton glanced away. "Of course, I'm glad they did."

Joshua couldn't respond. He still grappled with amazement and a peace that blanketed him when he'd prayed his fast prayer. God had heard him and delivered him.

Cudjoe came toward them. He pointed at Joshua. "Obeah man say you English man can't take beating and make ride to governor." Then his lips twitched in a wicked way. "Can't take a beating, but plantation will burn." Urgent voices rose behind him. "Get up. We send you now. You go to governor. If not return in two days with our treaty, we dig out king man's eyes."

Halton emitted a string of curse words and slumped against the rock wall.

Joshua stood and looked into the hard faces of the leader and those around him. God forbid. These desperate men were capable of doing everything they threatened.

Cudjoe stuffed the letter into Joshua's coat pocket and pushed him toward the cliff's edge and rope ladder. "These two will take you." A pair of warriors joined Joshua. One descended before him while the other climbed down after him.

It was a tough business to lower himself over the cliff edge and down the rocky wall in the moonlight. Every muscle and joint ached from his earlier bruises, but he finally reached the bottom at the river's edge. He sank to a sitting position, flexing his blistered hands.

One warrior poked him with his cutlass, and Joshua flopped into the river. His dress clothes, not yet dry from the earlier crossing, filled again with water and made his swim cumbersome. He emerged on the other side, slipping and sliding on the muddy bank, but got his feet planted and stood.

To his horror, the same mules waited at the edge of the forest. He would have to mount one of them again. His ponderous clothing weighed on him like heavy weapons strapped to his body. If only he *had* a weapon. When one guard pushed him forward, he swung a fist at the man and found himself tossed back into the water.

When he emerged, he mounted the mule. The moment he settled

on that razor back, he groaned aloud. The raw, saddle-sore places of his earlier ride burned in anguish. He gritted his teeth and gripped the scruffy mane. The two warriors mounted, one led Joshua's mule, and the other trotted behind as they started back across the rocky terrain.

Joshua concentrated on staying astride the mule as they traversed tortuous mountainous paths, pressed through thick forests where limbs bruised his knees, and splashed across bubbling creeks. Dawn came, but he scarcely took note. The few moments he dislodged his mind from the painful ride and the thirst that consumed him, he prayed. He prayed for Abigail, Jade, and for Rockford to be spared. Was God still listening to him?

They emerged onto a flatter terrain by the time the sun rose in its normal heat. Joshua, numb and weary, could stay astraddle the mule only by his best effort. He peered through blurry eyes beyond the mule's sweaty neck. This was savannah country, with its dry, warm smell of grass and plowed earth. Acres of sugarcane stretched across the horizon. A little farther down the way, between cane fields, they reached the edge of a simple farm roadway overgrown by grass and rutted by wagon wheels.

The two warriors stopped. One pointed to the road and spoke to Joshua. "You go on there."

"On that track?" he asked, trying to make his weary brain understand and his parched mouth speak words.

"Yes." The man handed Joshua the reins belonging to his mule, and the two Maroons turned their mounts and started back the way they'd come.

Joshua fought with his mule, which apparently didn't like the separation. One warrior returned and slapped the mule on the rump, and the animal took off down the road at a trot.

Renewed pain dulled Joshua's thinking, but he concentrated on keeping his seat. The rutted road ended an hour later at a crossroads amidst fields of sugarcane waving in the breeze. Joshua pulled back on the reins and squinted in all directions. Which way was home or Spanish Town? Pounding hooves from the left reached his ears, and soon three horses appeared with a cloud of dust billowing behind them. His mule shook his head and brayed. The loud sound between a whinny and a donkey's heehaw and the tossing head jarred Joshua and his grip on the animal's mane and he almost lost it.

British soldiers in dusty red-and-white military dress astride fine, lathered horses reined up in front of Joshua. One, wearing lieutenant insignias, stared, apparently tongue-tied for a moment, then doffed his hat, wiped his sweating forehead with his handkerchief, and cleared his throat. "Sir, is that you, Mr. Becket? Lieutenant Moore, at your service." His widened eyes expressed his surprise and pleasure.

"It is."

"I saw you at the ball with Lady Harcourt, leading the dinner buffet line behind the governor and his wife. May I say, I'm happy you're found. Was Lord Halton with you?"

"Yes. How was it discovered we were missing?"

"One of the kitchen slaves admitted he'd seen you and Lord Halton taken in the garden. The governor expressed great distress when this came to light." The soldier hesitated and looked down the rutted path behind Joshua. "But where is Lord Halton?"

Joshua exhaled a weary breath. "The Maroon kidnappers still have him, and I have to go to the governor right away with a message."

"Let us give you a decent mount, sir. And I will escort you back." The lieutenant spoke to one of his soldiers, who dismounted and led his horse toward Joshua. The man looked at the mule, and his lips tightened, but not a word of complaint passed his lips.

Lieutenant Moore turned to the other soldier with a command, and the soldier clamped his heels into the sides of his horse and galloped away. "I am sending him to let the military leaders know you're found."

Joshua slid off the mule and let the soldier help him mount the horse. "Military leaders?"

"Yes, sir. The governor called the militia out. We're scattered over the island in our search."

"Indeed?" That would add up to about a thousand horsemen in the militia and about the same number of infantry on foot. All for Lord Halton's sake, of course. "How far is it to Government House?"

"Thirty miles, sir."

Joshua groaned. How could he stay in a saddle, decidedly better than the mule's back, but for thirty more miles?

"Sir, my family's plantation is only three miles from here. We would be happy to harness up our carriage for you."

The man must have read his mind. Yes, a carriage. No more horseback riding. Not for a long time. "That would be fine, Lieutenant, and faster."

As they trotted down the road, Joshua wrestled with the desire to check on Rockford versus going to Government House. But the governor must be first. The Maroons said two days. Two days before a torturous death for Lord Halton and probably a full-scale war against the plantations. But was Rockford safe even now?

～

*A*bigail galloped down the plantation back road on Arabelle, huffing out an angry breath. Why did Jade often do the very thing she'd been told not to do? She searched the roadside and landscape as far as her eye could span. No sign of Jade or Buttercup. Just sugarcane fields and slaves toiling in the tropical sun.

Rounding a bend twenty minutes later, she jerked back on the reins, and Arabelle slid to a stop, snorting and tossing her head.

For a moment, Abigail couldn't grasp what her eyes saw. Jade and Buttercup came toward her, but strange black warriors with paint on their faces rode alongside her. Twenty-five men, at least.

Abigail's mouth dried up like a potsherd, and her heart pounded in her throat. She whispered a desperate prayer under her breath.

Lord God, what is this? Help me get Jade safely back home.

Arabelle snorted and pawed the earth as the group approached. Abigail patted the horse's warm neck and held her in tight rein. "Whoa, girl. Everything is going to be all right." She hoped and prayed.

The group stopped a few paces away, and Jade spoke. "Look, Abigail, here's Samson." She pointed to the muscular warrior beside her. "They were coming to burn our plantation, but I've stopped them." She turned to him. "You're keeping your word to me, aren't you, Mr. Samson?"

The man's fierce eyes softened when he looked at the child. He spoke to Abigail. "We not burn plantation today."

Mumbling rose behind him. The leader turned and spoke something, and the sound ceased. After those terse words, he reined his horse back in the direction they'd come, and all his men followed. They galloped away, leaving a cloud of dust behind them.

Abigail looked at the nonchalant child watching them disappear, and a volcano threatened to erupt from her governess lips. She sucked in a ragged breath. "Jade, you know I told you not to mount your horse until I joined you in the barn." Her voice came out harsh and shaking.

The child rode up beside her. "But, don't you see, if I hadn't gone ahead, Rockford might be burning right now."

Abigail just shook her head. "You have no idea the danger you were in, young lady, and we are all in right now. Come, we must get home."

On the gallop back to Rockford, frequent stories she'd heard in Charleston of Jamaican plantations being burned, their owners murdered by escaped slaves, came back to Abigail. Why did she ever come to the island? Where was Joshua Becket when his plantation needed him the most? And where was the British militia charged with keeping the island safe?

One question burned across her mind. At nightfall, would the Maroons change their minds about sparing Rockford?

Joshua Becket, where are you?

CHAPTER 14

*J*oshua exited the carriage at Government House, too tired to worry about his dirty, disheveled state. He must relay the message from the Maroons to the governor and get home to Rockford as soon as possible. The sun sat low in the sky, and long shadows fell across the street. He asked the driver to hold the carriage. He took two steps at a time toward the entrance of the imposing building. The guard jumped in front of him.

He bit back a curse word. "It's me, Joshua Becket." He wanted to add that he was back from the pits of hell but decided the young guard could not process it.

The soldier looked him in the eye and then lowered his musket and backed away. "Sorry, sir, I didn't recognize you."

Joshua strode down the long carpeted hall to the governor's office.

The secretary inside stood and gaped at him. "Why, Mr. Becket—"

Governor Smith came trundling through his open door in his blue silk waistcoat, white stockings, and full periwig. "Becket, by Jove, it's about time you showed up." He motioned Joshua into his office, slammed the door, and hurried behind his desk.

Joshua dropped into the nearest chair.

The governor sat and crinkled his nose. "What a mess you look and smell, my man. Now tell me exactly what happened. And where in tarnation is Lord Halton? I expect the British Navy to be on my doorstep if we don't produce him right away."

Joshua did not miss the edge of that authoritative voice. Did the man think him somehow responsible for the kidnapping or derelict in his duty to allow it to happen?

When Joshua finished his story and handed over the letter, he sucked in a deep, tired breath. How soon could he get away and home to Rockford?

The governor scanned the letter, then threw it aside. He stood and paced from his desk to the window, then back again. "You must be crazy to think I'd write up any kind of treaty like this. Why, I'd be the laughingstock of England."

"Sir, I'm only doing what the Maroons insisted. If there is no treaty, in two days, they plan to murder Lord Halton and burn as many plantations as they can." Rockford, most likely first.

The governor sank into his large chair, pulled a lace handkerchief from his sleeve, and wiped his brow. "Yes, yes. We have to rescue Lord Halton. Then the militia can take care of the rebellion." He stood and yelled for his secretary.

The man opened the door and stood at attention. "Yes, your lordship."

"Send fast riders out for my cabinet members. We must write up some kind of treaty tonight."

Joshua rose and glanced out the tall window at the setting sun. "Sir, I must get home to Rockford. I didn't tell you the leader, Cudjoe, especially singled out my plantation to burn. I have a borrowed carriage outside."

The governor glared at him. "And how will we get the treaty back to the place where Lord Halton is being held?"

"I will come back early in the morning, sir. They gave us two days." God help him find the mountain hideaway again when, both going and coming back, on the painful ride he was only half aware of the directions.

The governor flicked his handkerchief at Joshua. "Then go, but you be back here first thing in the morning, Becket, or I'll send officers to arrest you." He leaned back in his chair. "You should've never taken Lord Halton into the garden."

Bile rose in Joshua's throat. The man blamed him for the kidnapping. He swallowed and took a deep, exasperated breath. "I'll be back, sir."

Outside, he asked for a change of horses, then instructed the driver to head toward Rockford and not spare the animals. He gripped the handhold on the door of the conveyance as the horses galloped down the road in the falling darkness. Dust formed a cloud in their wake. Once Joshua leaned his head back on the cushion, weariness overtook him, and he dozed.

The smell of smoke filled his nose, and he awoke coughing. In the dim moonlight, he recognized the road to Windsor Park, Lady Harcourt's plantation, to the left. Rockford's entrance would be a mile or two beyond, although many acres separated the two plantations. He sat forward and froze. On the far horizon, flames flickered against the night sky. A plantation burned, as surely as he sat helpless in the dark, rocking carriage.

As the horses continued to gallop closer, the flames grew taller in the sky and the smell of burning stronger. Moisture gathered in Joshua's eyes, but not from the smoke. He mouthed a prayer. *Lord, it's me again. I know I don't have a right to ask, but I ask you to save Rockford. Save Jade and Abigail and all my people.*

~

*A*t dusk, Abigail stood on the upstairs front balcony of the library with Mrs. Pelfrey, Jade, Walter, and Lucy Dykes. Potcake sat at Jade's feet. The dog lifted his muzzle and emitted a mournful howl until Jade patted his colossal head. Abigail took a deep breath and pointed to the horizon. "What could that fire and smoke yonder mean?" She shuddered, remembering the painted Maroon warriors.

Walter, his eyes so wide the whites showed, shifted his heavy feet.

"Ma'am, it don't bode no good. That's toward Windsor Park as far as I kin reckon."

"Why would they be having a fire of any kind this time of evening?"

"I'se sure they ain't having it. Somebody doing it for 'em." Walter nodded as he spoke. "Some no-good folks bent on evil."

The Maroon Jade called Samson said they wouldn't burn Rockford today. Did they choose Windsor Park instead? A chill shot up her back. And was Joshua Becket still there and caught in the attack?

Mr. Dykes came running from the stables with Jeremy in his wake. "We've done seen some fire and smoke starting on the back fields of the plantation. Could be the mill and storage barns."

Abigail's breath caught in her throat. She glanced at Mrs. Pelfrey. Fear, stark and vivid, glittered in the housekeeper's eyes. Then a low moaning came on the wind from the slave village.

Isaiah Baker hurried across the lawn below and looked up at the balcony, worry etched across his dark face. "I believe them Maroons are on the warpath. What you're seeing on the horizon is probably Windsor Park burning. I'm praying for Rockford to be spared, but I've seen the fires near our mill. And our village people have seen it too, and they gone to try to fight the flames. That's the women and old folks who couldn't go who are moaning."

Jade moved forward and called to the plantation supervisor. "They said they wouldn't burn Rockford today. Samson promised me."

Isaiah shook his head and his lips tightened. "Little miss, I wish I could believe the word of a Maroon."

A carriage came galloping up the front drive. Joshua Beckett jumped from it before it came to a full stop. Abigail blinked back tears.

"Well, thank God, he's home." Mrs. Pelfrey turned and hurried from the balcony.

Joshua strode to Isaiah and Mr. Dykes standing below the balcony. Shock rolled over Abigail at his haggard, unshaven face and the ruined dinner clothes he had worn to the governor's ball. What had happened to him?

"The Maroons may come here next. We've got to make a plan." Joshua wasted no words as he looked from one man to the other.

"Sir, we're glad to see you back, praise God." Isaiah's voice carried.

"Yes, sir. Just tell us what we need to do." Mr. Dykes echoed the supervisor's thankfulness.

Jade leaned over the railing as far as she dared. "Papa, where on earth have you been? You look terrible."

He peered up at the child, and a smile crossed his weary face. He glanced at Abigail. "Glad you asked. The Maroons kidnapped me along with Lord Halton at the ball."

Abigail gasped and staggered back against the wall. How wrong she'd been.

"But how could they take you both? Didn't you fight? And how did you escape?" Jade peppered him with questions.

"We'll talk later. Right now we must prepare. Mrs. Welch, please take Jade to her room and keep her there." He turned back to the two men, and they hurried toward the stables.

Abigail took Jade by the hand and led her away from the balcony, her mind in a jumble. This was a story she wanted to hear. And was Lord Halton also rescued?

She put Jade to bed, read her a story until she slept, and then retired to her own room. She fell to her knees beside her bed and prayed for herself, for Joshua, and for Rockford's protection. When done, she arose and sat in her chair. A few minutes later, she received a summons to come to the parlor.

All the household servants stood about, but Joshua beckoned her to a chair near his and Mrs. Pelfrey's. Muskets, and a pistol Abigail recognized, lay on the tea table before him. He had changed from the ruined dress clothes he'd worn to the ball, but his face still mirrored weariness.

In quick words, he described how he and Lord Halton experienced the kidnapping, his escape, and the letter to the governor. And the risk now of plantations being burned.

"I've armed some of our men to guard the stables and the house in shifts. Now I want to arm most of you." He picked up the pistol and turned toward Abigail. "Do you still know how to use this?" His eyes flashed his seriousness, but a grin played at the corner of his mouth.

Heat climbed up Abigail's neck and spread to her cheeks. Of course, she still knew how to handle her very own pistol. He and his lieutenant had taken it from her when they stormed her ship. "Yes, Mr. Becket. I do."

He handed it to her, and she accepted it, as well as a powder flask and some lead shot.

He caught her eye. "I am charging you to protect Jade and your-self...if we fail to protect the house from assault." His serious voice sent a chill down her spine.

Gasps came from the house servants. Mira and Clarissa grabbed each other and cried in muffled sobs.

Mrs. Pelfrey walked over to them and patted their shoulders.

Joshua looked around the room and into each face. "I don't think we'll fail to protect the house, but it's best to have a plan." He lifted a musket and turned to Walter. "I believe you can handle this. Am I right?"

"Yassir. I can handle it. Just tell me where you want me."

"At the front door, your usual post. I will be beside you. We'll allow no intruders to enter. "

Lucy Dykes cleared her throat. "Sir, could I please have Jeremy with me in the house?"

"Yes. He'll be helping guard the back door of your kitchen with three other men I've stationed there. Your husband, of course, and two others will guard the stables."

He checked around the room again. "Everyone else, go to the place you feel safest in the house. But stay a moment, Mrs. Welch."

The rest filed out of the room.

Abigail stiffened as Joshua turned to her. He sat across from her, but the room seemed too confined with the others gone.

"I have something to say to you, Abigail, whether you believe it or not."

His eyes held a light she'd never seen before, and his use of her name shot warmth through her.

"When I was facing death at the hands of what I have to call frightened, desperate, angry men, I had a conversation with God. One I'm sure my father, Ethan, has prayed for me to have most of my life. I'm a different man. That's all I have time to say for now. Will you pray for our safety tonight?"

She took a breath of utter astonishment. "Yes, of course."

He smiled, and they stood. He reached out his hand to her, and she took it. The blood surged from her fingertips to her toes.

He pulled her to him in a gentle hug, and a delicious shiver of awareness pulsed through her.

Then he released her. "I was determined to make it back to Rockford for you, for Jade, and my people."

Her heart tripped at the sincerity in his voice. Could he mean he cared for her?

"Is the child sleeping?"

She forced her shaky knees to stabilize. "Yes."

"Please sit outside her door until you hear from me all is safe." He leaned forward and planted a kiss on her forehead. "Now we must hurry to our posts." He strode to the door, turned to smile at her, then disappeared down the hall.

Abigail walked up the stairs to the schoolroom in a daze. She touched the tingling spot on her forehead where he'd planted a kiss and pulled a chair in front of Jade's door. She sat with her Bible in her lap. And she prayed.

Father God, You are Almighty God. All power belongs to You. I ask You to station angels around this house and barns. Protect all lives and this property. Change the hearts of the desperate men who are threatening the plantations. Help Governor Smith know how to settle this rebellion wisely for all concerned. Deliver Lord Halton from his captors. She stopped a moment and reflected on what Joshua had told her. Was he sincere? *Lord, only You know if Joshua Becket has had a change of heart. If he has, I want to thank You.*

She alternately read Scripture and prayed until she lost all sense of time and dozed. The sound of carriage wheels and galloping horses in the front drive roused her. She stood and ran to the schoolroom window on the front of the house. She pulled back the drape.

A coach followed by a wagon carrying slaves stopped in front of the main entrance. Joshua came out the front door and down the steps at a fast clip. Abigail released a soft gasp as Lady Harcourt emerged from the coach. She ran and threw herself into Joshua's arms. They stood in the moonlight, arms wrapped around each other like two lost lovers reunited.

Of course, he was a changed man. But not so as you could see it. She dropped the drape back into place.

CHAPTER 15

$\mathcal{T}$he next morning, Abigail awoke in her chair in front of Jade's door when a loud knock sounded at the entrance to the schoolroom. She sat up and straightened her dress she'd dozed in through the fitful watch. The sunlight spilling through the windows lifted her spirit. They'd made it through the night of terror. She breathed a prayer of gratitude. *Thank you, Lord!* The knock sounded again.

"Come in."

Clarissa bustled into the room, her cheeks a rosy red—no evidence of the fear and tears of the night before. "Mrs. Pelfrey wants to know if you'll take breakfast here with Jade or in the dining room with Mr. Becket and Lady Harcourt."

Definitely not with Joshua and the lady. "Here will be fine." Abigail stood. "I'll awaken Jade."

The door behind Abigail opened.

"No, you won't. I'm awake and dressed." Jade paraded in, looking none the worse for the stressful night they'd gone through.

Clarissa put her hands on her hips. "Well, little lady, you missed the worst part last night. For a while, we didn't know if we was going to be burned out or not. But when Lady Harcourt came, she brought news that Lord Halton escaped his captors, and the militia has put down the rebellion." The maid faced Abigail with a swish of her skirts. "Of course, it wasn't in time to save her plantation. I heard her talking to Mr. Becket. Her great house is gone and her barns, but not her mill."

So that was why she'd showed up at Rockford. How long would she stay? Abigail blinked at her own coolness of heart. The woman deserved her pity and Rockford's hospitality.

"Well, Samson promised me he wouldn't burn Rockford, so I'm glad he kept his promise. Please bring me eggs, bacon, toast, and jelly." Jade sat down at the table in the schoolroom and sketched a drawing on her pad.

Clarissa shook her head and then winked at Abigail. "Ma'am, what would you like?"

"The same will be fine."

Clarissa hurried out the door, and her quick steps echoed down the stairs.

Was the danger truly over? Whatever the case, she would complete her toilette before breakfast, the Lord willing. A quick wash up and change of clothing would do much to lift the tiredness she fought from the night of fitful sleep.

A few minutes after finishing breakfast with Jade, Abigail received a summons to the parlor. She entered to see Lady Harcourt sitting on the divan, dressed for travel, and sipping on a cup of tea. Joshua sat across from her.

He stood as Abigail entered. "Mrs. Welch, you've probably heard the terrible news about Windsor Park."

"Yes." She turned to Geneva Harcourt. "I'm so sorry, but glad to see you escaped unharmed."

"And not by good luck. We escaped through a secret underground entrance I had the good sense to put in a few years ago. Saved me and my house servants. But, yes, the great house and my barns are gone." She lowered her cup and smiled at Joshua. "I knew Joshua would receive us, so I came here last night."

Joshua bowed. "And you're welcome to be our guest as long as you need, Geneva. We are glad to help any way we can." He arched an eyebrow at Abigail. "Is that not so, Mrs. Welch?"

Abigail swallowed. Why was he drawing her in on the offer? "Yes, of course. If there's anything I can do to assist you while you're here, Lady Harcourt, feel free to ask."

"Well, I'm headed to my townhouse in Spanish Town this morning. My military escort should be here soon. It would be nice to have a picnic lunch packed by Mrs. Pelfrey for me and my servants to take with us. Could you see about that while I talk further with Joshua?" The woman gave Abigail a bright smile, but it did not reach her proud dark eyes.

Abigail took a deep breath. The woman knew exactly how to underscore a governess's place in the household—just above a servant's role. "I'll be glad to alert Mrs. Pelfrey." She turned and left the room.

Later, in the kitchen, a trampling of hooves coming up the drive snared Abigail's attention. Geneva Harcourt's housekeeper and maids took the packed baskets and departed. From a window, Abigail watched the entourage board the coach and wagon and leave for Spanish Town. Her employer was nowhere to be seen.

～

*J*oshua galloped past his cane fields and to the mill and harvest barns still smoldering. He dismounted and walked around the burned structures. Could he salvage anything? That answer became obvious. They would have to be rebuilt. He sighed and kicked a corner beam ready to fall into the burned center of the mill. For the life of him, he couldn't spark any interest in tackling the rebuilding work. He closed his eyes, something new for him, to pray about decisions. *Lord, what's your plan? Should I rebuild or think about selling out and going home to Charleston?* Would Abigail go with him? Whether or not she cared for him, he'd still need a governess for Jade.

Charleston. The word echoed softly but with precision on the warm breeze behind him. He turned and looked around. Did he imagine it? In years past, he'd often heard his father and even his brother, Samuel, talk about God speaking to them. But would Almighty God speak to Joshua when he'd made such a mess of his life for years? When he'd even doubted God's existence?

He shook his head, remounted, and rode home. At the barn, he turned Haidez over to Dykes and headed into the house. In the hall, he stopped at the table where the butler laid the mail. He picked up an ivory envelope addressed to him. His heart skipped a beat. Its return address? Charleston. As he hurried to his study, he recognized Samuel's handwriting. It had been a long, long time, about fifteen years, but he still knew his stepbrother's scrawl.

He sat behind his desk and ripped the missive open.

Dear Joshua,

I hope this letter finds you well and healthy. I've taken the liberty to write to you and will not waste words. Our father is quite ill. He asks for you, and I promised to write. I know how long it takes letters to travel to Jamaica, so when you get this, can you come as soon as possible? We are praying for his recovery, but he continues in a weak state here at Salt Marsh. We brought him here hoping the fresh sea air will help recover his health. I do not know the state of your affairs on the island or how fast you might be able to leave. We pray nothing will hinder you. Father and I both, along with the rest of the family, will look forward to seeing you as soon as you can come. Surely, twenty years have settled any animosity. You can rest assured, I have none and look forward to your return.

Your obedient servant and brother,
Samuel

Joshua dropped the letter onto the desk, his jaw slack. The fact that Samuel had written him and in a conciliatory manner was surprising and gratifying in itself. After all it seemed like a lifetime had passed since that day Samuel had banished him from Charleston because of his sins—actually crimes—that had earned his banishment.

That his father was sick, maybe dying, split his heart. Whether he should return to Charleston was no longer a question. But was this letter a confirmation that it had been God's voice back at the site of the burned mill? He shook his head, still not quite ready to believe God spoke to him.

He scanned the law books on his lower shelves, but the book he needed wasn't there. He looked up, stretched, and pulled a volume from a taller shelf. The Holy Bible. He brought it back and sat down at his desk. Did God speak and confirm directions like this to individuals? He touched the thick leather cover and hesitated. It had been a lifetime ago that he had opened a Bible. He blew the dust from the spine of the book and parted it about midways. Isaiah. Hadn't his father preached from this book?

He turned the gold-edged pages with reverence until he came to chapter thirty. He read the first half and recognized himself in the rebellious people to whom the prophet directed his words. Yes, he bore deep guilt for his own selfish years. Still, did God give directions to individuals? Nothing seemed to connect to this question until he came to verse twenty-one.

Your ears shall hear a word behind you, saying,
"This is the way, walk in it,"
Whenever you turn to the right hand,
Or whenever you turn to the left.

He reread the verse aloud, and something akin to joy flowed through his being. Hadn't he heard a word behind him? *Charleston.* He took a quill, marked the verse, placed Samuel's letter in the space, and closed the Bible. He stood with a new purpose and energy flowing through him. How fast could he sell Rockford and be on his way to Charleston? A particular person had wanted Rockford for years. But first things first.

He hurried from his study and found Abigail in an upstairs window seat, embroidering in the sunlight.

*A*bigail moved farther into her corner of the bench as Joshua made himself comfortable beside her, filling the rest of the space on the padded seat. His masculine scent of spice tickled her nose. Her fingers refused to make another stitch, so she wrapped up her work and turned to face him. His dark eyes danced—in fact, his entire countenance glowed. He radiated a vitality that drew her like a magnet. What was on the man's mind?

He laid his broad hand on her hands, folded over her work in her lap. His touch sent a tingle up her arms. "Abigail, I have some big news I want to tell you...and get your opinion. Something I've just decided to do today."

She blinked. "Very well. What is it?"

"I'm going to sell the plantation and return home to Charleston. My mind's settled."

The words dropped like a cannonball. What had brought him to this firm decision? The Maroon rebellion and burning? And what of her new beginning she'd come to the island seeking? "Sir, if you've made your decision, why do you need my opinion?"

He turned and placed his hands on her shoulders, forcing her face close to his. She could hardly breathe. "Because I want you to go with me, Abigail. Will you?"

Confusion clouded her mind. Exactly what was he asking of her? His next words left no doubt.

"I, uh, I'm a great deal less than perfect, as you are probably aware, but for whatever it's worth, I'm trying to become a different man. I've had a change of heart. I care very much about you, dear little governess. And I know I'm some older than you, but could there be a place in your heart and life for me? I believe you and God can help me become the man I ought to be." He kissed her forehead and trailed a finger down her chin to her lips.

Her heart jolted and her pulse pounded. She moved back and gushed out the first words that came to mind. "What brought you to...this decision?"

He moved his hands from her shoulders and smiled. "The kidnapping and then seeing my burned mill and storage barns with the harvest destroyed set me to thinking. I couldn't picture myself trying to rebuild. And I began to think of going home." He ducked his head. "I prayed about it, and I think God confirmed it. But then He did so again when I returned home and found a letter from my stepbrother, Samuel. My father is ill, and he's asking for me. I need to go home and spend what may be his last days with my father."

He prayed and God confirmed the decision? Joshua Becket was full of surprises. He had bared his heart to her. Was he proposing to her as well?

Joshua stood and pulled her up into his arms.

Her breath swooshed out of her lungs, and a giddiness possessed her.

"What do you say, dear Mrs. Welch? This is a proposal." His piercing dark eyes roved over her face. The smoldering flame in them stole her breath. His closeness, so male, so bracing, engulfed her. He lowered his head and brushed her lips with his own. Then he kissed her again, this time a deep kiss, and she couldn't help responding— totally lost, floating in euphoria. Could she love again as she'd loved Philip? Everything seemed possible at that moment.

He lifted his head and chuckled. "Is that a yes, Mrs. Welch? You will go with me to Charleston? We can marry at Salt Marsh with my family around us, or we can marry now. What is your desire, my love?" He trailed kisses from her lips to her eyelids.

Everything in her wanted to shout with joy. *Yes, I'll marry you any place, any time.* But she pulled back, took a deep breath. Reality rushed in and struck against the romantic dream. This was her employer who had taken Lady Harcourt into his arms last night. This was the father of Jade, whose mother was a tavern doxy. Had he held that vulnerable young woman in his arms just as he held her now? Would he tire of her as he'd apparently tired of Jade's mother? Was he truly a changed man? His mesmerizing closeness fogged her mind. She put her hands on his chest to push back, but he kept her pressed to him. With a great struggle, she finally looked into his shining eyes and answered. "I—I need to think about your offer."

Joshua stiffened and released her so fast her knees threatened to cave. He clutched her shoulders and set her back on the window seat, his face a thundercloud. "Think about it, then. Meanwhile, I'm making plans to sell Rockford and leave for Charleston as soon as possible."

He strode to the steps, but before descending, turned back to her. His face and voice softened. "Abigail, even if you don't want to marry, I'll still need a governess for Jade in Charleston. Maybe that'll make it easier for you while you're deciding."

Still sitting in something like a state of shock, the slamming of the front entrance made Abigail jump. It was as if that door slammed on all her hopes and dreams of a new life, love, and security. The next moment, Joshua came into her view from the window. The man strode toward the stables with long, heavy strides, his fists clenched at his sides.

Abigail covered a sob with her hand and ran down the hall to her room. She threw herself on her bed, choking back tears and trying to make sense out of what had just taken place with Joshua Becket. She'd hurt his feelings when she hadn't immediately accepted his proposal. What else could she have done, given not just his past, but hers as well? Could she realistically hope to have a love again as wonderful as her first love had been? But, oh, why hadn't she said she needed to pray about it, instead of think about it?

She squeezed her eyes shut, but that didn't ease the memory of the thrilling moments she'd experienced in his arms. Her lips still burned from his kisses, and the blood coursed through her veins like a river awakened by warm spring rains. A river that had been slow for a long time.

Was there a second chance at true love and trust? Would it heal her heart so wounded by the loss of dear Philip, her first love, and then losing their precious child she'd named after him? Wasn't this why she'd come to Jamaica? To see if she could find healing, love, and security—a new beginning? Was God in Joshua's proposal?

The rest of the afternoon, Abigail moved in a daze. Joshua filled her thoughts. Jade, precocious child that she was, would have noticed her governess's preoccupation, but Clarissa had taken her charge in hand to play games on the back lawn with Jeremy.

Determined to stay busy, Abigail mended every rent in her sparse wardrobe and Jade's, sewed on missing buttons, repaired loose seams. Prayers rose from her heart as she worked with her nimble fingers.

She didn't see Joshua that evening at dinner. Mrs. Pelfrey remarked he'd gone into Spanish Town and would return late.

By bedtime, Abigail, weary from the battle in her heart, dressed for bed. She took her Bible from her nightstand, propped pillows to lean back on in bed, and searched the Scriptures. They renewed her troubled mind, and peace flowed through her being. Sleep pressed against her eyelids. She laid the Bible on her nightstand and blew out her candle. She had an answer for Joshua Becket.

CHAPTER 16

*T*he next morning, after finishing Jade's lessons, Abigail left the child with Clarissa and Mira, working on an inter-locking wooden puzzle. Potcake lay at Jade's feet, his tail thumping the floor. Joshua had brought several of the recently invented games called puzzles home from his travels. Jade and the maids loved the brainteaser pastime.

Already dressed in her riding outfit, Abigail proceeded to the stables. Joshua stood ready to mount Haidez in the corridor. She walked up to him and smiled. "Could I join you on a ride before lunch?"

He looked at her for a long moment, searching her face, then nodded. He called down the corridor. "Dykes, saddle up Arabelle."

The man backed out of a stall he was cleaning, propped his pitch-fork on the wall, and wiped his face with his handkerchief. "Yes, sir. That filly needs a good riding for sure after all the excitement we've had."

Soon Abigail rode beside Joshua down the back plantation road. She had to quicken Arabelle's normal pace to keep up with Haidez. They rode toward the Blue Mountains and took the same wooded path where they'd once had a picnic. A tingle flowed down her back, and she smiled. It was also where Joshua had first kissed her, and she'd almost left Jamaica.

They came to the clearing beside the creek, and Joshua dismounted. She did the same and followed to sit near him on one of the huge rocks. Birds twittered in the trees, and water gurgled over rocks beyond them. He pulled a weed stalk growing in a crevice and twiddled it between his fingers, then chewed on it.

"Now, Mrs. Welch, do you have anything different to say to me than you said last night?" His dark eyes blazed with intensity. Then he threw the stalk aside and his whole attitude changed. "Do you, at your younger age, know what a blow that was to me when you didn't jump at my proposal?" He smiled so wide a dimple creased his jaw. The heaviness of the air lifted with his words and grin. He looked straight in her eyes. "You're the first woman I ever proposed to, Abigail. Do you know how that would make a fellow feel at my age, to get rejected when he finally asks a woman to marry him?"

She smiled despite herself. "At your age? Yes, at your *great* age, I guess it would be a shock."

He stood, grabbed her hand, and pulled her up into his arms. The breath swooshed out of her lungs.

His handsome face pressed within inches of hers. His warm breath baptized her. "Better tell me quick if you've got an answer for me, Abigail." His lips brushed hers, and her heartbeat jumped into her throat.

"The answer is yes, Joshua, I'll marry you." Her words came out with breathy fervor.

"What did you say?" He kissed her, a firm, demanding kiss.

"I said yes," she responded, with a giddy sense of pleasure.

"And when? Here or at Salt Marsh?" He moved her back a few inches from his clasp, lifted her chin, and gazed into her eyes.

Was this some kind of test? But she could only give one answer, and she gave it in a softer voice. "At Salt Marsh with your family, Joshua. Wouldn't it be best to have all wrongs righted when we say our vows? You told me how you left Charleston."

He exhaled a slow breath and pulled her close again. She laid her head on his chest. Was he pleased or disappointed about waiting to marry until after they arrived at Salt Marsh and he made peace with his family? A fear nibbled at her heart. Had she made the best choice? Would he get angry and tell her to forget he'd ever asked her to wed?

He remained silent for a long moment. "You may be a few years younger, woman, but you've got the wisdom of Solomon." His words eased any worry the enemy could dash through her mind.

She looked up into his face, amazed at the joyful expression she'd so seldom seen. "Do you think it best we not announce our coming marriage right now?"

He frowned, then grinned again. "That might also be a good idea. After all, it's going to take all of our skill and energy to keep everyone happy when we disclose the sale and move to Charleston. One big change at a time."

He kissed her one more time, a breathtaking kiss, full of promise. Walking back to the horses, he swung her up in his arms and into the saddle. She couldn't help smiling all the way back to the great house.

~

*A*fter the midday meal the following day, with all the house servants and the Dykes present, Joshua stood at the head of the table, tall and handsome, and in full confidence announced his intent to sell Rockford and move back to Charleston.

Jade thrust out her lip. "But, Papa, I don't want to leave Rockford. And can I take Buttercup?"

He bent down to his daughter and kissed her forehead. "I promise you, you'll love Charleston. It's where I grew up, and you've got lots more family to meet there."

The housekeeper wrung her hands. "Well, sir, I don't know what I'll do. Will you need my services in Charleston?"

"Mrs. Pelfrey, I'll talk to you and the house servants again as soon as I have the sale finalized. I do plan to buy a townhouse there and will need you and other servants to go with us. It is my intention to practice my former law profession when we get settled."

Abigail resisted any show of surprise. Did he have that kind of money to get started? There was much she didn't know about Joshua Becket. Learning about this man who was to become her husband would be a challenge. She lowered her eyes and whispered a prayer. *And, hopefully, a joy, Lord.*

~

$\mathcal{T}$he next morning, the rattle of coach wheels announced the arrival of Lady Harcourt and an official-looking gentleman. He wore a short white wig and a silk waistcoat with lace at his neck and wrists. A saddle horse, tied to the back of the coach, pawed the drive.

Abigail frowned from the schoolroom window above. Lady Harcourt's tailored blue riding outfit fit her well and flattered her small waist. A matching, veiled hat sat atop blond curls.

Jade came to lean on the sill with her. "Look, Papa's going to ride with the pretty lady."

Indeed, Joshua rode up from the stable on Haidez and dismounted. While a servant held the stallion, he helped Geneva Harcourt mount the horse she'd brought with her. Both horses neighed and pawed the shell drive. The lady's voice rang out like a silver bell in laughter, and before Joshua could move away, she leaned down and whispered something to him.

He looked up at the woman, smiled, and shook his head, then mounted Haidez.

Abigail moved from the window and called Jade to her lessons. Even with the horseback ride Joshua was taking alone with Lady Harcourt distracting her, she finished the work with Jade by noon when Clarissa brought their lunch. After putting the child down for her nap despite protestations, Abigail descended to the first-floor library for a book. She browsed the shelves and finally pulled out a volume of poetry. As she started out the door to return to her room, familiar voices carried in the hall. Footsteps emerged from the study down the corridor. She eased back into the library.

"I will love this plantation just as you do, Joshua." Geneva Harcourt's silky tones could not be mistaken. What was she talking about?

"That's good to know." Joshua Becket's deep voice responded to the lady.

A male speaker Abigail did not recognize came next. "Lady Harcourt, I'll await you in the coach. Take as long as you like." The words carried the honeyed air of a man most likely used to dealing with aristocrats like Geneva Harcourt. His light steps receded down the hall and toward the front entrance. That must be the gentleman who'd accompanied the woman on her visit to Rockford.

"Well, aren't you going to kiss me goodbye?"

At Geneva's pouty inquiry, Abigail closed her eyes and laid her head against the library door. Why should she hide? Why not see exactly what was going on with this man who had just proposed to her? She yanked the door open and emerged into the hall.

The two of them stood close. But the lady had the upper hand. She slid her arms around Joshua's neck, pulled his head down, and kissed him.

Abigail sucked in an exasperated breath.

Joshua lifted his head and met her eyes. Red crept up from his throat.

She gave him a hostile glare.

He pushed aside Lady Harcourt's arms. "Abigail...I can explain."

Geneva turned and saw her. She shrugged and smiled back at Joshua. "Oh, it's only the governess."

Abigail marched past them and to the stairs, clenching her teeth. Of course, he could explain. Everything. No doubt. In her room, she fell across the bed. Shivers of shock and frustration rippled along her spine. Moisture gathered in her eyes, and she tried to blink it away. Finally, she gave up, and a blast of hot tears cascaded down her cheeks. She couldn't breathe and almost missed Joshua's plea at her door.

"Abigail, please let me talk to you."

She tried to ignore the voice, but it grew more insistent. He'd awaken Jade from her nap and alert the entire household.

Wiping her cheeks, she rose and opened the door. He stood there, sadness blanketing his features, like a little boy who knew he'd been naughty and wanted to make things right.

He entered and closed the door. In one step, he reached out and drew her into his arms.

She didn't resist but stood stiff in his embrace.

"I'm so sorry you saw that, Abigail. I promise you that last kiss from Geneva meant absolutely nothing." He leaned her back and looked into her eyes. "Listen, she's buying Rockford. She bought it today. That was her solicitor accompanying her, and we signed all the papers. But she won't take possession for a couple of months."

She bought Rockford? Abigail grappled with disbelief. She moved a step away, numb but with a plethora of emotions begging to be expressed. "And the ride today you two went on?" Her voice sounded icy, even to her ears.

"I showed her the plantation. That was the entire purpose of the ride." He placed his hands on her shoulders again. His eyes blazed with sincerity. Or was it with deception? Would she ever be able to trust him without doubting?

He pressed her close. "Abigail, I've already told you, I've not lived a God-honoring life." His voice turned hoarse. "But I am truly trying to change. Can you have a little more patience? I tried to tell Geneva today on the ride, and I thought she understood, that there could be nothing more between us, but then she pulled that act out in the hall. If you'd come up a moment earlier, you'd have seen she forced that kiss, not me."

Abigail relaxed the least bit in his arms. She had seen.

He drew her closer. "That, my darling wife-to-be, is the last either of us will ever see of the woman."

She chewed on her lower lip and lifted her head to steal a look at him. "Do you really mean that, Joshua?"

"Yes. She's given us the time we need to pack up and vacate the great house. I plan to do it as soon as possible." He kissed the tip of her nose. "Will you help me? We've a lot to do, including getting my ship ready to sail and deciding what to take, what to leave."

She swallowed hard, trying to manage the old fears and uncertainties that attempted to rear their heads in her mind. But the heart-rending tenderness in his gaze won out. "Yes, of course. What do you want me to do?"

"Glad you asked. Day after tomorrow, we'll walk around the house with Mrs. Pelfrey and decide the things we will pack and the things we'll leave. Will you please record the list? Tomorrow I must find my trusty friend Lambert and see about getting the *Eagle* ready to sail." Excitement laced his deep voice. "By the way, add my law books to take at the top of the list."

He bent and planted a warm kiss on her lips. And she shushed every resisting voice from her mind and heart. They would leave for Charleston as soon as possible, he'd said. She could scarcely believe it, but happiness flowed over her just the same.

One last crisis hit them, especially Jade, a few days before they were ready to embark on the *Eagle*.

Potcake died.

Jade found him on the floor beside her bed one morning—at his guard post to the end. She rushed into Abigail's room, sobbing. "Mrs. Welch, do you think he just didn't want to go to Charleston with us? Father said I could take him."

Abigail put her arms around the heartbroken child. "I think he was just tired, and it was time for him to rest. He was at a pretty good age for a dog, you know."

The girl, her eyes so much like Joshua's with their thick dark lashes now full of tears, looked up at Abigail. "Is there a dog heaven?"

Abigail cocked her chin, then blinked. Several texts in the Bible described animals in the prophetic future of Christ's kingdom. Horses definitely played a part. And if a lamb was going to lie down by a wolf, as Isaiah prophesied, might there not be a sheep dog there, as well? "I think there just might be, Jade." And she shared her version of the promises with her.

The child sniffed, and the tears slowed to a trickle.

❧

*T*welve days later, Abigail stood on the deck of the *Eagle* brigantine a day after it sailed out of the plantation harbor in Jamaica. She breathed in the fresh, salty breeze that flapped and snapped their white sails. The gently rolling ocean glistened like diamond dewdrops in the sunlight. She shaded her eyes with her hand and glanced up at the quarterdeck where Joshua and Lieutenant Lambert communed. Mr. Dykes and Jeremy viewed the capping waves from the elevated poop deck.

Happiness and excitement swelled her heart until she thought it might burst. They were actually on the way back to Charleston and a new life for her as Joshua Becket's wife. Her dream of a new beginning, love, and security hung like a forever promise within reach. The two weeks preceding their boarding had passed in a whirlwind of activity at the great house, choosing, then packing what to take with them. For Jade, the hardest part was leaving her horse, Buttercup.

At that moment, the child climbed up from the lower deck with Clarissa and Mira right behind her. She darted to Abigail's side. "When will we get to Charleston? How soon will I get a new horse? Will you still be my governess?" She popped out a question with each breath.

"Slow down, little lady. We just left the harbor yesterday, so it'll be about ten days before we reach Charleston, if the weather holds."

Abigail turned to the two maids. "Clarissa, Mira, how are you faring? Any seasickness?"

Mira, her face pale, held tight to the rail. "I've gotta go back to the cabin. Been a little sick, but not like Mrs. Pelfrey, thank God."

Abigail shook her head. Poor Mrs. Pelfrey took sick after the first few hours of sailing. Perhaps she should check on her again. "Clarissa, will you take Jade back to your cabin and work on a puzzle, maybe?

I'm going down to see about Mrs. Pelfrey. You know Mr. Becket doesn't want the child on deck without two adults."

"Yes, ma'am." The girl took Jade's hand and led her back to the hatch and down the steps.

Just as Abigail reached the entrance to the lower deck, Joshua called down to her from the quarterdeck. "Wait up, Abigail." He skipped down the quarterdeck steps and strode toward her. "I've something I want to put in your safekeeping."

She followed him to the lower deck, down the passageway, and to the door of his cabin. He entered and emerged in a few minutes, holding a small wooden box shaped like a miniature trunk. "I want you to conceal this among your things." He spoke in a lowered voice.

"You mean hide it?" She blinked at him, but he took her arm and headed toward her cabin. He entered behind her and pushed the door shut with his boot. Handing her the box with the carving across the top and a golden lock on the lid, he smiled. Then he pulled a key secured on a chain from around his neck and handed that to her as well. "This is the gold with which we will build our new life in Charleston. It's from the sale of Rockford. I want you to conceal it among your things until we get there. Only I, you, and Lambert know of its existence. And it needs to stay that way. Will you do this for me, for us?"

"Joshua, why...?"

He took the treasure from her hands and laid it on her small table, then drew her into his arms. "This is just a precaution."

Her heart started pounding. "Are you thinking something may happen to you or the ship?"

He kissed her forehead. "No, but I think it is wise to take this safety measure. Our ship has a small crew, including some I'm not too familiar with. Lambert thinks they're all trustworthy, or he wouldn't have hired them on. But he also thinks this might be a good idea, in case any of them have sticky fingers."

She took a deep breath. "If you think it best, I'll do it."

"By the way, I want you to know you can fully trust Lambert. He's experienced, wise, and can even sail this ship alone if he had to. And he knows how to deal with trouble if it should come." He smiled. "Not that I think any we can't handle might head our way."

She searched for the meaning behind his words. A wave of apprehension swept through her like a cold, northern wind. "Lieutenant Lambert could sail the *Eagle* alone if he had to? Do you expect you might not sail it yourself?"

"Now don't wrinkle up your pretty forehead like that. We're just talking about precautions, dear one. These waters still have some evil ships sailing them." He kissed her frown away, then claimed her lips for a quick, passionate kiss. "Now I must get out of here and away from temptation." He grinned until dimples creased his tanned cheeks.

Abigail wrapped her arms around herself and whispered a prayer. How terrible would it be to lose her dream of a new beginning for both her and Joshua with it almost in their grasp?

~

*J*oshua strode back toward the quarterdeck. He didn't tell Abigail what had alerted him to take safety measures. Lambert had shared with him about running into one of their old crewmembers when he'd searched for a crew, one they'd had trouble with before. Lambert didn't offer to rehire the man for the sail to Charleston. The pirate, half drunk, became angry and spat out some threats against Captain Jay until Lambert shut him up with a side clip to the man's slack jaw.

What could a lone pirate hope to accomplish with his threats? The man didn't even know Joshua's real identity. But the more he had thought about it since leaving Jamaica, the more he'd felt he should take the sort of precaution he'd just taken with Abigail and their funds.

After the midday meal, Joshua again stood on the quarterdeck, enjoying the slight breeze flapping the sails. Half the crew napped before their coming evening shift. Even Lieutenant Lambert slept below deck. He would relieve Joshua later.

"A sail. A sail!" The lookout's voice rang from the crow's nest.

Joshua whipped out his eyeglass and scanned the ocean. A large vessel sailed toward them at a fast clip on their port side. Could it be pirates or the Spanish? Then he saw their colors and lowered the glass. Neither. Why would a British patrol follow them?

Lambert appeared from the hatch and hurried across the deck, stuffing his shirt into his pants. He swung up on the quarterdeck. "I heard the lookout's yell. What's happening?"

Joshua handed him the glass.

"British. In fact, if I'm not mistaken, it's a man-of-war and twice our size. And it looks as though it's headed straight for us." Lambert's shocked voice pealed across the deck. He handed the piece back to Joshua, consternation creasing his brow.

Joshua kept his eye trained on the ship as it sailed closer. Yes, it was twice their size and with three times more guns. What were they doing this far out of their Jamaican waters? Surely, it would pass them.

Instead of passing, the British vessel sent a shot across their bow.

"What in—?" Joshua bit back curse words. Couldn't they see his English flag flying in the wind? Then a thought struck him like a fist in his gut. Perhaps they should've already changed to an American flag. They planned to do so the third day out. Since the American Revolution treaty had taken effect, England commanded their British captains not to fire on American ships. That flag might have offered him some safety.

He lifted the glass once more to his eye and looked straight into the glass of the captain on the man-of-war. An icy chill ran down Joshua's spine. Lord Halton, sent to the Caribbean to hunt down pirates. He'd never forget the face of the man kidnapped with him by the Maroons.

The leader of the other ship lowered his glass and cupped his lips with his hand. "Heave to, *Eagle*. Joshua Becket, you're under arrest by the British Crown. We have all our guns trained on you."

Joshua almost dropped his eyeglass overboard. He swallowed the bile that rose on his tongue and turned to Lambert. The man had turned pale under his deep tan. He touched his lieutenant's arm. "Go below deck. Hide. If anything happens to me, you must sail this ship on to Charleston. Make sure Abigail and Jade arrive safely to my family at Salt Marsh." His strangled words tore at his throat, and loss settled like a huge stone on his chest.

Lambert's nostrils flared, and he thrust out his massive chest. "No, sir. I'll stay and fight at your side."

"No, please, my man, if you've ever helped me, you must help me now. I think they'll only take me, unless they know or recognize you as my right-hand man. Go. Warn all our people to stay below deck." He looked into his friend's eyes.

Lambert stiffened, and his lips reduced to a tight, bleak line before he pivoted and hastened below deck.

CHAPTER 17

*E*very sailor on board the *Eagle* stood frozen at their various posts, their eyes glued on the huge British ship as it drew near. They stared from it to Joshua. He commanded them, "Men, you're not to fire a single shot or resist. It's me they want. The rest of you should be safe."

A rowboat lowered down the side of the *HMS Royal George* with the English captain and half a dozen armed marines aboard. They rowed to the *Eagle* with swift oars that left a trail of foam behind them.

Joshua walked toward the rail as Lord Halton of England's Royal Navy climbed aboard. Six robust marines followed him with guns drawn, and a hunch-shouldered, ragged pirate lagged behind them. Joshua stiffened. The former crewman about whom Lambert had warned him.

Halton stopped in front of Joshua. Clad in his spotless red-and-white uniform with medals and ribbons across his chest, he threw his shoulders back. His eyes glittered like shards of glass. "Joshua Becket, I have learned that you have operated under an alias—that of the pirate, Captain Jay."

Joshua forced a smile as heat flooded his face. "And how can you prove that, my lord?"

The man turned to the pirate, who shook in his boots when that beady stare landed on him. "Is this the man you served under in pirating escapades, and even against British ships?"

The pirate lowered his head, refusing to meet Joshua's narrowed eyes.

"Speak up, swine, or you'll suffer his same fate." Lord Halton spat out the words, his hand on the hilt of his sword.

The pirate lifted a shaking finger and pointed to Joshua. "Yessir, that's him, knowed him as Captain Jay on this here *Eagle*." He dropped his head again and moved aside, misery in every movement of his body. Why wasn't he exultant?

Lord Halton nodded, and the six marines surrounded Joshua and divested him of his sword and gun.

Their captain took a document from inside his coat. "Joshua Becket, alias Captain Jay, I arrest you for pirating and plundering ships in His Majesty's Caribbean waters, even English ships, a crime for which His Majesty has decreed the death sentence."

～

*A*bigail started out her cabin door after the firing of the warning shot across the ship's bow. She ran into Lambert as he hurried down the passageway. "Sir, what is happening?"

Lambert paused for only a moment, his face stiff and misshapen with worry. "Ma'am. I believe Captain Becket is...being arrested by the captain of a British man-of-war. He urged me to come below deck and warn all of you to stay here." His face hardened into battle lines. "I wanted to stay and fight by his side, but he has authorized me to sail this ship on to Charleston. You must be very brave, my lady, and help the others. Pray they'll not search the ship—or find and arrest me." He hurried down the passageway and lifted the hatch to the lower hold.

An icy knife ripped up Abigail's spine with pain like she'd never known. This was what Joshua had known could happen. Fear and anger both clamored for expression until she couldn't breathe. What would the British do to Joshua? How could they take him away from them? What was she supposed to do? Would they search and find his lieutenant or the treasure she'd hidden for their new beginning?

Jade and the two maids burst up the passageway. "Ma'am, what's happening?" Clarissa's voice echoed with fear.

Despite her confusion and anxiety, Abigail forced her mind and face into a semblance of order and peace. Drawing them into her cabin, she told them what Lambert had said.

"I ain't never liked them British soldiers. What will they do to us?" Mira spat out. Both she and Clarissa began moaning and wringing their hands.

"You must stop that right now and be brave, and start praying. And we must not go aboard deck until all danger is past. This is what Captain Becket would have us do."

Jade, pale as cotton, knelt beside Abigail's cot. "Lord Jesus, please save my father. Stop the men who took him." Her trembling voice dissolved into sobs.

The maids dropped to their knees, and Abigail knelt beside them. "Father God, please have mercy and protect and deliver Joshua. Give him words of wisdom." She blinked back moisture. "And help them not search the ship. Help us reach Charleston safe and bring him back to us." Her voice broke.

Forcing control back into her voice and demeanor, she rose and walked to look out the porthole. The others crowded in to get a glimpse. Jade stood on the cot. A rowboat reached the side of the ship with *HMS Royal George* blazoned across its hull. Abigail's heart fell to her feet as Joshua climbed up the ship's ladder, preceded by three large marines and followed by the same number, all heavily armed. In his white shirt and plumed hat blowing in the breeze, Joshua appeared harmless, unruffled. But when he arrived on deck, they chained his hands and feet and pushed him into the ship's interior with the butt of a musket.

Oh, Joshua. What will happen to you? Will I ever see you again, my love? She turned back to the maids and Jade and, with supreme effort, forced back the torrent of tears threatening to stream down her face. It was up to her to set a tone of hope. Could she find it somewhere? *Lord, help me find it.*

~

*T*he next morning Joshua sat on his cot in his straw-lined cell in the Jamaican Guard House and wiped perspiration from his brow. He whispered another prayer for Abigail and Jade and the *Eagle* to make it safely to Salt Marsh. It had both torn his heart and sped his hopes when, through a dingy porthole on the British man of war, he'd spied his ship making sail. Thank God it looked like they'd gotten away, and he could depend on Eric Lambert. But a lot could happen sailing north on the Atlantic.

The smell of sweat, unwashed bodies, and decay permeated the labyrinth of cells and sickened him. When a guard slid food under the opening at the bottom of his door, he pushed the watery soup and moldy hardtack back from where it had come and dropped onto his cot. With his hands propped behind his head, he examined his situation. He would have his day in court, if he knew anything about British law, and he knew a lot from his former practice in Charleston. Could he come up with any legal argument that might save him or give him more time? He racked his mind, but he'd not practiced law all the years he'd been in Jamaica. If only he had his law books.

The bars beside his cell rattled. "Sir, Capt'n Jay, I didn't wanna betray you, but them soldiers overhead me when I was drunk and mad."

His former, troublesome crewman with thin shoulders and ragged clothing peered from the cell next to him. Young, probably only nineteen or twenty. They'd often reprimanded him for too much drink on the *Eagle*. They'd kept him on because when sober, he was an excellent gunner. Wide blue eyes, fully alert, betrayed raw fear. His name came back to Joshua. Henry. A pitiful mess—like he himself had once been. Lost, foolish, and headed toward disaster—like Joshua again now.

Henry sank back onto his cot. "They said they'd release me, so I don't know why I'm here in a cell beside you." The man's voice quaked, and he turned and wrapped his fingers around the bars separating them. "I promise I was drunk, sir. I never meant nothing like this to happen. Why do you reckon they ain't released me?"

"Tell me one thing. How did you learn of my real identity, Henry?"

"I guess it don't matter none now to tell you. I fell in once with your old plantation overseer, name of Bishop, a while back. We had a few drinks together. After he'd had a few too many, he told me about seeing you coming in late at night with a cart of goods after we returned from a pirate raid. I put two and two together. After all, Rockford was one of the closest plantations to where you docked the *Eagle* in the bay." He leaned back on the wall, chewing on a straw. "I didn't tell your overseer my suspicions. He said he was saving his information for later, and I knew the man was wicked enough to do you damage." He took a deep, dejected breath. "But then I ran off at the mouth in the tavern when your man refused to hire me back on the crew. Two soldiers overheard, followed me out, and dragged me before Lord Halton." He leaned toward Joshua. "I wasn't going to tell them nothing, I swear, Capt'n, but they put me on the rack." He rubbed his shoulders and winced.

Joshua's nostrils flared. "I'm sorry to hear that, Henry." Poor devil. They would never release Henry. Not the pirate he'd admitted to being with his betrayal of his captain.

The guard came down the corridor, blowing out the few flickering lanterns, and thick, humid darkness descended, hindering further communication. Joshua leaned back on his cot with his hands behind his head. Finally, worn and tired to his very bones, he gave up the legal arguments he rehearsed in his head and fell into a fitful sleep.

At first light, a guard tromped down the corridor with other footsteps following. Joshua sat up and rubbed his eyes in time to see the minister, Mark Gardner, being admitted to his cell.

"Hello, Joshua. How are you faring? I just heard about your arrest last night when I attended a party given by Lady Harcourt." Somehow, he managed to sound both cheerful and sad, and he sat on the edge of the cot beside Joshua. His presence brought a measure of peace.

"I'm surviving. For now." Joshua expelled a deep breath and moved to dip a drink of fresh water from the bucket in the corner the guard had just deposited. Then he sat back down beside the reverend.

"Is there any truth to these pirating charges, my man?"

Joshua glanced into the man's steady gray eyes. "Not if you understand letters of marque."

"I do. Did you have a letter of marque from another country giving you license to attack and capture ships of their enemies?"

"I did, but I can't produce it. It's in the trunk I had to leave on my ship. But I don't think the British Court would accept it if I could present it. It's from their arch enemy, France. Also, if they beat the bushes around Montego Bay, they may flush out a few more witnesses that worked on my crew." He kept his voice low. Behind him, Henry still snored in his sleep.

Concern lined the minister's face. "I'm sorry to hear this. Is there anything I can do?"

"You can pray."

Gardner cocked his head. "Really?" His brows rose. "So you believe in prayer?"

Joshua rubbed the two days' growth on his prickly chin. "There are some things you don't know about me, Reverend." He told the man about his minister father, then how he turned from his godly teachings and pursued his own way until a few months past.

The man's eyes grew wider at each turn in the story, especially at how God confirmed Joshua's sale of Rockford and return to Charleston. When Joshua finished, Mark chuckled and slapped his knee. "What a wonderful tale. Thank you for sharing it with me. Might I ask, did Abigail Welch have anything to do with your change of heart?" His eyes lit up when he spoke her name.

Had the man also fallen in love with Abigail? *Well, give him the truth.* "I have to admit, she did. She always lived out a true Christian life before me, encouraged me to make peace with God, return home, and do the same with my family. Though several years younger than me, the woman has a lot of wisdom."

"Mrs. Welch is a wonderful person. Where is she now—and your house servants? Did they come back to Jamaica after the British inter-cepted your ship?"

Joshua stood and paced across the cell. He balled a fist and slammed it into his opposite palm.

That sound roused Henry from the next cell. The young man sat up, yawned, and then remained quiet after glancing at Joshua's visiting minister.

What was safe to tell the minister? Had the ship reached the safety of American waters by now? Lambert would've raised the patriot flag as soon as he took command of the *Eagle*. Could he trust the minister not to tell the British where his ship was headed in case they decided to pursue and confiscate it?

"Mark, I understand you're of the Baptist faith. Are you also American?"

"Sure am." A wide smile creased the man's face.

Joshua came back and sat beside him. He leaned toward him and lowered his voice to a whisper. "They did not force my ship to return to Jamaica, thank God. Hopefully, Abigail and Jade are on the way to my family in Charleston. I left my excellent assistant and best friend on board to do just that." Should he also tell him he and Abigail were secretly engaged, and their plan was to marry at Salt Marsh, his step-brother's plantation? Again, he felt prompted to reveal the truth, this time about his relationship with his governess. "Abigail and I planned to marry after we arrived in Charleston."

Shutters fell across the minister's eyes for a moment, but he recov-ered fast. "I'm glad you shared that, Joshua. It clears the air."

"Clears the air?"

The minister ducked his head. "I would've asked her to marry me if you hadn't, but I didn't know when you were leaving. I've been feeling I missed my opportunity after I heard you'd set sail." He lifted his face and looked straight at Joshua. "Now I know it probably was not part of God's plan for me."

Joshua's shoulders relaxed. Mark might be a minister, but he was also a real man and a genuine friend to open his heart as he did.

Mark stood. "Listen, I'll do anything I can to help you. Just tell me.

Can I bring you something decent to eat this evening? I don't mind coming back at all, and I've favor with the guards here." A smile spread across his smooth, tanned face.

"That would be great. The food here is...pretty terrible." He kept his voice just above a whisper. No need to invite retorts or revenge from the guards.

"That's right, Mr. Minister, it is. Could you add me to that food offer?" Henry clutched the bars between their cells and looked hopefully at Mark Gardner.

"I'll bring extra. You can count on it." He turned to leave.

"Mark, one more thing. Can you bring me a Bible? I had to leave mine on the *Eagle*."

The minister's eyes lit up, and he grinned at Joshua. "Of course. I'll be happy to." He rapped on the cell bars, and a red-coated guard came to escort him out of the Guard House.

❧

*J*ust before the midday meal, a commotion sounded from the prison entrance, and a delegation soon paraded down the corridor to Joshua's cell. He stood and looked into the three hard faces of Lord Halton, Governor Smith, and the Lord Chief Justice whom Joshua had met once at the government ball. All the men wore full white wigs. The governor boasted his usual silk waistcoat, this time a pale blue, and spotless white silk stockings, and shining, buckled shoes. Lord Halton wore his full military uniform, and the judge, his long black robe. All three held lacy handkerchiefs to their noses.

Governor Smith spoke first. "Joshua, I am sorely shocked and saddened by your crimes of piracy while living among us as a loyal British subject and planter." His voice started in sadness but migrated into anger. "How could you do such a thing?"

"Come, now, governor. You remember I was born in Carolina. I was never a British citizen." Joshua smiled at the man, who huffed, puffed, and threw out his ruffled chest at the retort.

Lord Halton shook his fist at Joshua. "You won't be so saucy when you're hanging on that post at low tide as we've got planned for you."

A moan erupted from the adjoining cell. "Sir, my Lord Halton, you don't...you don't plan to put me on one of them horrors, do you? You promised..."

"Yes, you will share your captain's fate—and every other pirate's who served with you. We're going to flush them out of this island."

So they would hold the two of them until they found more witnesses they could compel to testify. That would give Joshua more time to think, to plan his defense.

The judge's dark eyes bored into Joshua, so he asked the man a question. "Would you judge me before I've had a trial?"

"No, you will have your trial, Joshua Becket." His eyes hardened into steel. "I'm astounded that you—supposedly a man of honor, a man of fortune, and one that has had a liberal education, even in the law, I understand—could sink so low." The judge shook his head.

The three men stamped back up the corridor, mumbling.

Joshua frowned. Those last words reminded him of the famous court case against Major Stede Bonnet, a titled gentleman in Charles Town in the early 1700s. The militia arrested, tried, and hanged Bonnet for piracy. That chief justice had noted a similar description of the gentleman pirate.

Joshua pressed his lips tight. Yes, he'd been all of those things at one time—a man of honor, fortune, education. He'd had many blessings but lived like a pagan in more ways than the piracy with which he was charged. How could God forgive all he'd done?

He turned and dropped back onto his cot. Had his past caught up with him, regardless of his repentance? Would he suffer the full sentence for piracy British courts handed out? To escape would take a miracle.

A dark cloud settled about him and failed to dissipate, even when Mark Gardner returned with decent food and the requested Bible.

CHAPTER 18

*A*bigail stood on the deck as the *Eagle* advanced through the bay toward Samuel and Georgia Ann Vargas's island planta-tion. Her breath caught as the Salt Marsh dock came into view. Thank God they'd made it back to Charleston. Her heart tripped with relief that soon dissolved into despair. Memories of her time spent at the place two years earlier for John Vargas and Anna Grace's wedding flowed across her mind—a happy time. Like this one should've been. How different this arrival would've been with Joshua at her side. She blinked back tears.

A young black boy jumped up at first sight of their approach and swung his wooden hammer against the dock bell with enthusiasm. Its peals rang out across the bay. The white columns of the imposing house, shrouded by tall trees draped in silver moss, loomed into sight. Figures piled out of the entrance and down the shell-strewn path to the sea.

Quite a group had gathered on the dock when Lieutenant Lambert dropped anchor in the bay and lowered a rowboat to disembark.

Taking Jade's hand, Abigail lined up to be in the first load with the child and their luggage. Their house servants would follow. She scanned the welcoming faces as they rowed toward them. Anna Grace pushed out to the front and waved at her.

Abigail disembarked with Jade beside her and fell into her friend's arms. But she moved back fast as Anna's extended stomach protruded between them. "My goodness, Anna, I hadn't heard about this. Are you doing well, my friend?"

"I'm fine, Abigail. It's wonderful to see you. Sorry I didn't write. It's been hectic here with Grandfather Ethan so ill." She glanced back at the rowboat and a servant setting the luggage on the dock. "Where is...Joshua?" She noticed Jade and smiled. "And is this his little girl?"

Jade held out her hand. "Hello, I'm Jade Becket. What's your name, ma'am?"

Anna bent down and hugged the child. "I'm Anna Grace Vargas, and we are so happy to have you here, Jade." She glanced back at Abigail with a questioning look. "And Joshua?"

"A British warship arrested my father," Jade explained. "But I believe God is going to take care of him."

Anna Grace's eyes widened, and she looked at Abigail with a sobered face.

Abigail flicked a tear from her cheek and touched Anna's arm. "It's a long story. Please, let's get to the house, and after a little rest, we can talk. I'll need to tell your family what has happened."

"Of course. In fact, the midday meal is ready. Let's wait until after that, my friend."

She started up the path to the house with Jade and Anna at her side. Servants followed with the luggage.

After dining, Abigail put Jade down for a nap with Mira and Clarissa dozing in nearby chairs. She walked into the parlor where Samuel Vargas had assembled the family and Lieutenant Eric Lambert. Marisol, they told her, was sitting with Ethan.

Vargas, a tall man, his dark hair and beard streaked with gray, glanced around at his gathered clan and acknowledged each one. "Now we are all ready to hear what has happened to Joshua. Who's going to start? You, Abigail? Or Eric?"

Abigail sat forward. "Sir, before we do that, please tell me about your father, Ethan. Is he...? Joshua wanted so much to get back in time."

"He's still with us, Abigail, and actually took a turn for the better when he heard Joshua would be coming home." He smiled at all assembled. "And that Joshua wrote he'd had a change of heart. I don't know if we'll disappoint Father until we have all the facts about why his prodigal son didn't make it home with you. But tell us what happened." He took a seat beside Georgia Ann.

Abigail told of her arrival at Rockford and her surprise later to learn her employer was Ethan's son. She shared about Joshua's decision to sell out and come home, some about his change of heart, and the British man of war stopping the *Eagle* to arrest him, allegedly for piracy. She didn't share about their marriage plans. How could she without Joshua beside her?

Eric Lambert added what he knew, including that Joshua had a French letter of marque under which he sailed. "Course, the British will never accept a French authorization of any kind, if Joshua does try to use it in his defense."

Samuel nodded. "You're right about that. Not from their long-time enemy."

John Vargas, who knew Lambert from his visits to Joshua in Jamaica earlier, leaned forward. "So what you're telling us is that Joshua has been arrested for piracy and is right now facing trial before the British crown in Jamaica?" Anna Grace's husband appeared a neat combination of his father and mother's traits. He had his father's height, dark hair, and emerald eyes, but his mother's cupid bow lips and wide forehead.

Lambert nodded. "That's what I understand from what Lord Halton shouted from his ship as they approached the *Eagle* and fired a warning shot over our bow. I wanted to stay and fight by Joshua's side, but he insisted I go below and be available to sail the ship to Charleston if the British arrested him. That's what I've done."

Samuel spoke then. "Yes, and we are deeply thankful you've succeeded, Lieutenant. You've brought our dear friend Abigail and my wonderful first niece safely here." He glanced around the group. "This morning that child gave me the warmest welcome I've seen from a young'un."

Georgia Ann and Anna Grace, sitting on the large sofa with Abigail, murmured similar thanks and patted Abigail's hands knotted in her lap.

John turned to Lambert, his green eyes so like his father's, blazing. "Eric, I'm for formulating a plan to rescue Uncle Joshua. Are you with me?"

Eric balled a fist and smashed it into his other hand. "By all means, my man. I was just waiting for you to ask. We can do it. I know we can."

Anna's hand flew to her cheek, and her brow constricted. A tear slid down her cheek. "But John...the baby."

He stood, strode to her, and dropped on one knee beside her chair. He took her hand in his. "My dear, that is the one regret I'd have doing this—leaving you at such a critical time." He turned to his mother, who sat with her eyes closed. Then he glanced at his father. "But we all know Joshua will get a death sentence. What should we do?"

Heaviness settled in the room.

Abigail's heart lurched, and her mouth dried up like sawdust. Yes, a rescue attempt of her beloved would be a most dangerous undertaking. The rescuers, if caught, could suffer the same sentence as Joshua. Could she wish that for Anna's husband and Lambert, especially with the Vargas's' first child due in a matter of weeks?

Georgia Ann Vargas tucked a loose blond curl back into her upswept hairdo and laid her hand on Anna's and her son's hands clutched together. She took a deep breath as if she'd just whispered a prayer. "This is a critical decision for our family. For sure, Joshua's life is at stake, even if he did sail under a letter of marque. Also there's so little time, considering the distance to Jamaica, to even have a hope of an escape plan succeeding. Let us agree to pray tonight for God's sure direction and decide in the morning. God will never guide us wrong. And where He guides, He will always provide. We've lived by this principle all our lives. Let's not stop now."

The group nodded, and the women went out. Abigail put her arm around Anna Grace as they walked up the steps to their respective rooms. What could she say to her friend? She gave her a quick hug at her door and left without a word.

Before retiring that evening, Abigail spent quality time in prayer and searching the Scriptures. She could have no part in the decision Joshua's family made. The two men would take a dreadful risk. It must be their choice—and the family's. But she could pray and find a promise to stand on. In the fourth chapter of Philippians, she found peace.

Be anxious for nothing, but in everything by prayer and supplication, with thanksgiving, let your requests be made known to God; And the peace of God, which surpasses all understanding, will guard your hearts and minds through Christ Jesus.

She prayed, released the situation into God's hands, then closed her Bible and slept.

At breakfast the next morning, Abigail, with Jade at her side, greeted her hosts, but conversation lagged as they placed food on their plates from the buffet and sat at the table.

Jade wolfed down her porridge and egg and latched her bright green eyes on their host. "I want to see all your horses, Uncle Samuel. Do you have one for me? I had to leave my beloved Buttercup at Rockford."

Mr. Vargas smiled. "I'm sure we can find a new horse friend for you, Jade. Your Mr. Dykes and Jeremy are down at the stables now. Perhaps someone can take you there this morning."

"Yes, I'll get Clarissa to go with her." Abigail rose to call the servant. Jade, chattering about the new horse she'd find, soon scurried out the kitchen door with the young woman.

Abigail sat back at the table and glanced around. Where was Anna? And John and Eric Lambert? Only Samuel and Georgia Vargas had come down to breakfast.

Samuel wiped his mouth with his napkin. "Abigail, if you're wondering where everyone is, John and Eric set sail at dawn for Jamaica."

She gasped, and conflicting emotions flowed over her—joy that a rescue attempt was on the way and anxiety at the terrible risk. Was Anna upstairs grieving that her husband had gone on such a dangerous mission? She laid her napkin beside her plate. Should she go to her?

Georgia Ann smiled at Abigail. "Anna wanted to sit with her grandfather a little this morning, along with Grandmother Marisol. We had quite a time of prayer last night and believe God is going to protect our men and bring Joshua home safe. Anna agreed with John going."

Abigail blinked, swallowed the lump in her throat, and lowered her head. She didn't trust herself to speak without breaking into grateful tears. She clutched her hands in her lap.

Samuel poured himself another cup of tea. "Those two brave men, even if one is my son, came to my room last night with a plan that just might work. John's ship, the *Sand Dollar,* is a sloop, Abigail. It's small, fast, and can outrun any British ship." He patted her hand. "So don't live in constant fear while they're gone, is my advice." He glanced at his wife. "Joshua wrote that you two planned to marry. Is that right?"

Abigail took a deep, shaky breath and placed her folded hands in her lap. "Yes. And I'm thankful and relieved to hear about your son's fast ship and his willingness to accompany Lieutenant Lambert on this dangerous mission. I'm in full agreement with your family's prayers for their safety and success."

~

*J*oshua lay back on his cot after his final day in court. The sentence came as no surprise. He was to be hanged three days hence. The trial had lasted six weeks, probably because the court had never prosecuted a member of the assembly like him. They made sure they met every legal requirement. The Crown had rounded up four more of his crew who testified against him. Nothing Joshua had said made any difference, even his admitting to attacking British ships only during the American Revolution. The prosecutor pointed his long finger at him and screamed. "But you were living here on this island, parading as a good British citizen, while destroying every ship of ours you could."

When the evening shadows stretched across the cell from the high, barred window, a deep, darker feeling descended on Joshua. Mark Gardner came by with food, but Joshua could eat very little. Even Mark praying with him before he left didn't lift Joshua's spirit.

When full darkness descended in the Guard House, Joshua stared into the gloom, and a chill ran up his spine. Would he suffer the full penalty for his sins? Had God left him?

Yes, you're no good and God couldn't care less about you.

Joshua sat up. The mocking voice came from the fetid air permeating the cell. He slammed his fist into his hand. If only he could read the Bible Mark had brought, but the guards allowed no light in the prison at night—probably to hide their evil deeds of accepting bribes, gambling, and stealing prisoners' goods. He picked up the Bible and held it against his chest in the thick darkness.

A verse of Scripture flowed across his tortured mind, one his father had preached on several times. *For we wrestle not against flesh and blood, but against principalities, powers, rulers of darkness, and spiritual wickedness in high places.*

He stood and prayed. Time stopped as he entered a terrible wrestling. Contemptuous voices attacked his mind with doubt and fear. He fought them with Scriptures that came forth from his earlier years, giving him relief until it started all over again.

At dawn, a strange peace enveloped him. He determined to spend the entire day reading Scripture—his last day before the sentence would be carried out.

After Mark came with food that evening, prayed, and left, Joshua continued to read, praying the light from the window wouldn't fade early.

Muffled sobs rose from Henry in the next cell. Suddenly, he shook the bars. "Capt'n, sir. Kin you tell me why you're so peaceful and us fixin' to be hanged tomorrow?"

Peachy fuzz covered Henry's troubled youthful face. Why, the boy hardly had enough beard yet to shave. He held up the Bible. "This is why, Henry. Are you a believer?"

"I know my mama was. She went to church every Sunday, and she was a good woman. But I never had much use for religion after she died."

"It's not religion, Henry." Joshua sat nearer to the boy. "It's about deciding you don't want to live a sinful life anymore. You want to pray and ask the Lord Jesus Christ, who loves you, to forgive all your sins and help you make the best decisions." What would his father think of how Joshua was explaining salvation to a lost, frightened prisoner facing hanging like himself? Would he be proud?

"Well, I've done a few of those sins for sure. I guess God's done give up on me." Henry slumped back on his cot.

Something akin to joy bubbled up in Joshua. "No, Henry. He has not given up on you. If you simply pray right now and ask Him to forgive you and to come be the Lord of your life, He'll do it. I promise."

"You sure that's all? Seems mighty little." A small ray of hope lightened Henry's voice.

Joshua warmed to his subject. "That's because Jesus, God's Son, has done all the work, Henry, when He died on the cross and rose from the dead so we could be forgiven." Amazing how quickly his father's teachings came back. He remembered more than he'd thought.

Silence came from Henry. He sat with his arms folded and eyes clenched shut. A moment later he said, "Well, I did it, like you said, Capt'n, and seems I feel some better." Then his face paled, and he shook the bars again. "But I'm still skeered bout that hanging. Ain't you?"

Joshua took a deep breath. "Probably anybody is scared when it's time to die, but God wrote some words in the Bible to help us. Would you like me to read them to you?"

"Yeah, go ahead. Ain't got nothing else to do."

Joshua read aloud the twenty-third Psalm. As he finished, the last rays of light faded from the window. He shut the book and reclined on his cot with the Bible lying across his chest. Henry's soft snores soon came through the bars. So the young man had found enough peace to sleep. Joshua smiled.

〜

Fighting his way up from a pit full of sinking sand trying to pull him to his death, Joshua came awake in the heavy darkness. Sweat poured from him, and his heart pounded like a galloping horse. He opened his eyes. Someone stood in his cell in front of his open door. He bolted up.

"Take it easy, Capt'n."

That voice. Lambert?

In a whisper—"Me and John, we've come to get you out of this stinking British prison. You ready to go?"

Joshua swung his legs from the cot without making a sound, every cell in his body alert. "Yes, you're just in time, old friend."

A movement in Henry's cell drew Joshua's attention.

Lambert stiffened.

"Sir, take me too. Please, take me too." The soft, desperate whisper went no farther than the two cells.

Joshua looked at his lieutenant.

The man held out the guard's key ring and grinned.

Joshua leaned toward Henry. "All right, my man. But don't make a sound."

Within minutes, Joshua, Lambert, and Henry—swiping at tears—tiptoed up the corridor and out of the Guard House entrance. Three guards lay in a heap beside the steps, their ragged breathing proving they still lived but wouldn't arouse for some time.

Lambert led them away from the building and down a dark alley to the edge of a field. A wagon covered with hay stood waiting.

Its driver whispered a greeting. "Good to see you, Uncle Joshua." John Vargas sat on the headboard holding the reins.

Joshua grabbed his nephew's extended hand and squeezed it hard.

"Come, both of you, get under this hay fast. We've got a lot of riding to do 'fore dawn." Lambert was already at the back of the wagon, pulling back the hay strewn between large milk jugs.

Joshua and Henry lay on their backs in the wagon, and Lambert covered them with a blanket, then the hay. The milk containers, filled with rocks to stabilize them, stood at their sides.

For sure, he'd never forget that strange ride under the hay in the dark hours after midnight. They traveled slowly until they reached the edge of town and the smooth road gave way to a bumpy path. Where were they headed? There'd been no time to discuss the plan with his rescuers. Joshua prayed the wagon would not attract attention. How wise for Lambert and John to choose a milkman's conveyance, as farmers drove to supply the city with milk early each morning.

Henry twitched beside Joshua. "Capt'n, I want to thank you for letting me come. I'll never forget it, and you'll not regret it." His hoarse whisper warmed Joshua's ear.

The smell of the sea alerted Joshua when they were nearing the coast. The wagon stopped with the wheels skidding in sand.

Lambert and John pulled the hay off their passengers and helped them jump from the wagon. Joshua looked around and recognized where they were even though darkness still hung heavy. Rockford's dock. And John's *Sand Dollar* bobbed in the bay.

With no words spoken, each man knew what to do. While John unharnessed the horses and released them, Joshua and Lambert readied the ship and the sails to depart.

In a matter of minutes, the *Sand Dollar* moved out to sea.

By the time a streak of dawn lined the eastern horizon with deep shades of pink, the ship, with its sails snapping, passed out of Jamaican waters on its way north to Charleston. Exhilaration mixed with deep peace swept over Joshua. He was heading home to Abigail, to Jade, to his family. He stood with John on the quarterdeck and scanned the smooth ocean beyond the hull's frothy trough.

As the sun rose into the sky, the lookout's shout alerted the *Sand Dollar* crew. "A sail. A sail."

John Vargas whipped out his eyepiece. "Uh-oh." He handed it to his uncle.

Joshua pointed the glass toward the ship emerging fast on the horizon. His heart fell to his toes. A British warship. And worse. Lord Halton's pennant flew beneath the English colors.

CHAPTER 19

*H*enry darted up the quarterdeck steps and stopped before Joshua with his ragged, dirty hat clutched in his hands. "Sir, please let me send that British ship a message they ain't looking for. I ain't got no hankering to be taken back to that island prison and the hangman's noose. I can stop 'em in their tracks. I know I can. You know I'm a great gunner." His words poured out in a rush, and his amber eyes flashed fire.

John glanced at Joshua. "Is this true?"

"Yes, it's true. He's a good gunner." Then he addressed Henry. "We will only have a moment before they recognize us and come close enough for our cannon to do any damage. Their guns outnumber us ten to one. They can blast us out of the sea if they want to."

Henry balled his fist. "But you got a long nine cannon. It's got a lot better range. Plus, you got two other pretty good cannons. I know I can hit them, sir, before they know we're even trying. Just give me two of your crewmen to keep the cannons primed. They won't be able to pursue us." Excitement laced his voice.

Joshua turned to his nephew. "John, this is your ship. What do you say?"

"I say, let the man do what he's trained to do. We can't risk hoping that warship might ignore us, thinking us an insignificant, small sloop. Even flying our American flag, they might just decide to check us out. Then where would we be?"

He'd not even told John the ship sailed under the command of Lord Halton, the very man who'd arrested him before and would recognize Joshua at first sight. Should he tell him?

Joshua took a deep breath. In earlier years he would've never worried about lives being lost, but now things were different for him. "Very well, Henry, go do your worst. With one condition. We just want to stop their pursuit, not blow them out of the water...or kill and maim a bunch of the crew. You understand?"

Henry stared him a moment, a question on his face, then nodded "Sure, you're right. I can do it."

John leaned over the rail and shouted for two of his crew to assist the gunner.

Henry's first shot blasted over the water and hit the stern tip of the ship, not quite below the water line.

Joshua watched the scurrying on the other deck through the eyepiece. He could imagine the surprised curses flowing through the ranks. A gnat attacking a buzzard. Heavy cannons screeched as they were pushed through gun ports. Many cannons and gun ports. All would be over in a matter of moments for the *Sand Dollar* if Henry's next shot didn't make it to something vital on that ship. He whispered a prayer.

A cannonball careened through the air, then in quick succession, a second shot boomed from Henry's small gunner team. A tremendous explosion followed by a loud cracking sound erupted from across the water. The main mast of the British ship trembled then fell forward and sailors scurried from its crashing descent to the deck.

Joshua's mouth gaped open.

John Vargas emitted a loud whoop. "Tarnations, Uncle. How did your man manage that?"

"He's good, but still I'd say it's something akin to a miracle."

"Yes, by all means. A miracle."

Joshua wiped the sweat from his face. Why did he ever doubt the possibility of miracles?

❧

*T*he *Sand Dollar* sailed into the Salt Marsh bay and dropped anchor. No bell sounded to announce their arrival, not even when Joshua and John rowed up to the dock and disembarked.

They looked at one another and frowned, then headed up the path to the house.

"It's too quiet, Joshua. Reckon what's going on?"

They both increased their pace. When they reached the steps to the plantation house, a woman's plaintive cry came from an upstairs room.

John's face paled. "The baby." He pushed through the door, ignored the servants gathered in the hallway, and took the stairs two at a time.

Joshua entered and stood at the bottom of the steps. He glanced around at the expensive furnishings in the elegant parlor and the unique hanging staircase John flew up. Stepbrother Samuel had done all right for himself. Several servants, two maids and a footman, standing in the hall stared at him with wide eyes but said nothing. Someone hurried past them down the hall toward him. He smiled. Mrs. Pelfrey, with Lucy Dykes right behind her.

"Mr. Becket." Their voices rang out in unison. For a moment, he thought they might hug him, but they stopped and curtsied instead, smiles wreathing their faces.

"Well, ladies, this is an awful quiet house in the middle of the afternoon." He gestured up the stairs. "Is anything happening up there?"

They smiled at each other. Mrs. Pelfrey leaned forward and whispered. "Why, Mrs. Anna is having her baby, that's what. Mr. Samuel told everyone to be quiet. It started early this morning."

"Joshua." He turned. Abigail stood at the top of the staircase, her face bright as sunlight after the rain.

He had almost forgotten how beautiful she was. He smiled and held out his hand.

In a brief moment, she was in his arms, sobbing.

"Hello to you, too. Can I get a smile, maybe? I've missed you something terrible, Abigail Welch, soon-to-be Mrs. Becket." He lifted her chin, kissed away the tears, then claimed her lips.

Mrs. Pelfrey and Lucy backed away, as did the other servants. In a moment, Joshua and Abigail stood alone.

"Oh, Joshua. I prayed and prayed, but this last trial sorely tested my faith that I'd ever see you again."

He kissed her forehead.

John Vargas appeared at the top of the stairs, his tanned, youthful face aflame with pride. "Uncle Joshua, come see my fine son. We got back just in time."

He walked up the steps with his arm around Abigail's waist. It seemed so right, and gratitude overflowed his heart. How could he ever thank God for all the mercy and grace He'd extended to him?

TWO WEEKS LATER

*A*bigail awoke, stretched, and smiled. So much had happened since Joshua and John had returned from Jamaica. She blinked back moisture as she remembered the reunion she'd witnessed between Joshua and his father. Her heart had blossomed with love for her husband-to-be and a father who never gave up praying for his son. Then there was Joshua's reunion with his brother, Samuel, and his stepmother, Marisol. A lot of tears flowed from the women in the house, including her.

Jade's excitement over learning that her father and Abigail would marry filled the house with joy and made the servants smile. In addition, she delighted in discovering so much family she could claim as her own. She had to go up to see Grandfather Ethan at least once a day, and he appeared to be growing stronger and doted on the child.

Abigail pushed back the blanket and swung her feet onto the soft rug. She glanced at the clock on her dresser. Already nine o'clock.

Goodness, Joshua must wonder what had happened to her. He wanted to take her into Charleston for a surprise, he'd said.

After sailing across the channel, they disembarked at Gadsden's Wharf, and Joshua hired a carriage. Abigail's heart rejoiced as they traveled down familiar lanes of the city. Sunshine lit the cobbled streets, and spring blossoms hung over garden walls. When Joshua directed the driver to Charlotte Avenue, she gaped at her fiancé. Did he know she'd grown up on the street?

When he had the driver pull up at her family's former townhouse, her hand flew to her mouth. "Joshua, why are we here? Do you know this used to be my home?"

He chuckled, stepped out of the carriage, and helped her down. He walked to the little gate, now needing a coat of paint, and escorted her through.

She stopped in the walk leading to the porch she knew so well. "Joshua, why have you brought me here?" Despite the overgrown garden, the steps needing repair, and the house itself practically begging for various kinds of maintenance, it was all so familiar, her heart turned over.

"Abigail, I thought of waiting until our wedding to tell you, but I couldn't do it."

"Tell me what, sweetheart?"

"This is your wedding present. I'm already talking to repairmen. We'll soon have this house looking better than it did when first built. And I'm repairing the stable for Jade's horse and ours."

Her breath caught in her throat. "Oh, Joshua. Nothing could've made me happier. But aren't you planning to rent law office space somewhere also? Can we afford both?"

"I've been inside. That front parlor will work fine for my office, dear one." He lowered his head and whispered in her ear. "And money will not be a problem for us, wife-to-be. The sale of Rockford will carry us for quite some time—until my law practice is established."

Moisture gathered in her eyes. She squeezed his hand. "You have completely surprised and pleased me, Joshua."

On the way back to Salt Marsh, her heart sang. A new beginning,

THE SUGAR BARON'S GOVERNESS

but with good things from the past reclaimed. How good could life get? And Jade would love growing up in Charleston. There was so much to do and see. They'd start their new family right here in their home city.

~

THE WEDDING DAY

*A*t two o'clock on the third day of May, Abigail, with the help of Clarissa, dressed in a lovely lavender gown bought at one of the better stores in Charleston. Georgia Vargas had accompanied her shopping since Anna Grace was still recovering from the birth of baby John Ethan. That healthy boy had brought joy to the entire household, and especially to Jade, who called him her little brother. The first time she'd made that remark, Joshua had looked at Abigail and winked. "She can always have more than one brother."

Ethan Becket had rallied so much since Joshua's return, they'd asked if he'd perform their ceremony. He'd accepted, his eyes sparkling. "I may have to sit in a chair to do so, but this will be a family marriage I wouldn't want to miss having a part in."

Abigail's image in the dresser mirror reflected how happiness had lifted lines from her face. Love truly worked miracles.

"You look beautiful like a bride should, dear friend." Anna Grace sat on a chair watching while Clarissa worked on Abigail's hair. Soon, every shiny, dark curl performed its part in a lovely, flowing hairdo. Then Clarissa placed the pearl bridal headpiece on the crown of Abigail's head with its gossamer lavender veil flowing down the back.

Anna stood, smiled, and headed out of the room. "I'll see you downstairs, Abigail. Happy, blessed wedding day."

At three o'clock, Abigail left the bedroom and met Jade at the top of the stairs holding the basket they'd made. Her lavender dress fit her well, with its lace ruffles cascading down the sides. Mira held the child's hand as instructed.

Jade looked back at Abigail. "You look like a fairy princess, mama-to-be. And when do I get to scatter my rose petals?"

Abigail's heart swelled at the title. Mama. Had Joshua told her to say it? "Start when you get to the bottom of the stairs and continue right up to Grandfather Ethan's chair in the parlor, as we practiced."

Samuel Vargas stood at the bottom of the steps, grinning and handsome in his blue waistcoat. He had been happy when asked to give Abigail away.

The visiting musician played a harpsichord. The music resounded through the plantation house. This was Jade's signal to go down, and she walked slowly, careful not to stumble on the hem of her dress. After the last step, she reached into her basket and scattered pink petals on the floor.

Abigail descended and took Samuel's extended arm. When she entered the parlor, her heart swelled at the sight of her new family gathered to celebrate her and Joshua's wedding.

Marisol Becket sat on one side with Anna Grace and little John Ethan in her lap.

On the other side, Mrs. Pelfrey and Lucy sat together. Mr. Dykes, Jeremy, and Henry clustered behind them. With a wry expression, Henry wiggled a finger beneath his new cravat.

Ethan Becket sat in a tall chair at the front of the room. Joshua came to stand nearby, and drew her full attention. In a black silk waistcoat, white shirt, and fluffy lavender cravat, he was more handsome than she'd ever seen him. His eyes met hers and blazed with love. Eric Lambert walked up beside him, grinning.

Abigail's heart could burst with happiness as Samuel led her to Joshua, then took his seat beside Georgia.

She lifted her gaze to Joshua. He winked and placed his arm around her waist. When Ethan cleared his throat, they both turned their attention his way.

Ethan Becket had to sit, but there was nothing wrong with his voice. It rolled over the room as he read from the worn pages of his Common Book of Prayer.

"'Dearly beloved, we are gathered here in the sight of God, and in the face of this Congregation, to join together this man and this woman in holy Matrimony, which is an honorable estate instituted by God signifying unto us the mystical union that is betwixt Christ and his Church.'"

Abigail, lost in happiness, heard the rest of the words as though in a dream, but replied when her response was needed.

Joshua's father prayed a wonderful blessing over them. "'May God the Father, God the Son, God the Holy Spirit, bless, preserve and keep you, and surround you with favor and grace so you may live happily together in this life, and in the world to come, have life everlasting. Amen.'"

Joshua pulled her into her arms and kissed her until she felt faint. Clapping came from the servants peering in from the hall. Someone, most likely Henry, gave a shrill whistle.

Jade pressed against them. "All right, Papa, let her go so we can go eat."

Abigail was still regathering her wits as Anna, Marisol, Georgia, and Samuel came to hug them and offer their congratulations.

They flowed into the dining room for a plenteous feast of roasted pheasant, baked ham and smoked turkey, okra, sweet potato pie, rice pilaf, squash, cabbage and peas with stewed tomatoes, and an array of fresh fruits. Joshua's cook, Lucy, and Georgia's cook had outdone themselves. Two beautiful cakes made with fruit and molasses sat enthroned on the sideboard. Abigail smiled, remembering Clarissa had told her there had been a bit of dissension about which of the two servants would bake the cake. They ended up both baking the special cake. Was any kitchen big enough for two proud cooks?

After the meal, Joshua hurried Abigail upstairs. He requested she change into more simple clothing and pack a small overnight bag. She looked at him, surprised, but did as he requested.

Soon he led her down the path to the dock and into the rowboat tied there. Eric Lambert helped row them to the *Eagle* anchored in the bay. He never spoke a word.

When they climbed aboard, Eric rowed back toward the Salt Marsh dock and waved. "See you in the morning, Capt'n."

Joshua placed his arm around her waist and drew her to his captain's cabin, that wonderful place that had so surprised her when he'd rescued her from the pirate ship on her arrival in Jamaica. She'd been sure it was a pirate's secret hideaway.

Silk still lined the walls and covered the large bed with its colorful, fringed pillows. Everything, though, seemed freshly cleaned and sparkling in the evening sun cascading through the row of windows. A lantern hung next to the door, and another glowed on the bookcase shelf. The sound of the surf lapsing against the sides of the anchored ship filled her with peace and well-being.

A small table sat in the middle of the room with two chairs. A steaming silver teapot and a variety of small cakes, sandwiches, cheese, and fruit lay across its top.

She turned to look into Joshua's face. He'd been watching her.

He swept her into his arms. Her heart thudded in her ears, and she found it hard to breathe. The tenderness of his gaze baptized her with joy. "Husband, you've astounded me. Are we to spend our wedding night aboard your ship?"

He whispered into her hair. "Would you mind?" He kissed her brow, the tip of her nose, and trailed kisses across her cheek toward her ear.

"You haven't answered me. Do you mind?"

The intoxicating, spicy scent flowing from him filled her with delight, and his kisses kindled feelings of fire. "No, my love, my former pirate captain, sugar baron, and lawyer-to-be. I think it's a wonderful idea."

"Good. We don't have a way back to the dock till morning."

Did you enjoy this book? We hope so!
Would you take a quick minute to leave a review where you purchased the book?
It doesn't have to be long. Just a sentence or two telling what you liked about the story!

Receive a FREE ebook and get updates when new Wild Heart books release: https://wildheartbooks.org/newsletter

VOCABULARY APPENDIX

1) Wood's colt

    A child born out of wedlock. The term originated from the unplanned breeding of horses allowed to roam in unsupervised areas and woodlands.

2) Queue

    British soldiers and sailors during the 18th century wore their hair in a queue. While not always braided, the hair was pulled back very tight into a single tail, wrapped with a piece of leather, and tied down with a ribbon at the back of the neck. The hair was often greased and powdered in a fashion similar to powdered wigs, or tarred in the case of sailors. It was said that the soldiers' hair was pulled back so tightly that they had difficulty closing their eyes afterwards.

3) Sugar cane growing and harvesting in the Caribbean in the 1700's & today

Sugar cane took 12 to 18 months to mature and grew best in the wet months from June to November, ripening in the dry months of January to May. Planters staggered the cultivation so that the cane did not all mature at once.

Slaves planted, either by digging a trench and laying old cane cuttings end to end, or by digging holes and inserting cuttings. The cane was fertilized with animal manure. When the cane ripened, the workers cut it by hand with broad curved machetes and loaded the stems on wagons to be taken to the mill.

There, enslaved workers fed it through wooden or metal rollers to extract the juice. From the mill, the raw cane juice was channeled to the boiling house where it flowed into clarifiers (large metal pans). Lime and ashes were added to the juice to remove impurities, and then it was further heated to reduce and thicken it.

Next, when the syrupy sugar was close to crystallizing, it was poured into large wooden barrels in the curing house, where it finally turned into golden-brown muscovado sugar. The hogsheads of muscovado were then shipped to Europe for further refining into white sugar crystals. (Muscovado sugar, which is different from regular brown sugar, can be bought today at most major grocery chains.)

Today, sugar cane is grown and harvested mainly by machines, but some is still done by hand. Brazil, India, and China are the largest producers and exporters of sugar. The United States is by far the largest consumer of sugar. The average American consumes 140 pounds of sugar, corn syrup, and other natural sweeteners per year, up from 114 pounds in 1967. 50 percent more than the French and Germans and nine times more than the Chinese. Americans also consume 61 pounds of high-fructose corn syrup a year.

Note: Sugar beets are slowly displacing sugar cane because they can be grown in countries where sugar is consumed. Sugar beets are cheaper to produce because they can be planted and harvested using machines and are less labor intensive. They produce the same white crystals.

4) Chifferobe

A chifferobe is a closet-like piece of furniture that combines a long space for hanging clothes with a chest of drawers. Typically the wardrobe section runs down one side of the piece, while the drawers occupy the other side. It often boasts a mirror on the door of the wardrobe.

5) Jamaican Maroons & slavery

When the British captured Jamaica in 1655, the Spanish colonists fled, leaving a large number of African slaves. These former slaves created free settlements in the mountainous areas of the island. Runaways from the later large British sugar plantations joined them over the years. They intermarried with a group of indigenous people, the Arawaks. They spoke an English-based but Creole language unique to Jamaica and still in existence.

The Maroons survived by subsistence farming and periodic violent raids on plantations to take what they needed. They became strong warriors using camouflage and guerilla warfare before these tactics were widely known. They battled the British in several Maroon wars for their rights through treaties.

Caribbean witch doctors called Obeahmen often offered guidance and help. The planters' violent measures used to subdue the Maroons from burning plantations and murdering owners is thought to have accelerated the process of emancipation by the British Parliament.

The Slavery Abolition Act (1833), an act of Parliament that abolished slavery in most British colonies, freed more than 800,000 enslaved Africans in the Caribbean—including Jamaica—and South Africa, as well as a small number in Canada. It took effect on August 1, 1834.

It's interesting to note that English emancipation took place almost thirty years before Lincoln signed our Emancipation Proclamation and America fought the Civil War (April 12, 1861 – May 9,

1865). England had some mighty abolitionists—Wilbur Wilberforce, John Newton, and their colleagues.

One further note about slavery—**it still exists in the 21st century.** What countries still have slaves? As of 2018 statistics, the countries with the most slaves were: India (18.4 million), China (3.86 million), Pakistan (3.19 million), North Korea (2.64 million), Nigeria (1.39 million), Indonesia (1.22 million), Democratic Republic of the Congo (1 million), Russia (794,000), and the Philippines (784,000).

6) Obeah man or woman/Witch Doctor

Obeah is Jamaica's spiritual folk practice, used either to ward off evil or bring harm to someone else. Some compare it to Santeria or Haitian Voodoo or North American Hoodoo. The primary social function of an Obeah man or woman is said to be that of healer. In this capacity as healer, Obeah men and women are often called upon to provide protection from any number of spirits that inhabit the living world.

The origin of the word *Obeah* is thought to be connected to the Greek word for serpent. Snakes of some kind, real or carved, are often part of the Obeah man's paraphernalia.

Jamaica passed laws starting in 1845 against the practice of Obeah. Today, visitors who arrive at the Norman Manley International Airport in Jamaica's capital, Kingston, will find a visit to customs reveals a strict rule: *All publications of de Laurence Scott & Company and of the Red Star Publishing Company of Chicago in the United States of America relating to divination, magic, cultism or supernatural arts are prohibited from entering the country through the ports.*

7) Pirate versus Privateer

What usually set a privateer apart from a pirate was a paper known as a Letter or Marque. (See the next entry). Privateers—a term that referred to a ship, a captain, or a crew—preyed on the merchant ships of a specific country's enemy. In exchange for providing the privateer with a safe haven and license to attack, the issuer hoped to share in the profits. Sometimes privateers turned to piracy during times of peace.

While Henry III of England was the first to employ privateers, they fought in European and North American wars into the 19ᵗʰ Century. Since the United States Navy owned few ships, privateers played a key role in the War of 1812.

Many British naval seamen eventually became privateers to get away from the harsh treatment of seamen on British ships. When Britain was not at war, these men had few opportunities to find work on the sea unless they signed onto a merchant ship, a privateer, or pirate ship. History does record that privateers often turned to piracy. Blackbeard is an example. Supposedly born in Bristol, England, he served first on a privateer ship. When peace came to Europe, he embraced piracy and became the charismatic legend history records.

8) Letter of Marque

A letter of marque and reprisal (French: *lettre de marque; lettre de course*) was a government license in the Age of Sail that authorized a private person, known as a privateer or corsair, to attack and capture vessels of a nation at war with the issuer. Popular among Europeans from the late Middle Ages up to the 19th century, cruising for enemy prizes with a letter of marque was considered an honorable calling that combined patriotism and profit.

Such privateering contrasted with individuals conducting unlicensed attacks and captures of random ships, which was known as piracy. Piracy was almost universally reviled. In practice, the differences between privateers and pirates were often at best subtle, and at worst, a matter of interpretation. (Resource: Wikipedia "Letter of Marque")

FROM THE AUTHOR

Dear Reader,

In *The Sugar Baron's Governess*, I wanted to show Joshua Becket's redemption and relate it to his father's ceaseless prayer for him. The son of Reverend Ethan Becket in Book 2, and stepbrother of Samuel, Joshua was not a good guy, and he was quite jealous of his brother. The first crime in the Bible (Genesis 4) came as a result of Cain's jealousy of his brother Abel.

But Ethan Becket never ceased praying for his son Joshua to turn to God. A Christian parent may lose *physical* authority over their child, but we never lose *spiritual* authority that we exercise through prayer and spiritual warfare.

For more explanation on spiritual warfare, I invite any reader interested to check out my non-fiction mini-book on the believer's authority in Christ—*Power Over Satan*. Grab this brief Bible study about powerful prayer on Amazon for only 99 cents. If the booklet proves a blessing to you, would you consider writing a brief review on Amazon? I thank you in advance.

Blessings,

Elva

Don't miss The Lieutenant's Secret Love, book 5 in the Charleston Brides series!

Chapter One

1786
CHARLESTON

The dark lines of the master's brow and his loud drunken command shot tremors through Ezekiel as he stood in the doorway of the master's study. Cuddling a newborn wrapped in a blanket in his black, bony arms, he lowered his head, and a long, heavy breath gushed from his lips.

"I said take that baby and leave it far out in the woods to die. I'll not have another female in my house. This 'pose to be a son." Carter Seymour's harsh words echoed through the plantation house. He sat forward behind his desk and pointed his finger. "You hear me, boy? Don't think I'm too drunk to mean this." He slumped back in his chair where he'd spent the night as his wife struggled to give birth before she died.

"But, sirrah. She's a healthy one." Ezekiel's large hands shook, holding the small bundle from the previous night's birthing. He bent his gray head down to look once more at the girl child with her curly blond wisp of hair, wrapped in a Seymour white baby blanket. "I'se real sorry about Miz Seymour. And look, this baby's got that crooked little finger just like her mama." He held up a little hand with its miniature fingers spread. The smallest finger on the left hand bent at the middle joint.

Seymour's eyes widened when he saw the peculiar trait of his wife. "Take it out of my house. I never want to see it again," he thundered and reached for his whiskey bottle.

The child stiffened at the loud, angry words, and Ezekiel clasped her closer. He looked down at the tiny infant wrapped in the lacy covering with a C and S embroidered on one corner. The little one whimpered and pushed a tiny fist toward her rosebud mouth. Turning, he stumbled out the door, shaken in mind and heart. He had no choice but to obey his master. His old heart hammered in his chest and made his legs heavy and slow.

Ezekiel passed down the long hall lined with servants who'd heard the master's loud, drunken command. The maids and footmen stared at him with rounded eyes and stunned faces.

He walked through to the kitchen where his wife Molly stood wringing her hands. Tears streamed down her face, and she handed him a sugar tit she had dipped in milk. Ezekiel took it and gave it to the baby who began in earnest to suck the little ball of old linen with a spoonful of sandy sugar gathered in its center. He headed out the back entrance of the large house and swiped a tear that trickled down his weathered cheek before it dripped from his chin onto the little one in his arms.

Leaving the plantation grounds, he trudged deep into the woods. Scents of pine, sweet cedar, and the damp earthy smell of decomposing leaves flowed around him and the child. The morning sun moved higher in the sky with the promise of more heat to come. He pulled a handkerchief from his pocket and wiped the sweat from his brow.

The baby slept after the sugar tit ran out, but soon awakened and began to cry. He fell down on his knees next to a dirt road at the edge of the forest. "Lord Jesus, you knows I don't want this baby to die. I ain't no murderer. I needs your help. Show me what to do, Lord!"

The squeaking wheels of a wagon and clip clop of horses' hooves approaching interrupted his prayer. Quickly he placed the little bundle up against the trunk of a large oak that sheltered the roadway. The baby began to cry in earnest when his arms no longer held her. Ezekiel scrambled behind bushes and hid.

He heard a surprised feminine voice. "John, will thee stop the wagon? I'm sure I hear a baby crying."

Ezekiel peeked from his concealed spot. A bonneted woman in a plain gray dress with a white collar sat in the wagon holding a sleeping child in her arms. Another youngster sat on the wagon floor at her feet clutching her skirt with one hand, sucking a thumb with the other.

"And it's not our Michael or Adam." The mother lifted her eyes and searched the shaded forest and wild growth encroaching on the roadway.

"Could be a baby goat, you know, caught in a vine or something," the man holding the reins replied.

"I believe it's a baby. Will thou please go search, husband?"

The man stopped the wagon and climbed down. He walked in the direction of the sound toward a large oak.

Ezekiel pushed back into the undergrowth not daring to breathe.

"A baby for sure, dear Sarah, and it looks like a newborn," the man called out. He bent and picked up the bundle with care and looked into the tiny, porcelain face. The crying stopped. "And it's got violet eyes, the like of which I've never seen." The next moment the little countenance wrinkled up and heartrending cries again filled the air.

He hurried back to the wagon, shaking his head. "Who in tarnation would do a thing like this and leave this tiny helpless one out here in the woods?"

His wife laid her own sleeping child into the basket beside the toddler at her feet and reached for the sobbing infant. She rocked it in her arms. "Yes, I do believe it's a newborn and probably about to starve." She touched the snowy blanket and fingered the lace. "But its coverlet seems to be from rich folk." Without another word, she opened her bodice, pressed the little one to her bosom, and began to nurse it. Suckling sounds and the gentle whisper of the wind in the trees replaced the cries of the child. "Husband, please see if you can find anyone about."

The man looked up and down the road and walked a distance along the sides. "Hullo, is anyone out there?" He peered into the trees and called out several times.

Ezekiel shrank into the shadows.

The woman spoke from the wagon. "Will thou take us home, John White? Someone did not want this wee one, but God saw fit to have us come along in time to save it." She pulled back the blanket and a joyous cry broke from her lips. "It's a girl. What a blessing for us to finally have a lassie after losing our Hannah. God has sent a replacement. Shall we call her Hannah after our poor lost lamb the Lord has in His good care?"

The man smiled and nodded, swung back up into the buggy and snapped the reins on the backs of the two horses. "Home, my four-footed friends, home." The horses moved forward at a brisk pace as if they understood the word.

Ezekiel stood from behind the bushes and wiped the tears from his cheeks. He raised his hands toward heaven. "Thank ye, Lord. Thank ye."

~

1803
SEVENTEEN YEARS LATER

Hannah White traipsed through the forest to the secret place she loved, a hidden pool with moss-covered banks where deer and her other animal friends came to drink. She could spend hours just sitting and watching the parade of thirsty creatures. Besides deer, a raccoon and a fox often came by, as well as several kinds of birds. They would fill the nearby trees and move lower and lower in the branches, ever watchful, before hopping to the edge of the water to sip a drink.

As the sun climbed higher and the animals finished drinking, she undid her braided hair, wiped the perspiration from her brow, and slipped out of her boots and muslin dress. She gasped as she stepped into the cool, clear pool. The refreshing wetness wrapped around her feet and rose up her waist as she walked farther in, soaking her thin chemise. She didn't mind. She'd lie on the mossy hillside until it dried before returning home. Today was a glorious summer day, but most happy because her older brother Adam would be returning from his three-year stint at sea, fighting President Jefferson's Barbary Wars. How she'd missed her strong, cheerful, handsome sibling.

She emerged from the pool and sat on a warm, moss-covered rock.

SNEAK PEEK: THE ABANDONED DAUGHTER

After squeezing the excess moisture from her thick tresses, she lay on her back to dry her chemise. Drowsiness pressed against her eyelids.

The sound of hoof beats coming near roused her and she sat up, startled. No one ever came this far into the wood.

To her dismay, a horse and rider appeared in front of her before she could reach for her dress. And not an ordinary horse or person. The beautiful, glossy black stallion lowered his head and sniffed in her direction with pricked, fine-shaped ears. The young man in the saddle dressed in a green silk waist coat and breeches, grinned at her, and his eyes devoured her.

Heat flooded her cheeks to be seen in her undergarment. She tried to move around the two of them to fetch her dress, but the rider reined the animal to block her path.

"Sir, I beg of you. Let me pass."

"Why should I, you lovely forest nymph."

She placed her hand on the velvet nose of the horse and whispered to him. The animal moved back, but the rider swung down from the saddle, grabbed her around the waist, and pulled her to him.

Hannah pushed him away. He fell back against his mount, and the horse snorted.

She slipped past them both and reached for her dress. But as she bent to retrieve it, he caught her from behind.

He turned her about and tried to kiss her.

She kicked his shins and scratched his cheek.

The young man cursed and twisted her arm behind her back. "Now I have you, little tigress, and you will not escape this time.

She cried out in pain.

He pressed her close and looked into her face. "What? Violet eyes? I've never seen such."

"Turn her loose, you scoundrel, or you'll see death like you've never seen either." Her brother Adam's strong voice, heavy with authority, made her heart fly.

Thank you, Lord.

Dressed in his smart, blue and white American naval uniform, he burst through the trees with a drawn pistol gripped in his thick hand.

Her attacker released his hold on her and faced the newcomer. The youthful surprise blanketing his face stiffened into haughtiness. He adjusted his silk waistcoat and frowned. "Who do you think you are, sailor?" He spit out the last word with derision. "Get off my property. I'm Saul Seymour and this is Seymour Plantation land you're trespassing on."

"No it's not. This particular spot belongs to my father, John White. He tenant farms for Whitehall Plantation." Adam lowered his pistol and grinned at the young man, as if he were dealing with a misbehaving child.

Hannah slid her dress over her head, pulled on her boots, and hurried to stand beside her brother.

"We'll see about that, you squid." With one more hot glance at Hannah, Saul Seymour turned on his heel and mounted his horse. He pressed his legs into the animal's sides and galloped away.

Hannah sighed. "Adam, I'm pretty glad you came along when you did." She reached up and hugged his thick neck. "And we're so glad to have you home. Mother will be so happy."

Adam pulled her arms from around his neck and looked into her face, frowning. "Are you okay, little sister? Did he harm you?"

"No, I'm fine." She gave him a big smile to relieve his worry. "You know I think Saul Seymour is about my age, and probably spoiled and been given everything he's ever wanted. He's another of the Lord's many lost sheep."

"Now don't you go excusing the rascal, you tender-hearted one." Adam picked up his sailor's ditty bag where he'd dropped it and hefted it to his shoulder.

They turned and started back toward home. "Hannah, would you promise me not to come out walking alone anymore this far from the house?"

She looked up at him with wide innocent eyes as if it never occurred to her to be afraid or worry when immersed in the wonderland of nature she loved. "Why?"

"I don't think we've seen the last of Saul Seymour."

~

Adam White's frown stayed glued on his face in spite of his effort to relax it. Besides the shock of walking up on the scene he'd just dealt with, he couldn't stop thinking about how Hannah had grown up in his absence. He'd left her three years earlier as a thin waif of a girl, more bones than flesh and thick, unruly dark blond hair neither she nor their mother seemed able to keep managed more than a few minutes.

The girl who'd just thrown her arms around his neck and hugged him was a woman with curves in all the right places. Her hair had become the color of sweet sorghum syrup that glistened like gold when it caught a ray of the sunshine blazing over the trees. She was, in fact, everything and more, he'd dreaded her becoming—and local, unscrupulous men discovering. And, to make matters worse, Hannah appeared unaware of her charms. How would he ever protect her when he was committed to long naval stints at sea away from their family's small farm? Especially when she was determined to be a free spirit traipsing over the countryside?

They reached the yard of the cottage and a baby goat danced and skipped from behind a shed toward Hannah. "Hello, there, Rupert. Are you glad I'm back?" She bent, picked the young creature up, and hugged him and then set him back down. He playfully butted at her leg with the soft horn nubs barely visible on his head.

A cry came from the kitchen window, and Adam's mother Sarah came running out to them. "Adam, my son. Thee made it home." He dropped his sailor's bag and opened his arms to embrace her.

Their two freed servants, Mammy and her daughter Ida, stood on the porch looking on and smiling. He walked up and gave a hug to Mammy who'd helped raise him. She patted his muscled arm. "Lawsey me, Master John. You done got thick and hard. What kinda work they give you on them ships?"

"Way too much, Mammy, that's for sure."

Supper was a blessed affair with his father and his mother, and younger brother Michael and Hannah sitting around their wooden table. John White led in the blessing.

"Father God, we thank you for bringing our son Adam back safe. We ask you to bless this food now and keep us strong for our labors and your kingdom work. Amen."

John grinned. His father knew how to pray a brief prayer when folks were hungry. Cabbage, corn, and chicken had never tasted so good to him.

After the meal, Michael, especially, wanted to hear about every port Adam's ship had sailed to and whatever adventures had come his way. His father listened, smoking a pipe.

Mammy and her husband Samson and daughter Ida, who lived above the stable, sat in the kitchen doorway happy to be invited to hear, too.

Hannah sat at Adam's feet on the braided rug and never said a word. Her dark eyes didn't leave his face.

Finally, his mother Sarah stood from her rocker and laid her sewing in the basket at her feet. "Now, children, thou may stay up as long as thou wantest to but remember it's still a workday tomorrow and the harvest won't wait."

His father grunted an assent, stood, and knocked the burned ashes from his pipe into the fireplace. The servants left by the back door.

The next few weeks passed quickly as corn, wheat, and vegetables made it from the fields and garden into the barns or to the kitchen larder. John made the most of the three month's leave he had to help with the harvest. He also bought a pistol for Hannah and trained her how to use it. Another gift he found for her brought the most joy—a mixed mastiff puppy that would grow into, he hoped, a huge guard dog. She named the pup Hercules, and the two of them became instant friends and inseparable.

In spite of his warnings, Hannah continued her walks into her wooded spots, she called "happy places" after she completed her day's work or at the crack of dawn before it began.

One day she came back from a long jaunt with the half-grown

SNEAK PEEK: THE ABANDONED DAUGHTER

puppy at her heels and confided to Adam. "I never see anyone, but I do have the feeling at times I'm being watched."

He placed his hands on her small shoulders, uneasiness lined his brow. "There, can you understand now why I'm asking you to please stop going so far out, dear sister? He dropped his hands. "You're too pretty to be safe out there alone. How will I ever have peace about your safety when I have to go back to sea?"

She grinned. "Okay, I promise to curtail my longer treks until Hercules grows up to help guard me. Will that make you happier?"

He took a deep breath. "And I'll be praying daily for you, Hannah, to be wise and stay safe."

One morning after breakfast, two weeks before Adam's planned departure, two horses with riders pranced into the yard. John White opened the door and greeted the Seymour Plantation owner and his son, both dressed in silk waistcoats and polished black boots. When they dismounted and came up on the porch, he invited them into the sitting room, his face tight. Adam knew his father had never had any dealings with the largest plantation owner in the parish. They all sat in the simple straight-backed chairs around the fireplace.

Hannah and her mother stayed in the adjoining kitchen with Mammy and her daughter.

After the usual pleasantries about weather and planting, Charles Seymour took charge of the conversation. His son had not said a single word, but he kept throwing glances at Adam. Michael was already at work in the south field with Samson.

"Now I guess you're wondering why we've come. Well, here it is." He gestured to his son, whose face brightened to pink. "Saul here wants to take your daughter Hannah as his wife. I know they're both young, but she'll have everything she could possibly want and one day will be mistress of Seymour Plantation. What do you say?"

Adam suppressed a snort, but his father's face turned pale.

Finally, John White cleared his throat and spoke. "Sir, I cannot imagine why you've come here with such a request today. Hannah...will probably marry one day, but she doesn't even know your son as far as I know."

Hannah stepped into the room from the kitchen with her mother behind her.

"Father, I've met Saul Seymour once." She eyed the young man. "And I have no desire whatsoever to marry him now or ever. I must decline."

Saul smiled a strange smile at her, as if her words carried no weight.

Adam's heart swelled at Hannah's simple, confident response.

John White took a deep breath. "There, you have your answer, sir. Hannah will have the freedom to make her own choice of marriage partner when the time comes."

Charles Seymour frowned, and redness crept up his neck. He stood and slapped his riding crop across his boot. "No, that's not the end of it, Mr. White."

"What do you mean, sir?"

His father's voice held the least bit of tremor that Adam was surprised to hear. Seymour was nothing but a bully, maybe a wealthy one, but still a bully.

Adam stood. "You've heard my sister's response and my father's, sir. I don't think you and your son have any more business to conduct here."

Charles Seymour turned a hard, accessing eye on Adam. "Well, let's just see if I have." He walked to the window and tapped it with his riding crop. Several horses entered the yard from the woods, stamping and neighing. Seymour stood aside. "Come see." He motioned to John and Adam, and they stepped to the window.

His father's eyes widened, and Adam ground his teeth at what he saw in the yard. Four riders milled there, armed to the teeth and carrying unlit torches, desperate men you could pay to do most anything from the looks of their scraggly clothing and unkempt beards.

A wicked smile creased Seymour's face but never met his hard eyes. "Yesterday I bought your tenant farm from Whitehall's owner. The girl comes with us, or we'll burn this place to the ground, the barns, too, and shoot the animals. You'll only escape with your lives."

Adam made a move to reach the musket hanging over the fireplace, but Charles pulled his pistol and barred his way. "I only have to give the men outside thumbs up, and two of them will light their torches, and two of them will begin shooting every animal on the place. You ready for that?"

Hannah cried out and fell at the man's feet. "No, please don't do any of that. I'll come." She burst into sobs, and young Hercules came to flop down beside her and whimper.

Sarah White, her face calm, walked to a trunk in the corner. She rummaged down to the bottom and brought out a baby blanket.

She walked regally to Charles Seymour and held the soft fabric up with the two embroidered initials, C and S, clearly in view. "Sir, doest thou recognize this baby blanket? Hannah is the baby girl we found wrapped in it seventeen years ago at the side of the road at the far back of your property."

Charles Seymour's hard face turned to chalk. He stumbled into a chair.

Saul came to him. "Father, are you all right? Who cares how they found her as a baby. I want her." His petulant voice rose higher with the last phrase.

Charles brushed him away. "Girl, Hannah, show me your left hand." His voice came forth in a harsh whisper.

Hannah lifted her left hand with its bent little finger.

"Dear God." Charles Seymour lowered his head into his hands.

Adam's breath caught in his lungs, and every muscle in his body tensed. Hannah was not his blood sister?

GET *THE LIEUTENANT'S SECRET LOVE* AT YOUR FAVORITE RETAILER.

GET ALL THE BOOKS IN THE
CHARLESTON BRIDES SERIES

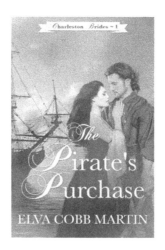

Book 1: The Pirate's Purchase

Book 2: The Sultan's Captive

Book 3: The Petticoat Spy

Book 4: The Sugar Baron's Governess

ABOUT THE AUTHOR

Elva Cobb Martin is a retired school teacher, a mother, and grandmother who lives in South Carolina with her husband and high school sweetheart, Dwayne. She grew up on a farm in South Carolina and spends many vacations on the Carolina Coast. Her southern roots run deep.

A life-long student of history, her favorite city, Charleston, inspires her stories of romance and adventure. Her love of writing grew out of a desire to share exciting love stories of courageous characters and communicate truths of the Christian faith to bring hope and encouragement. She always pauses for historic houses, gardens, chocolate, and babies of any kind.

If you'd like to keep up with Elva's escapades, find her and a newsletter sign up at http://www.elvamartin.com or stalk her on Facebook, Twitter, and Pinterest. She'll be glad to alert you when

future books are available, including Book 5 coming soon in this Charleston Brides Series, *The Abandoned Daughter*.

And guess what? She loves to hear from readers! Feel free to drop her a note at elvacmartin@gmail.com

In addition to the Charleston Brides Series, Elva Cobb Martin is author of:

The Barretts of Charleston Series
Book 1: In a Pirate's Debt
Book 2: Summer of Deception

Non-fiction
Power Over Satan: A Bible study on the believer's authority

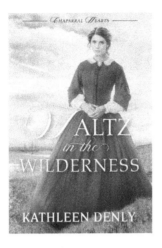

Waltz in the Wilderness by Kathleen Denly

She's desperate to find her missing father. His conscience demands he risk all to help.

Eliza Brooks is haunted by her role in her mother's death, so she'll do anything to find her missing pa—even if it means sneaking aboard a southbound ship. When those meant to protect her abandon and betray her instead, a family friend's unexpected assistance is a blessing she can't refuse.

Daniel Clarke came to California to make his fortune, and a stable job as a San Francisco carpenter has earned him more than most have scraped from the local goldfields. But it's been four years since he left Massachusetts and his fiancé is impatient for his return. Bound for home at last, Daniel Clarke finds his heart and plans challenged by a tenacious young woman with haunted eyes. Though every word he utters seems to offend her, he is determined to see her safely returned to her father. Even if that means risking his fragile engagement.

When disaster befalls them in the remote wilderness of the Southern

California mountains, true feelings are revealed, and both must face heart-rending decisions. But how to decide when every choice before them leads to someone getting hurt?

Lone Star Ranger by Renae Brumbaugh Green

Elizabeth Covington will get her man.

And she has just a week to prove her brother isn't the murderer Texas Ranger Rett Smith accuses him of being. She'll show the good-looking lawman he's wrong, even if it means setting out on a risky race across Texas to catch the real killer.

Rett doesn't want to convict an innocent man. But he can't let the Boston beauty sway his senses to set a guilty man free. When Elizabeth follows him on a dangerous trek, the Ranger vows to keep her safe. But who will protect him from the woman whose conviction and courage leave him doubting everything—even his heart?

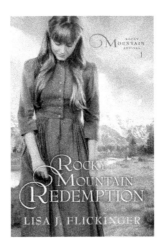

Rocky Mountain Redemption by Lisa J. Flickinger

A Rocky Mountain logging camp may be just the place to find herself.

To escape the devastation caused by the breaking of her wedding engagement, Isabelle Franklin joins her aunt in the Rocky Mountains to feed a camp of lumberjacks cutting on the slopes of Cougar Ridge. If only she could out run the lingering nightmares.

Charles Bailey, camp foreman and Stony Creek's itinerant pastor, develops a reputation to match his new nickname — Preach. However, an inner battle ensues when the details of his rough history threaten to overcome the beliefs of his young faith.

Amid the hazards of camp life, the unlikely friendship growing between the two surprises Isabelle. She's drawn to Preach's brute strength and gentle nature as he leads the ragtag crew toiling for Pollitt's Lumber. But when the ghosts from her past return to haunt her, the choices she will make change the course of her life forever—and that of the man she's come to love.

CPSIA information can be obtained
at www.ICGtesting.com
Printed in the USA
JSHW040946100622
26904JS00006B/147

9 781942 265603